I0691649

By ZAHRA OWENS

NOVELS
Diplomacy
Façade
The Hand-me-down

CLOUDS AND RAIN STORIES
Clouds and Rain
Earth and Sky
Floods and Drought
Moon and Stars

NOVELLAS
Balance
Charity Starts at Home
Happiness for Beginners
I Can See Right Through You
Isali Dreams

You Can't Choose Your Family
You Can Choose Your Friends

Published by DREAMSPINNER PRESS
http://www.dreamspinnerpress.com

Moon
and Stars

ZAHRA OWENS

Dreamspinner Press

Published by
Dreamspinner Press
5032 Capital Circle SW
Suite 2, PMB# 279
Tallahassee, FL 32305-7886
USA
http://www.dreamspinnerpress.com/

Moon and Stars
© 2013 Zahra Owens.

Cover Art
© 2013 Cover Art by Anne Cain.
annecain.art@gmail.com
Cover content is for illustrative purposes only and any person depicted on the cover is a model.

ISBN: 978-1-62798-173-6
Digital ISBN: 978-1-62798-174-3

Printed in the United States of America
First Edition
September 2013

To Anne Regan and Julyssa Diaz for making me realize the plot was all there and I just had to put it down on paper.

To Ariel Tachna for the extended pep talk (twice!).

To Damon Suede for kicking my ass (and making me see that if he can have writer's block and get past it, so can I).

And not least, to Elizabeth North for her infinite patience.

—1—

THE first time Cooper Nelson felt his blood flow faster again after many years was when he bumped into Kelly Freed in town.

For the last eight years, he'd survived by keeping his head low and his eyes averted. It was the only way to live in a small town where he'd been the subject of a big scandal. So why hadn't he moved away? He'd had his reasons at the time—reasons that no longer seemed valid, but were replaced by loyalty to the owner of a big-ass ranch who'd harbored him when the rest of the town would have much rather lynched him.

Although Coop kept to himself, he'd found a home on the Blue River Ranch and a kind of family, still, he didn't let the men he worked with come too close. He got along with everyone, but very few people knew the man behind the scruffy exterior and often grumpy manner.

And now a part of his past—one older than the scandal—had walked into town, and it unsettled Cooper more than he could have ever predicted.

When Cooper had walked out of the clothing store, he had his hat on, and out of habit, he hadn't looked the stranger in the eye as they'd crossed paths. His hand on his Stetson, he'd shielded his eyes from the stranger's gaze, masking it as if he was tipping his hat at him, and to this day he didn't know what had triggered his memory. Was it a smell or a particular movement? He'd never know, but he'd felt compelled to turn around to take a better look.

Kelly Freed looked barely older than how Cooper remembered him. Had it really been fifteen years? Kelly wore a tan deputy's uniform, pants with a perfect crease down the front and his shirt tucked into them, a belt breaking up the two. Cooper couldn't resist remembering the body that filled up the rear of those slacks so perfectly, the bubble butt he'd worshiped all those years ago. When Kelly turned slightly, resting his hand on the counter as he waited for the shop girl to pick something out for him, there wasn't even a hint of a beer gut visible around the tight belt and gun holster. Cooper felt his jeans grow tight, and only then realized he was staring at the man, so he hurriedly averted his eyes and continued on his way, letting the door of the store fall shut.

He returned to the truck, his mind still on the man at the store.

"You look like you saw a ghost. You okay, Coop?"

Cooper looked up and remembered why he was in town. Izzie Conroy was smiling at him from the passenger seat, bags and packages all around her. "Yeah, I'm good," Cooper replied, not even believing it himself and hoping Izzie wouldn't inquire further. She was the foreman's wife and the owner's sister and Cooper liked her a lot, but she was a little too inquisitive for Cooper's taste. "You need to stop at Calley's?"

"Yup," Izzie replied. "She said the apples would be in today, and I want fruit for the kids. You know, maybe we should plant some apple trees by the river. The blossoms would look nice in spring, and we could probably grow enough for all the kids and the men at the crew house too. Everyone likes a nice juicy apple, right?"

"Sure," Cooper answered flatly. What he liked about Izzie was that she kept rambling, and as long as he nodded to agree with her from time to time, he didn't need to reply. For now, the talk about the ranch kept his mind off Kelly Freed. At least partially.

"Could you go inside, Coop? I'm all settled in here with everything else I bought. She knows what I ordered."

Cooper stopped the truck in front of the grocery store owned by Calley Haines. She delivered to the house, but occasionally, when her wholesalers were late, she had to come by a second time. Since they were in town now anyway, Izzie had decided they'd pick up the missing item from the delivery list.

Andy and Vicky, Calley's twins, were playing in the yard next to the shop and Noah, Calley's foster son, was leaning his bike against the side of the fence.

"Hi, Noah," Cooper greeted the seven-year-old. "How was school?"

Noah smiled. "I like my teacher."

"Well, that's a start. Is Calley inside?"

Noah shrugged. "Just got home from school."

They walked in together, where Noah's sixteen-year-old brother was stacking apples.

"Hey, Ryan." Cooper pointed at the apples. "I'm here for those. Don't know how many Blue River ordered, but I came to pick some up."

Ryan stopped what he was doing and walked behind the cash register, his actions the only acknowledgement that he'd actually heard Cooper. Ryan picked up a folder and started leafing through the contents, then put the folder away again before walking back to the apples and filling a small crate.

Cooper knew better than to try to coax words out of Ryan. Ryan occasionally lent a hand at the Blue River when they were short a few men, so it wasn't like they were strangers. It paid to give Ryan space. If you didn't get on his case, he was a hard worker. When Ryan handed him the crate, Cooper tried to make eye contact, but he didn't insist. Cooper knew all too well how to avoid it himself. "Thanks, Ryan. Tell Calley I stopped by for these, so she doesn't need to deliver them."

Ryan nodded almost imperceptibly, and Cooper walked out with his apples. He put them in the back of the truck before climbing in again.

"You planning on feeding an army with those apples, Izzie?"

Izzie grinned. "Six kids eat a lot of grub, Coop. And we do try to feed you guys *some* healthy stuff occasionally too."

Cooper just smiled and watched the road.

A sheriff's car passed them, and Cooper found himself trying to see whether it was Kelly behind the wheel. The truck was too high compared to the car, though, so he couldn't tell. He shook his head, trying to dispel the wicked thoughts that entered his mind.

"Are you in some kind of trouble, Coop?" Izzie asked, genuine concern in her voice.

"Nope," Cooper answered dismissively.

"I saw you looking at Deputy Freed when you walked out of the clothing store, and now at that car. Like you're worried about something."

"It's nothing, Izz." He couldn't just come out and tell Izzie that he knew what the deputy smelled like up close, how he felt under his hands, how he moaned…. Cooper closed his eyes just for a moment, then stared intently at the car driving away from them.

Izzie was the most open-minded of the women at the ranch. She'd been instrumental in her brother Hunter's acceptance of his love for Grant and had always stood by him through thick and thin. She was also the only one of the women who actually worked the ranch, although that had changed some after she'd had her two girls. Still, whenever they were hands short, she'd be the first to braid her impossibly long hair and saddle her horse to ride with them.

If Cooper could tell anyone at the ranch about his feelings, it would be her. She knew he was gay. Everyone who lived anywhere near St. Anthony eight years ago knew about the scandal, and after that, no closet was big enough to hold Coop. Izzie was no exception, yet they never talked about his private life. Basically, because he had none. Like most people who knew Cooper in his former life, Izzie never opened that can of worms. Unlike Tim, Izzie's brother-in-law, Cooper didn't go to the one gay bar he knew of, and he didn't usually go to the Barrel Run with the other ranch hands on Saturday night either.

"Kelly Freed seems nice enough. I think I'll vote for him," Izzie said resolutely. "He's cleaning up around here now Sheriff Hanson is retiring, and I think I trust him more than the other guy, who only seems to be moving back here for the election."

"Freed's not from around here either," Cooper said.

"I know," Izzie replied, apparently not perturbed by what Cooper said, "but he seems more genuine, and he's younger, more energetic. The other one looks like he'll park his butt in his chair and never leave it again. Deputy Freed is always around town, talking to people, helping them out, even with the smaller things. He rescued Davinia Lloyd's cat the other day, after she was stuck in a drainage pipe."

Cooper couldn't resist smiling. So Kelly was still doing that. Always helping people. He used to tease Kelly about that when they were still in law school, and at the time, Cooper's intentions of becoming a lawyer weren't exactly fueled by something as altruistic as helping his fellow man. After having grown up in abject poverty, he wanted to make money. Lots of it. Unlike Kelly, who was always going to be the one to rescue the kittens. Anything to make people like him. It had taken way too many years for Cooper to see things Kelly's way, and now it was too late. Now he had the life he deserved and so did Kelly. Karma was definitely a bitch.

Cooper chewed his thumb and then realized Izzie hadn't said anything in a while. He looked over at her. The window was rolled about halfway down, and the wind was blowing her dark-brown hair away from her face. She was smiling, her eyes narrowed against the sunlight and gusts of wind coming through the open window. Cooper's mood lightened when he thought about how much the image of Izzie reminded him of Tim's rescue dog, Maul, who looked just like that when he sat in her place. Must be nice to be so content, Cooper thought as he turned into the driveway to the Blue River Ranch. Suddenly, another image flashed through his mind, of Kelly borrowing a friend's convertible to drive them to the countryside between the end of term and Cooper's graduation from law school. Since Kelly had another two years to go, they knew their ways would part, but they wanted one more blissful day together. It was the end of an era for Cooper, although he didn't know it then.

Cooper felt his throat constrict, so he cleared it before parking the truck next to the biggest homestead.

— 2 —

KELLY FREED didn't like going on the campaign trail, but since he'd decided to run for office, he knew it was necessary. He always felt useless and wasteful while he was shaking hands and handing out flyers around the local shops in town. But today was Founder's Day, and everyone would be out in droves to walk the stalls and shop with a discount, so he'd get to introduce himself to a lot of people in a short time.

Kelly would much rather be working so he could let his actions speak. He had excellent contacts with the press, as they readily picked up on him arresting a criminal or busting someone for fraud. For them it was something to put in the local paper, and for Deputy Freed it was an opportunity to show the electorate that he meant business.

Kelly hadn't been a resident of Fremont County for that long, which was the reason he needed the exposure. Sheriff Hanson was retiring at the end of his term, and he'd made it abundantly clear to everyone who wanted to hear that he wanted Kelly to step into his shoes, but there was competition. Mario Bareillas had moved back to the county after leaving with slamming doors four years earlier, and he wasn't pulling punches. The fight with the current sheriff wasn't that long ago, and most people still remembered it, so anyone not entirely happy with how Hanson ran his ship was going to stand behind Bareillas.

Although Kelly Freed had been chief deputy for over a year and was basically doing Hanson's job, he wasn't a local boy like Bareillas. He'd forged himself a solid reputation for being forthright and honest, but he knew that doing the right thing didn't always get noticed right away, and karma took a while to kick in. So he smiled at the people he'd become familiar to in the last year and made sure they knew he was running for sheriff. By the time the election came around, he'd know whether moving here and working the way he had was paying off.

"Please vote!" he said to anyone taking a flyer from him. "Even if you don't vote for me, please show up. Make your vote count." He knew voter turnout was generally low for something like this, so he had to get them to fill out a ballot.

"Please vote!" Kelly looked up from the weathered hand that had just accepted the red-and-blue piece of paper, to the man it belonged to. "Cooper. Hi."

Cooper Nelson touched the brim of his Stetson and nodded. "Deputy Freed."

"Oh, come on. Call me Kelly. You make me feel like my father."

Half a smile appeared on Cooper's face, softening the lines and creasing the slightly coppery scruff surrounding his mouth. Although Cooper's general appearance showed evidence of a hard life and premature aging, Kelly had always been taken by the man's pale-blue eyes, which were never devoid of light. And he still had that perfect row of teeth that made the ladies swoon, something Kelly knew Cooper didn't give a hoot about.

"It's been ages since I've allowed myself to think of you that way, Kelly," Cooper replied.

"Like my father?"

Cooper chuckled. "Like my Kelly."

So Cooper was still a flirt. Who would have guessed? "Are you in town for a while or just picking up supplies?"

Cooper gestured over to the clothing store. "Need to pick out something decent to wear for the Conroy wedding."

Kelly nodded. "Tim told me about his brother coming back to the ranch to get married. You're invited, then?"

"No, I thought about crashing it. Since Old Mac's death, I'm the oldest ranch hand at the Blue River, and I figured I was entitled." He groaned. "Of course I was invited. Everyone who works there is invited."

"I've been asked to show up to keep the reporters at bay. Apparently Jack Conroy is tabloid fodder?"

"Country singer fresh out of rehab? You bet. But he's still the same old Jack."

"Good to know." Kelly wanted to keep on talking to Cooper, but he knew they both had better things to do.

"So are you bringing…?"

"No," Kelly answered curtly, knowing exactly what Cooper was aiming at.

"Did she move up here with you?"

"Yes, of course," Kelly said, not wanting the conversation to go that way. "Listen, I'm only going to be there in an official capacity, okay?"

Cooper nodded, his mouth tightening for a moment, and then it was relaxed again. "I'll see you around."

Kelly watched Cooper walk off, admiring his sinewy frame encased in worn jeans and a shirt that looked too big. He wondered what Cooper would buy to wear at the wedding and then shook his head. He didn't want to go there. He'd left those thoughts behind a long time ago and it was no use dwelling on them now, so he turned around and handed a flyer to another passerby, putting on his best game face.

LATER that night, all alone in bed, Kelly couldn't stop thinking about Cooper Nelson. When he moved to St. Anthony, he knew he was bound to bump into him sooner or later, but he'd been surprised it had taken him almost a year. Maybe the stories of Coop keeping to himself and practically living as a recluse were true. It was strange seeing Cooper again after fifteen years and realizing time hadn't been kind to the man.

The Cooper Nelson Kelly remembered was quite different from the one he'd bumped into that afternoon. Both the younger Cooper and the more mature one were hard to resist, though, so it was easy to let his mind stray to the first time he laid eyes on Cooper, back in law school.

Even before reaching the study hall, Kelly could hear a boisterous voice rising above the others.

"Yeah, but then you'd walk into the hallway, and there would be Tanker Overhead. I swear Overhead was her real last name, and she looked like a tanker, so the nickname stuck. She'd prowl the hallways and corner you at the lockers, so there was no way you could be late, or she'd report you. I swear...."

The door to the study hall squeaked when Kelly pushed it open, and all conversation stilled at the same time seven pairs of eyes looked his way. The silence was killing him. "Is this the study group for Professor Finkelstein's class?"

"And you are?" a guy sitting on top of a long mahogany table asked.

"Kelly Freed."

"Are you sure you're old enough to be in law school? College is on the other side of town."

"I'm twenty-two."

The guy stretched out his legs and jumped down from the table. With an insanely wide, bright white smile across over his face, he walked over to Kelly and held out his hand. "Cooper Nelson, and I'm a few years older than you. Welcome to the only way to succeed in Fink's class."

"Yeah, Coop, you should know. This is the fourth time you're taking it," one of the other guys said.

Cooper turned around. "That's why you need me here. I know all the loopholes by now. And it's not like I haven't passed his class before. I'm just doing it again to get a better average. Thanks to me, all of you will only need to take this class once."

"That's what you said last time, Coop," one of the girls said. She got up and walked over to Kelly. "Don't listen to him. He's got a high opinion of himself and absolutely no reason for it. He wants to do corporate law, because that's where the money is, but I told him he should become an ambulance chaser instead, because the way he lies without batting an eyelash—"

"I just sugarcoat the truth, darling," Cooper intervened, *wrapping his impossibly long arm around her tiny shoulders. "The world would be a prettier place if more people did that."*

"Hi, I'm Nina," the pretty dark-haired girl said as she shook Kelly's hand. *"Don't mind Cooper. He means well but forgets how he comes across sometimes."*

"So what are you going to be when you grow up?" Cooper asked, looking at his study hall group when a few of them laughed at his statement.

Kelly didn't like being the butt of anyone's jokes, but he'd been told this group was his best chance at beating the notoriously impossible Professor Finkelstein at his own game, so he knew he had to grin and bear it. "Law enforcement," he replied, trying to sound casual.

"Well, sheriff, sit down, listen, and learn."

Kelly turned his face into his pillow to stifle the grunt that escaped his lips as he came hard into his hand. He hadn't even made it as far as the memory of what happened after that first study group, of Cooper pushing him against the wall of the men's room and devouring him with a kiss that had made him come into his fine dress pants as if he was a teenager.

Kelly had been strangely enticed by Cooper's self-assuredness, which seemed to cross the boundary into arrogance all the time. They'd become friends, and occasionally Kelly had been allowed a glimpse into the quieter side of Cooper Nelson.

He got up from the bed for a quick wash and to check on the occupant of the room next door.

Nina was sleeping comfortably.

—3—

KELLY knew he didn't have time to lose. He was driving in the direction of the Blue River Ranch to see Cooper with the sole purpose of asking for his help. Damn, why didn't that man own a cell phone?

The last couple of hours had been tense, to say the least. Being called by Tim Conroy to a house where Rory McCown was holding John Delco at gunpoint was something his childhood dreams had been made of. All his years in law enforcement had taught him reality didn't live up to those dreams, though. For one, as shitty as his life was sometimes, he valued it too, and he didn't want to end up a statistic. He'd learned to be confident and calm in tense situations, but he knew, where guns were concerned, especially held by two men with impulse control issues, you could never be too careful.

Everything had turned out okay, with nobody seriously hurt, Delco in custody and Rory sent home with Tim on the promise he'd present himself to his parole officer the next day, but he knew this was only the beginning of the story.

When Kelly had first met Tim, he'd taken a liking to him almost immediately. Tim was so concerned about Rory. Kelly thought it was endearing, and he'd seen an opportunity to go a little beyond his job description. He'd promised Tim he'd keep an eye out for the people trying to make life hard for the ex-con Tim had obviously fallen hard for. The feeling that Tim loved Rory was even more clear when he'd helped rescue Rory from a flood by taking him to the hospital in his chopper.

When Tim showed up at the sheriff's office asking for help because Rory had gone after Delco, who'd been taunting him since he'd been let out of prison, Kelly immediately jumped into action.

Maybe that wasn't one of his best ideas, but fortunately he'd been able to defuse the situation and managed to keep the two men from shooting each other.

Questioning both men at the police station, he'd realized Rory was quiet and shy, apologetic to everyone for letting the situation get out of hand and oh so sorry. Delco, on the other hand, was a psycho, so convinced of his own right and so full of hate toward Rory that he'd made Kelly's neck hair stand up. He was going to do his utmost to make sure Delco was going back to jail.

Which left Rory's predicament.

The fact that Kelly had seen Rory wield a rifle was enough to send him straight back to prison. He was just five days shy of the end of his parole, but nevertheless, he was in violation of this parole, and his parole officer was a guy who didn't pull punches. Kelly, as a future sheriff, had to lean hard on known criminals, which was what Rory was considered to be. Yet all he wanted to do was cut Rory some slack. More than the parole officer, Kelly believed in rehabilitating ex-cons, and from what he'd seen, Rory was doing an amazing job keeping to the straight and narrow after a life filled with petty crime. Until that afternoon. Now Rory was going to need all the help he could get, which was the reason he was driving to the Blue River Ranch to see Cooper.

Kelly stopped his car near one of the barns where he still saw light and killed the engine. He hoped Cooper would at least talk to him.

When he walked into the barn, he saw Grant, the ranch owner's live-in lover, wiping down his horse by the light of the bare bulb hanging from the rafters. "Hey, Kelly, what's up?"

"I'm looking for Cooper Nelson."

Grant pointed his thumb over his shoulder. "Woodshed. We spent most of the afternoon taking down a big tree, so he's probably finishing up in there."

"Thanks," Kelly said, tipping his hat and turning to walk out.

"I heard there was trouble with Rory this afternoon," Grant said.

Kelly turned around again, nodding hesitantly. "Can't say much. But yeah, he's in trouble. If it were up to me, I'd let it slide, but there are others who don't agree with me. Talk to Tim."

Grant nodded and let Kelly leave.

KELLY found his way to the woodshed by walking toward the bright yellow light shining from its open door. When he walked in, Cooper was sweeping the last of the woodchips from the back of the tractor trailer. Despite the quickly cooling autumn air, he looked sweaty and hot.

"What are you doing here?" Cooper asked gruffly after letting Kelly wait for several long seconds.

"Looking for you. Can we talk somewhere? Privately."

"What is this about?"

Kelly couldn't help hearing the unspoken dismissal. Cooper clearly had no desire to talk to him. He decided to cut to the chase. "It's Rory McCown. He broke his parole this afternoon, and he needs your help."

"That's what public defenders are for," Cooper replied as he continued to sweep the floor.

"And his public defender is Sean Goddard," Kelly said without further explanation.

"Norm's son? Is he even out of diapers yet?"

Kelly chuckled, more out of nervousness than because he found what Cooper had said funny. "Just passed the bar. You know his dad, right?"

Cooper nodded. "Sure I do. He was my biggest competition when I first came to town. Big shark of a small-town lawyer, but he was gracious enough to not fight me over my piece of the pie."

"Well, Sean's a little out of his depth against Emmett Love."

"Jeezus," Cooper replied. "Emmett Love? Carries the name, but doesn't know what it means. He used to hold the record for the most parolees returned to prison. Don't suspect he got any more lenient in his old age?"

"Nope," Kelly replied. "And he's got it in for Rory's hide."

"Figures."

"Rory needs your help, Coop."

"Can't do it. I'm not a lawyer anymore."

"You'll always be a lawyer, Coop. You were the most amazing legal mind I've ever met."

Cooper looked at Kelly from under his hat. "The emphasis on 'were.' They disbarred me, Kelly. Stripped me of my rights. I couldn't represent Rory if I wanted to. And I don't want to."

"You don't need to represent him. He just needs some advice. And to know someone is on his side."

"We're all on his side," Cooper was quick to reply, standing tall, his broom by his side. "He's Tim's man. He used to work here. I like him. But I don't see what I can do for him."

Kelly smiled. If his memory didn't betray him, the sparkle he saw appearing in Cooper's eye was the first sign of Cooper becoming excited about something, although the rest of his body still dismissed him. "He needs someone to show him he's worth fighting for. And he needs someone to talk Emmett Love under the table. According to your reputation, you're the only guy in this town who can do that."

"Naah," Cooper said, putting his broom aside. "I was never interested in him enough to talk him under a table." Cooper wiggled his eyebrows, and Kelly was transported back to the law library, their study group, and their favorite place for sex. On top of or under the long tables.

Damn, Cooper!

"Pretend," Kelly ordered. "Just this one time and just for Rory's sake. Love is hell-bent on sending him back to state prison for a year. I'll settle for him serving the remainder of his parole, not his prison sentence, in county jail."

"But it's not your call, is it?"

"No, that's something the county prosecutor has to decide, but he'll listen to Love. If Love recommends the shortest possible sentence, he'll follow, and then all Sean Goddard needs to do is agree with it. The judge will follow the prosecutor. You know that."

"I suppose it's worth a shot."

Kelly had the overwhelming urge to wrap Cooper in his arms and kiss him senseless. He thought he could smell Cooper's sweaty, manly scent from where he was standing, but considering the overwhelming woodsy aroma emanating from everything else in the shed, he figured it was just his imagination. When he took one step toward Cooper, the man tensed up, though, so he decided a butch punch to the arm would be enough. "I knew I could convince you."

Cooper shrugged. "Emmett Love probably won't even let me in."

"Don't know if you don't try. And if he doesn't, at least Rory will know you support him."

"Fair enough," Cooper said. "What time do you want me there?"

—4—

GOD, it felt good to stand up to Emmett Love.

When he was still a lawyer, Cooper had talked the arrogant parole officer down from his pedestal more than a few times. In fact at one point, Cooper had overheard Emmett mutter whether Cooper couldn't find someone else to harass. That was the time when Cooper could simply smile at him and feel smug. Nowadays he'd probably feel guilty. Then again, it did feel good to challenge him again, to make him think about his personal crusade against repeat offenders and see Rory McCown for what he was: a guy who'd been dealt a bad hand all his life and who was now trying very hard to defend what he'd been fighting for since his last release.

Cooper had a soft spot for Rory. Not in a romantic or even a lustful sense, but he admired the guy. He'd defended a lot of petty criminals in his day, and he'd never met a guy like Rory. Rory had no problem getting up early and working hard. He kept his head low and never complained. Rory wasn't the greatest team player, but Cooper had respect for that too. Most of the time, Cooper also preferred working on his own. And Cooper liked men who said little but picked up on everything. Rory had gained a lot of respect with the other ranch hands when two horses and a foal had broken loose during a violent thunderstorm, and he'd kitted out an entire barn and arranged for breakfast too. Rory had a good head on his shoulders, which was why Cooper was surprised he always seemed to get caught whenever he did something wrong. And why he figured Rory needed a break.

Silently, Cooper also liked that Rory had found some happiness with Tim Conroy, who had always been his favorite of the Conroy brothers. He had no doubt that Tim's glass-half-full attitude was what had kept Rory on the straight and narrow all this time.

Well, Cooper had had his say, and now all they could do was wait for the judge's decision. His mind was on Rory and Tim, though, so he kept himself busy with mindless work, like mending tack.

"You're a hard man to find sometimes."

Cooper looked up with a start. This was the second day in a row that Kelly had shown up at the ranch. He scanned Kelly quickly—sheepskin coat, jeans, boots, hell, he looked more like a cowboy than Cooper did—and Cooper knew he couldn't let his gaze linger. "It's a big ranch, but a hand like me can only be found in a few places," Cooper said, somehow managing to make his voice sound like he wasn't surprised to see the deputy.

"I had to ask around for you. Again," Kelly replied, with a slightly embarrassed smile.

"I'm going to get a reputation, which isn't a problem for me, but you're a married man, Deputy Freed. And you're running for sheriff."

"Listen." Kelly's face turned sad, Cooper thought. "Your boss's man doesn't seem like the kind to spread rumors. I think I'm safe. Besides, I don't need to lie to say that whatever rumors get spread are untrue."

"Fair enough." Cooper felt Kelly deserved to be cut some slack. It was kind of nice to see he was still as much of a softy as he'd been in college. "So why are you here?" Cooper didn't wait for an answer but turned around to put the saddle he'd just mended back on the rack.

"I wanted to say thank you. For talking to Emmett Love."

"Won't be much use if he sends Rory back to prison for a year. It would gut him. And Tim too." Cooper turned back to the table to clear away the saddle grease and the rags he'd used for the job. "I admit it was nice to be there for them. They both deserve the break." He looked straight at Kelly. "Now why are you really here?"

Kelly raised his eyebrows in surprise. "I…. You…."

Cooper chuckled, breaking the tension.

It gave Kelly time to recompose himself. "I wanted to ask you over for dinner. Saturday. I told Nina about you, and she wants to see you."

"So it's Nina and not you?"

"I didn't say that, Coop."

Cooper chuckled. He didn't mean to let Kelly see his feelings like that. He could only hope that Kelly was still as obtuse about what Cooper felt for him as he had been at the start of their relationship. Back in college, Cooper had needed to spell it out for Kelly as well. "What time do you want me there?" He had to admit he wanted to see Nina again. He couldn't imagine her as the dutiful sheriff's wife who baked and cooked and followed her husband around to wherever he got work. He was sure she had ways of keeping busy, and it wasn't with kids. Cooper had asked around, and the future sheriff didn't have offspring. "So give me a time, and I'll be there."

"Whenever you're done with work," Kelly replied.

Cooper nodded. "I'll be there," he said again and watched Kelly leave. He started clearing up the rest of his stuff so the barn was immaculate again.

KELLY walked out and brought his hand to his nose. Was saddle grease becoming the smell he associated with Cooper? On a whim, he'd grabbed one of the cloths Cooper had used from the small table when Cooper turned around to put the saddle away. The barn had smelled of saddle grease when he'd walked in, and it had given him a strong memory flash of teaching Cooper to ride at his parents' ranch.

When Kelly met Cooper, he'd found out he was a city boy and not from the right side of town. He was the oldest son of a blue-collar single mother who worked three jobs to keep her head above water. Cooper's reaction had been to get a stellar grade point average at his less than stellar school, and he'd applied for a scholarship at an Ivy League university. Although he'd had to work his ass off all through college, his determination was singular, and he hadn't looked back.

Kelly came from the right side of the tracks, with a father who had married a rich rancher's daughter and had given up a burgeoning law enforcement career to take over his father-in-law's place. Their kids were spoiled rotten, and middle child Kelly was no exception. He'd gone to a posh private school and had made his dad proud by doing well enough at his father's alma mater to be let into law school.

Although his grandfather had dreamed of a big-shot lawyer grandson, Kelly had followed in his father's footsteps and had declared interest in law enforcement rather than a law practice.

One spring break, Kelly had taken Cooper back home to the ranch with him. They'd been inseparable for the whole year and didn't want to be without each other away from school either. They'd had to sleep in separate rooms, of course, and keep their hands off each other while they were in the company of Kelly's family, but the sneaking around had its own merits. Kelly had taught Cooper the basics of mounting and riding a horse so they could go trekking to the more remote areas of the ranch where they could indulge in some more intimate interactions, like skinny-dipping in the lake and fucking al fresco.

That was how they were found out. Betsy, Kelly's sister, had caught them together naked. They weren't doing anything too intimate, but she'd freaked and run home to Daddy, who had given Kelly a stern talking-to later that evening.

Kelly clearly remembered the awkward conversation with his father.

"Why did you bring that boy here, Kelly?"

"He's not a boy, Dad. He's five years older than me, and I stopped being a boy even before I went away to college. You said so yourself."

"He's put things in your mind. Things.... Things a young man shouldn't know about."

"What are you talking about?"

"Going skinny-dipping, and.... What your sister saw." He dismissively shook his hand at Kelly.

"What did Betsy see? We were swimming in the lake, that's all she saw, I swear! If she said she saw more, she was lying." He wanted to add that nothing more had happened, but that would be a lie. Nothing had happened that afternoon because Betsy had caught them before anything could happen, but he knew from earlier days that if she'd come half an hour later, she would have caught them fucking.

His father frowned. "There was more to see?"

"No! Dad, we were swimming."

"Naked."

"We didn't bring trunks. Cooper doesn't even have any. And we hadn't counted on going swimming."

"Why did you ride there, then?"

"To show Cooper around. And to practice his riding." Well that wasn't a lie. At least not if you considered all forms of "riding."

"What are you smiling at?"

Kelly hadn't even realized his expression had changed. "At how stupid it was of Bets to come running to you about this," Kelly said, glad he'd gotten a lot of practice talking himself out of a difficult spot in mock court this last year. "You'd think she'd be used to seeing a man naked now she's practically married herself."

His father was fuming. "I don't know the kind of women you hang with at law school, Kelly, but Elizabeth is a respectable girl. Of course she was shocked! There's a difference between seeing your brother naked and seeing a strange man."

Kelly tried to keep his face neutral. His oldest sister was a prude, so he could believe she was shocked at seeing them naked. She used to run away screaming when they were kids too, and Kelly and his youngest sister would run around naked between their bedrooms and the bathroom. "She'll get over it, Dad."

Freed senior shook his head. "I want Mr. Nelson out of here. Tonight. Before dinner. Give him some money for the return trip and some extra to get dinner on the bus."

"What?" Kelly shouted.

"He's not our kind of people, Kelly. Even you can see that."

Kelly forced himself to reply calmly. "He's going to be the most amazing lawyer to come out of his class. He's so smart it doesn't matter that he didn't come from a private school, Dad. He tutors me, so don't look down on where he comes from. He knows what it's like to work for what you want." He knew he was giving away too much by defending Cooper so vehemently, but dammit, he loved this man. He took a deep breath to calm himself, though. "And he's a guest in this house. You don't throw a guest out of your home. That wouldn't be very polite."

"Oh, Kelly," his father lamented. "You make it sound like he hung the moon and the stars." He turned to face the window. "My mind is made up," he said with unmistakable finality. "Go change so you're ready for when your mother calls you to dinner, but ask Mr. Nelson to leave first."

"No," Kelly said.

"No?"

"No. If he leaves, so will I."

Kelly smiled at the memory of his show of bravery. He'd packed his bags and told Cooper they were going back to school. During the long car trip, the real reason had come out slowly. It had taken a lot of persuasion on Cooper's part to make Kelly say it. After that, Cooper had grown quiet. Kelly remembered not knowing how to react to Cooper's silence. Once they were back at school, everything returned to normal. They never talked about the incident, and Kelly knew better than to take Cooper home again. He limited his visits to the Freed homestead to just enough to keep his mother happy, and after Cooper graduated, the problem solved itself. Kelly's relationship with his parents never quite recovered, though, not even after he brought Nina home with him. The reason for that was simple. Kelly stopped seeing his father as the god he'd been for all of his young life. He just saw a narrow-minded, bigoted man who would never accept his son for who he was.

—5—

As HE got into one of the Blue River Ranch trucks, Cooper took in a cleansing breath. He felt uncomfortable in his new pants and shirt, and his jaw itched from shaving his scruff off.

The full impact of the invitation hadn't sunk in until Kelly had left. He hadn't seen Nina in fifteen years, and he and Nina went back further than Kelly and Nina did. Up until the time they met Kelly, Nina had been his partner in crime. They'd met in college and had been accepted to the same law school. She was hell-bent on saving the world. She wanted a career in politics so she could represent "the people" and would do that via the proven route: by becoming an assistant district attorney, and then she'd run for office. She had it all planned out. Back then, Cooper didn't understand her. Why go to all the trouble of being first in your class only to take on a job that paid peanuts? He was aiming for the big money. This didn't mean he didn't like her or even respect her. She was so persuasive, he was sure she could have talked him, Cooper, gold-card carrying and very "out" gay man, into her bed. She never did, though, and Cooper was sort of glad of that. It was as if she wasn't interested in Cooper that way. Maybe having a gay man in her bed wasn't good for her resume, or maybe he couldn't do enough to advance her career. He didn't know and didn't care. She was a great friend anyway.

And the direct reason why he left Kelly behind.

Okay, one of the reasons.

Nina and Kelly had hit it off immediately. The first few weeks at law school, Kelly followed Nina around like a puppy, and Cooper often wondered if the man would ever have the balls to make it in the real world on his own. She got him into the editing staff of the Law Review and helped him pick his electives, then got him a very low-key job at the law firm she was interning at, saying it would look good on his resume. Cooper watched it all with amusement and then went for the kill. Within a week, Kelly was in his bed instead of Nina's, and they became the three musketeers of their law campus.

Fifteen years ago, Nina was pretty, but too petite to be a killer in the looks department. She wore insanely high heels and flashy makeup, which always looked immaculate, and it gave her that edge. Her short dark hair and miniskirts made her look quirky, but nobody messed with her. Although she only just reached his shoulder, she had once decked a fellow student who was a bit of a jock and had made snide remarks about female lawyers and how they slept their way into the big law offices. They always watched their words around her after that. Last he'd heard of the jock, he was writing briefs for some minor corporation.

Cooper smiled as he turned out of town and down the road that led to Kelly's house. It was going to be strange to be together again, the three of them. He'd been the one to leave, and he knew Kelly and Nina had stayed together, even gotten married. He'd read about it in the law school alumni news, mostly because, by the time of their marriage, Nina was well on her way down her chosen career path. He had no idea what had happened after that. Nina had clearly not run for office. No matter how estranged Cooper was from the world of law, he'd have noticed that. In fact, Kelly was the only one who had gotten his dream, now that he was a shoo-in for the sheriff's position.

Parking the truck, Cooper eyed the house. It was a beautifully maintained wood ranch house, all one story. It had a porch all around, but no flowers or other embellishments. The yard looked like it could use some maintenance, but Cooper figured Kelly had other priorities. When he killed the engine and got out, a young man Cooper didn't know exited the front door and walked along the porch to where Cooper was standing.

"May I help you?"

"I'm Cooper Nelson. Kelly and Nina invited me to dinner."

"Of course," the young man said, nodding. "I'm Teo. Come right in. Can I get you a drink?"

"A beer would be nice, thanks."

Teo held the door open and let Cooper in. "It's straight through to the back." He pointed down the hallway and disappeared to what Cooper thought was probably the kitchen. After the door closed behind Teo, leaving Cooper alone in the hallway, Cooper walked toward the back of the house. Passing through a screen door, he arrived on the back porch. He turned around after hearing a whirring sound.

"Hi, Coop."

Cooper felt his throat constrict. There, with her back to the wall and strapped into a high-tech electrical wheelchair, sat a woman Cooper would have barely recognized if it hadn't been for her short raven-black hair, immaculate makeup, and bright-red nail polish. She was only a ghost of the friend he'd left behind fifteen years ago.

"Nina," Cooper replied, swallowing away the lump.

"I know," she said, clearly with some effort. "Not the reunion I expected either." She paused to take a few breaths. "But I wanted to bite the bullet and get it over with."

Cooper nodded, trying to find words that somehow eluded him.

"At least I silenced you. Not something I've ever been able to do."

Cooper took a tentative step forward. Damn! This was his friend. And she was suffering. Why couldn't he just cheer her up like he always used to?

"Sit, Coop. I don't bite. Anymore."

Cooper chuckled, and at that moment, Teo walked in with Cooper's beer. He put a coaster on the table and set the sweating bottle on it. He held out a glass to Cooper. "Will you pour, or shall I?"

"No, that's okay. I'm a ranch hand. We drink from the bottle."

Teo nodded. "Nina, is there anything you need before I leave you two to talk?"

"Just a refill." She gestured her head at a glass with a straw in a holder near her shoulder.

"Be right back," Teo announced as he took the glass and retreated to the kitchen.

"Okay, ask," Nina ordered, looking directly at Cooper.

Cooper sat down on the chair next to Nina and took a swig from his beer to stall for time. Teo quickly returned to replace the cup, and turned the straw so Nina could reach it before disappearing again.

Cooper didn't know what to ask. He wanted to know everything that had happened, but at the same time he realized that a lot of time had passed, and no single question would cover everything and let Nina feel he still cared. He settled for "I never realized I missed you until now, Nee."

"Bullshit," Nina replied, chuckling without moving her shoulders. She then turned serious. "Bet you didn't miss me half as much as Kelly missed you."

Cooper regained his composure, realizing that, underneath the fragile-looking shell in the wheelchair, she was still his college friend. "Now who's talking out of her ass?"

"Oh no, that was always *your* talent, Cooper."

Cooper raised his hand, wanting to put it on top of Nina's, but then pulled it back. He looked up at her, realizing what it must have seemed like.

"You can touch me, Coop. I won't break. I like being touched. I guess that comes from not being able to touch anyone on my own anymore."

A little hesitantly, Cooper put his hand over Nina's emaciated one. To his surprise, it felt warm, so he snaked his fingers underneath hers until he was truly holding her hand.

"That's nice."

Cooper smiled. "You always used to have such cold hands. I couldn't count the amount of times I had to warm them."

"Massachusetts winters are cold," Nina said with a smile.

"So are Idaho winters."

"I know," she said. "I've lived through my first house confinement. The wheelchair doesn't like snow, but I do. I feel sorry for poor Teo for having to dig through the sludge to get groceries, though."

"So Teo is your nurse?"

"Nurse, minder, housekeeper, cook, companion, you name it."

Cooper thought she looked a little sad, so he gently squeezed her hand.

"Kelly takes good care of me, but a husband shouldn't be a caretaker too. You can't argue with the person who needs to wipe your ass."

Cooper smiled, but the conversation made him uncomfortable. He hated seeing Nina so vulnerable. And although he had always known how much Nina loved Kelly, it was a painful reminder when she called him her husband.

"He's here," she announced. "Kelly," she explained. "I'm not surprised something came up that needed his immediate attention around the time you were going to arrive. I think he wanted to give us a little time to get reacquainted."

"He's inside?" Cooper asked, feeling like an idiot because he'd been so preoccupied with his own emotions he hadn't even noticed.

"He's talking to Teo. One thing that still works about me is my hearing."

Cooper tried to hear what they were saying, and then Kelly briefly came into view through the screen door separating the kitchen from the porch. Kelly was smiling teasingly, dodging a towel Teo was flicking at him. Cooper felt a pang of jealousy ten times larger than the one he'd felt earlier with Nina. Was this Nina's compromise? A boy toy for Kelly and a nurse for her all in one?

"Cooper?"

It was Nina's voice, so Cooper looked at her.

"Everything okay?"

"Yeah, yeah."

At that moment, the screen door opened, and Kelly walked out, wearing jeans and a plaid shirt and looking every bit the cowboy. "Teo said you'd arrived already." He looked at Nina. "And you've had a chance to catch up some with Nina?"

"A little," Cooper answered. He peeled his eyes off Kelly, knowing Nina would catch on immediately if his gaze lingered.

"So he knows what happened to you?" he asked Nina.

"No, we hadn't gotten to that point yet."

Kelly took Nina's hand in his and caressed it lovingly. "Maybe you should, because the tension here on the porch? Damn, you could cut it with a knife."

Nina smiled, and Cooper took another swig from his beer bottle. When he put it back on the coaster, Teo walked in with a platter of tortilla chips and salsa. Cooper wished he'd stay in the kitchen so they could get the talk over with.

"Dinner will be ready in about half an hour," Teo announced.

"I'll bring Nina inside then, so you can concentrate on the food," Kelly told Teo, and Cooper was glad that this meant it would probably the three of them for at least half an hour.

"Does anyone need more drinks?" Teo asked.

"I'll get them if we need them, thanks," Kelly replied with a million-watt smile.

Nobody said anything until Teo was back inside. Then Nina took in a breath. "I have motor neuron disease," she announced. "Stephen Hawking, but without the spectacular mind."

"That's debatable," Kelly quipped.

Cooper noticed there wasn't the sadness in Kelly's eyes that he expected. He didn't know much about what Nina had, but looking at her sitting there, he'd be devastated if it were his life partner afflicted like that. He looked at Kelly's thumb, caressing the clearly visible tendons of Nina's still hand.

"I got it younger than most people, and it progressed slower than with most people too," Nina continued. "Which simply means the torture lasts longer. When I was diagnosed, they gave me three years, but that was eight years ago. I'm still more mobile than Mr. Hawking, although pretty soon my neck and facial muscles will start to give out and I'll need a ventilator. But as you can see, I'm not dead yet."

Nina was still smiling, and Cooper realized her smile crushed him more than it would if she'd looked sad. "I'm sorry" was all Cooper could manage.

"Sorry I'm not dead yet, or sorry this happened to me?"

If this question had come from anyone other than Nina, it might have sounded accusatory, but this was Nina: brash and in your face.

Cooper took it to mean he was still part of the inner circle and could be yanked around a bit more than the average stranger. "Sorry you got sick," he corrected himself. "Not sorry to see you still alive. I'm glad we could get together again."

"The three musketeers unite," Kelly said with an overly broad smile. "Have some salsa."

Cooper took some out of politeness, but he didn't feel hungry. Nina, his Nina, their Nina, was living on borrowed time, and all he could think of was that he'd missed out on so much.

"Do you want to know the whole story or just the highlights?" Nina asked.

Cooper swallowed hard. How long was the torture going to last? Then again, this was the torture Nina and Kelly lived with every day. The least he could do was let them tell their story. "Anything you want me to know is fine."

Kelly offered Nina a corn chip, but she declined wordlessly. "You promised you'd eat, Nee."

"Yes, I did, but not this. Besides, Coop needs to know the whole story, and it's hard enough for me to talk a lot, let alone if I need to spend energy eating as well."

"I'll chime in when you get tired," Kelly assured her.

"It all started when I got pregnant. I was working for the DA's office, and we didn't exactly plan the pregnancy." She looked at Kelly, who squeezed her hand, then moved her eyes back to Cooper. "I was tired all the time and felt weak. Sometimes I could barely make it up the stairs, and courtrooms have a lot of stairs. The doctors kept telling me it was because of the pregnancy and promised me it would all get better by the second half, but it didn't. They started testing me for everything from lupus to MS, but nothing turned up. Then our son was born."

Cooper swallowed and hoped they hadn't noticed. So they had a son together. Where was the child now?

"He was born early, and there was clearly something wrong with him," Kelly said, taking over from Nina. "He lived for only a few hours."

For the first time, he saw sadness in Nina's eyes, but Kelly's were actually brimming with tears. Kelly rubbed Nina's hands more vigorously.

"They asked us for an autopsy, and I said yes," Nina continued. "I wanted to know what was wrong. As luck would have it—if you can call it luck—they figured out he had congenital motor neuron disease. I gave my bad genes to him, and it killed him."

Cooper didn't know more about genetics than what he'd picked up during a few medical trials he'd done, but he knew the basics. "But if you gave the gene to him, that means you were born with it too."

"Mine was a spontaneous mutation and didn't express as much as in our boy," Nina explained. "I got symptoms much later than he did. It's more complicated than that, but to fully understand it you need a medical degree."

"I'm sorry you had to go through that." Cooper hated that all he seemed to do was apologize, but he didn't know what else to say.

"It was a long time ago, Coop."

Kelly got up from his seat. "Let's get you inside. Teo will have dinner ready, I think." He moved the chair he'd been sitting on so Nina could maneuver her wheelchair with the most minute movements of her hand.

Cooper stayed on the porch as Kelly helped his wife to go inside. He didn't know if he could survive an entire evening with them. He still loved Kelly so much it hurt, but he loved Nina too, and he could see the love they had for each other. There would never be any room for him, not when Nina needed Kelly this much. And Cooper knew he'd never come between them.

"Hey, you coming?"

Cooper looked at Kelly holding the screen door open for him. His knees were shaking, but he managed to walk toward Kelly without swaggering. When Kelly put his hand between his shoulder blades, Cooper wanted to turn into the embrace, sink into Kelly's warmth, but he didn't. Instead, he put on his game face and walked forward.

—6—

KELLY picked Nina's light frame up out of her wheelchair, spun around, and gently put her on the bed Teo had turned down before Kelly had told him he had Nina covered. Although most days Teo took care of Nina's evening routine, Kelly's movements showed the fluidity of years of practice. While he undressed her and changed her into her nightgown, his thoughts were on the road they'd traveled together from the first symptoms to the state she was in now. He was grateful he'd never really had a physical attraction to her body, because what was left of it was none too appealing, and it made it easier for him to care for her. It didn't mean he didn't love her. Even when they still slept together, he enjoyed the physical closeness, the warm body, and the way she looked at him much more than the sex. She was a true companion and a great conversationalist. It wasn't an ordeal to spend time with her, and he'd never regretted marrying her.

"You miss him, don't you?" Nina asked, returning Kelly's thoughts to the present.

"Who?"

Nina sighed, her eyes closing slowly only to open again much faster. "Cooper, you dork."

"Cooper was just here." He tried to sound cheerful, although he didn't feel it, because Nina was right. Cooper had barely left, and he already missed his presence.

She looked at him as if he was an idiot, and Kelly felt like one for trying to hide his feelings from Nina.

"It's nice to be living closer to him again."

Nina shook her head, as if to say she knew he was still not telling the truth.

"Yes, I missed him, Nee."

"So, go after him. You'll probably catch him before he goes to bed. Tell him how you feel."

"What?" Kelly shook his head. "That's stupid. It's been fifteen years. He left and met the love of his life. If he looks mournful, it's because he's still grieving his DA."

Nina's mouth went thin. "If I could, I'd grab your shoulders and shake you."

Kelly grabbed the oxygen mask from its peg and tried to put it over Nina's mouth.

"Don't you dare gag me with that, Kelly Freed."

Kelly pulled it away from her face.

"I know you don't want to hear this, but I'm not going to be around forever. If you don't talk to Cooper now, you'll regret it for the rest of your life. I'm giving you permission to pursue him, Kelly."

"But you're my wife. I vowed to take care of you in sickness and in health." Kelly swallowed away the tears he'd been fighting successfully for most of the stressful evening. He knew he was losing the battle now.

"And as selfish as I am, I know you'll do just that. But don't let Cooper get away this time. You two need each other, and Cooper and I have always been close. He'll have to tolerate me, but somehow I don't think that'll be a problem."

"And how will that make *you* feel?"

Kelly couldn't hold her gaze, because instead of answering right away, she was piercing him with her eyes.

"I've always been your second choice. I've been fine with that thought for fifteen years, Kells. When my sister still dared to show her face, she always told me how she was jealous of me being married to my best friend. I never dared to tell her I had two best friends. Before you, there was Cooper. When Cooper seduced you, I resigned myself to being the fag hag. Everything extra was a bonus. When he left and we remained close, I figured I still had you. You're the best husband I could have ever had."

"You deserve better. You deserve a man who really loves you. All of you."

"And how long would that perfect man have stayed around after I got sick?"

Kelly shrugged.

"My sister was right, you know. A good friend is better than a lousy husband. You stayed around when I got worse. You're still here, taking care of me, and I hope you won't leave me now either." She stopped to catch her breath. It betrayed how much it moved her. "I think I owe it to you to tell you to go get your man. You've waited long enough."

Kelly was standing next to Nina's bed, cheeks wet with tears. He let go of Nina's hand to wipe his face, but it didn't make him feel better. He couldn't run out of the room to go to Cooper, no matter how much he yearned to. Nina was his rock, his anchor, and he couldn't leave her, no matter how much she urged him on. "I'll talk to him tomorrow."

Nina sighed. Even though her limited mobility didn't allow much body language anymore, Kelly could tell she was frustrated with him.

"Nee, *if* he returns my feelings, then they'll still be there in the morning. *If.*"

"Just don't forget to give him a chance for the *when* too."

Kelly nodded, holding up the oxygen mask Nina needed during her sleep. "Night," she dismissed him. He kissed her on the lips before setting up the breathing aid and tucking her in warmly. Then he walked back to his own room, where he changed into his pajamas and crawled into his own bed. As he lay awake, all he could think about was Cooper and how he needed him back in his life, but also about all the time that had passed and everything that had happened. Was Nina right? Did Cooper still have feelings for him? And if he did, could they start up their relationship again? What would the town think of their sheriff being gay? Not to mention married and not asking for a divorce. No, divorce was out of the question.

Sleep kept evading Kelly, so he got up again and walked to his closet. At the bottom stood a cardboard box he hadn't unpacked yet. His journals. He picked out 1996 and opened it, knowing what he'd find. He hadn't looked at the pictures of the three of them since Cooper left. There they were, all three of them, skinnier, healthier, and without gray streaks in their hair. Especially Cooper looked a lot younger, with reddish-brown hair that curled over his forehead and a wicked smile on his face. His arm was around Nina, but his hand was in Kelly's dirty blond hair, and the way he looked at Kelly over Nina's shoulder spoke volumes. That was way back when they loved each other so much they couldn't stand being apart for more than a few hours. The memories spread warmth through Kelly's stomach, but chills on the back of his neck. At the time, it seemed only natural that they were going to spend the rest of their lives together. But just a few weeks later, Cooper accepted a job halfway across the country and left Nina and Kelly behind. Kelly was so gutted, he almost blew his year, and if it hadn't been for Nina, he would have.

That's why he couldn't go back to Cooper. He needed someone he could depend upon, especially if he was going to start something with a man again. No matter how much Cooper had reawakened his flame, he couldn't risk it.

Kelly went back to bed and rolled himself into his duvet. He grabbed the second pillow and hugged it, feeling warm and secure enough to fall asleep.

—7—

ALTHOUGH Kelly had been to the ranch two nights in a row before the dinner invitation, after the Saturday visit to his house, Cooper hadn't seen Kelly all week. He'd been busy, getting the Blue River Ranch in tiptop shape for the society wedding of the year, but it had still given him time to miss his favorite deputy. It didn't matter that, after meeting Nina again, he'd told himself he couldn't pursue Kelly anymore. Kelly was still on his mind more than he liked.

As the day of the wedding neared and overnight guests started arriving, Cooper became more anxious. Kelly was going to be there, and since it wasn't a huge wedding where guests were concerned, a lot of not-so-welcome guests in the form of reporters were expected to turn up. It was Kelly's job to keep them at bay. Once they'd been given a small glimpse of Jack Conroy and his bride and Kelly and his men had orderly escorted them off the property, Kelly would have to stick around to make sure they didn't return. At that time, Cooper was sure he'd bump into the man, intentional or not. Part of him was looking forward to it. Another part was thinking of skipping the wedding altogether.

On the day itself, Cooper stood to the side, hugging a glass of champagne and just observing the crowd. This used to be one of his favorite pastimes: people watching. It had taught him a lot about what made people tick, and this had come in handy in his former life, when he was still a litigator. Those days were long gone. Life was a lot simpler now, and there was a lot less need for observation. Occasionally he couldn't help himself, though, especially when he was trying to alleviate boredom or like this, when he was an outsider in a large crowd of people, most of whom he barely knew.

At one time he would have been the life of the party—at college he often was—but too much had happened between then and now, and these days he preferred blending into the crowd. It was less stressful and meant he could leave when he felt like it.

Right now, Cooper didn't want to leave, though. His line of vision was interrupted by Deputy Sheriff Kelly Freed, in full dress uniform, kindly but firmly telling the reporters trying to get sound bites from the newlyweds to buzz off. He was patient and calm, but sported a don't-mess-with-me look that convinced even Cooper. Even after all these years, Cooper could still be surprised by Kelly. Fifteen years ago, he would never have guessed Kelly could have such a commanding presence and such infinite patience.

Even after all this time, Cooper could still imagine what Kelly looked like out of his uniform. He knew because at one time he'd mapped all of the man's delicious contours with both his hands and his mouth. They'd unashamedly spent hours in bed together when they should have been preparing arguments and counterarguments, studying for tests, or preparing papers to be presented to their peers and professors.

Although Cooper felt his dress pants grow tight, he knew it was futile to remember those times. Kelly looked even better than he did at law school. He now resembled the Norse god Cooper had only seen the makings of back then, because then Kelly didn't have the confidence he exuded now. Cooper even liked Kelly's crew-cut hair and close shave and wondered what it would be like to kiss him again. Cooper knew he'd never find out. Time hadn't been kind to Cooper, but then hard times and way too much hard liquor had turned him into a gray, gruff, and disheveled ranch hand, while Kelly had turned from a naïve, enthusiastic puppy of a law student into a sheriff with a commanding presence. Maybe choosing law enforcement instead of criminal law was easier on a man's looks? Then again, being disbarred wasn't something Cooper wished on anyone.

Cooper shook his head and turned away from the enticing picture of Kelly. He gathered discarded napkins and other debris guests hadn't bothered throwing into the waste buckets they'd placed in strategic areas. Although he wasn't at the wedding to work, he still preferred to stay busy. One thing that hadn't changed about him was that he didn't like standing idly around.

"I like what you picked out from the store."

Cooper looked up into Kelly's mischievous blue eyes and bit the inside of his lip. "You don't look half bad yourself."

Kelly chuckled. "It's standard issue."

"It's a dress uniform, and it fits you like you were poured into it, Kells."

"You always did have a soft spot for uniforms."

Cooper cocked his head but couldn't look Kelly in the eye now. "I have a soft spot for you," he murmured. He realized Kelly had heard him when he looked up and saw Kelly was blushing. He averted his eyes again and took a sip from the glass he was holding, only then realizing it wasn't even his own drink. He turned around to put it on a tray with other discarded glasses.

"Can we go for a walk or something?" Kelly asked.

"I thought you were on duty," Cooper said more than asked, without turning to face his partner in conversation.

"The others know what to do. I can't stray off too far, but I have my phone. If they need my say on something, they know to call me."

Cooper wanted to. He wanted to do more than go for a walk. He wanted to take Kelly behind the barn and kiss him until they were both out of breath. Or saddle two horses and ride off to the lake like they'd done at Kelly's parents' ranch. He knew he had to stick to his guns, though. Kelly belonged to Nina, and heaven knows Nina needed him, so Cooper had to keep his hands to himself and his lustful feelings safely tucked away. "We can talk here, right?" Cooper eyed Kelly from the corner of his eye.

Kelly sighed. "I just want some time with you, Coop. At the dinner, we barely got to talk. Every time I show up here, you act as if I need a good kick up the behind and you're the one to dish it out. Tell me what I did wrong, Coop?"

Hearing Kelly grovel like that softened Cooper's armor. "You didn't do anything wrong. It's just hard when you're still the guy I fell in love with in law school, only now you're all grown up and more than a little off limits." Cooper tried to keep his face in check but felt his cheeks twitch and his lips grow thin from the tension. Damn, when had it become so hard for him to hide his feelings? Then again, hiding them from Kelly had always been hard.

"That's why I wanted to talk to you," Kelly replied, turning so he stood shoulder to shoulder with Cooper but facing the other way.

Cooper realized it wasn't an entirely uncomfortable position to be in. He could enjoy the vista of long, stretched out meadows with horses grazing on them and had Kelly's sexy, low voice in his ears. No, Kelly's voice in his ears. For his own sanity, he tried to dispel the idea that it was sexy. "So talk."

"I came to Idaho for you, Cooper."

Cooper swallowed away the giant lump in his throat. "I thought you came here for a job."

"I'd been trying to find you for a while. I knew you'd gone out west."

"Portland."

"Yes, Portland," Kelly acknowledged. "So that's where I started my search. Law firms are surprisingly tight-lipped about ex-employees."

"And so they should be." Cooper tried hard to keep a level tone, but he wanted Kelly to get on with his story, just so he could hear more of that slightly raspy, low voice.

"But you had the tendency to get your face in the papers, so I managed to track you that way. Even here in St. Anthony."

"Especially here in St. Anthony," Cooper corrected with a sigh. He was flattered that Kelly had clearly gone to great lengths to find him. It also meant there wouldn't be much to explain. Not that he trusted the newspapers to get the whole story, especially not about what happened when he got disbarred, but at least Kelly knew the broad strokes of what had happened to him.

"Yeah, there was lots to read on the matter of your fall from grace in this little town," Kelly said.

There was an uncomfortable smile on his face, and Cooper didn't mimic it. Not that he felt like Kelly was mocking him. It was simply a very dark time in his life, and he didn't enjoy bringing it up again. Cooper decided to change the subject. "So after all that, you still came to this town because of me?"

"Nina found the opening for the job. I can still hear her say 'Isn't that the town where Cooper lives now?' She also figured out Hanson was ready to retire and probably looking for a successor, which made it the job I was looking for. You being here was the cherry on the cake."

"And what if I'd turned into this bitter old man?"

"You mean you didn't?" Kelly said with a serious frown.

For a moment, Cooper thought Kelly was actually serious, but then a smile broke over his face, and this time Cooper couldn't help smiling back. The joking felt good, but Cooper realized Kelly had definitely grown up. Back in law school, he'd never have dared something like that, since he worshiped the ground Cooper walked on back then. Now they felt more like equals. Cooper figured it was more because he'd fallen off his pedestal than because Kelly had grown up, but it simply felt too good to deny. "I'm just a few drops short of bitter, Kells. I'm definitely not your shining example anymore."

Kelly nudged Cooper with his shoulder as he leaned against the table behind him. It made him a little shorter and therefore closer in height to Cooper. "My father used to tell me I thought you hung the moon and the stars. I denied it, but he was right. I would have followed you to the end of the world, so when you pushed me away, I was so lost I didn't know where to turn. If it hadn't been for Nina, I wouldn't have finished school." He paused, leaving a pregnant silence between them. "Nina knows how much I ached for you, Coop."

"Glad you're talking in past tense."

"That must have been a slip of the tongue. She knows how much you still mean to me."

"I'm no longer the man I used to be," Cooper replied, hearing the pain seep into his words.

"Still like him, though," Kelly said casually. "Occasionally the old Cooper resurfaces. The passion with which you defended Rory at his parole officer's brought it all back. Controlled passion, mind you. You haven't lost any of your touch. I'm not letting your rough edges fool me."

It seemed that every time Kelly came near him, Cooper just wanted to wrap him in his arms and never let go again. Despite the fact he couldn't do it here, in public, with Kelly in his finely pressed uniform, he also couldn't drag him behind a barn and do it there. He'd never survive walking away again. He couldn't get between Kelly and Nina like he had when they were younger. In law school, he didn't mind so much. Nina was Miss Independent there and would surely have found herself some hotshot to marry, but things were different now. "Trust me, those rough edges chafe," Cooper grumbled as he turned away from the table and walked away. He couldn't turn around, didn't dare look at Kelly's face after the clear brush-off, but he had to keep walking or Kelly would surely see his eyes glistening.

Cooper walked past Calley, who was smiling at her kids playing in their new clothes as she talked to Gable and Flynn, but didn't acknowledge them. He had to leave. The party was over for him.

—8—

"HEY there, Calley," Gable greeted his friend as she left her truck and walked across the driveway toward the Blackwater ranch house. Flynn, Gable's partner, appeared from behind the truck carrying two three-year-old children. He'd hoisted Andy, the boy, on his shoulders and had Vicky, his twin sister, on his hip. Both children seemed overjoyed to see the younger of the two men and tried their hardest to see who could smother Flynn first. Gable smiled at the spectacle and noticed another small boy trying to hide behind Calley's skirt and a taller, lanky youth following close by with a large box filled with groceries for the ranch's occupants.

"Brood's growing, Cal," Gable remarked. "Is that Ryan?" He nodded at the young man with the heavy-looking box, who looked stern and didn't seek eye contact.

"Yes, and you met Noah, Ryan's brother, at the wedding," Calley answered, pushing the young boy forward. He resisted, though, and Calley stopped pushing him. "They used to live with Leah, but since she moved to another state, they live with me. I'm bringing them along on my rounds so my new shop girl can work in peace," she said conspiratorially. "They get bored at the shop, anyway."

"Let's get the box inside, Ryan," Calley said to the kid before turning to the little one. "Why don't you go play with Vicky and Andy?"

Noah looked up at her, and she smiled warmly. "It's okay. I won't forget to pick you up before we leave."

"I'll take them to go see the horses," Flynn suggested. "The foals are growing big already."

By the time Calley and Gable turned to go inside, Ryan had exited the house and walked back down the porch, where he stood waiting.

Calley didn't speak until they were inside. "He's a strange one," she commented, nodding at the kid outside. "Noah's sweet, but very shy. I suppose never having had any parents doesn't give you much sense of security."

"So are they with you permanently now, Calley?" Gable asked as he poured her a cup of coffee.

"Not sure. I'm only their foster mom, so things may change. Leah used to say she got the creeps from Ryan. They were with her since Noah was two, but before that they lived in four or five different homes. Every time, Ryan did something to get them thrown out."

"What do you have to do to get thrown out of a foster home these days?" Gable asked, sipping his coffee. "Is it drugs?"

"Don't think so, and neither does Leah. He's a hard worker, doesn't do badly at school, although he's definitely an outsider. Leah said he didn't have any friends, and it does seem that way." Calley looked sad. "He works hard at the shop, and I sometimes give him a little extra money, but I've hardly heard his voice. He just nods his thank-you and walks off to school. I can't fathom him."

"He doesn't creep you out?" Gable asked.

"Naah. I agree he's a little strange and his social skills could use a little polish, but he's not a bad kid. He's worked for me every day before school since I was pregnant, and I never caught him doing anything bad. He's never even stolen any candy or anything."

Gable smiled. "Well, if he needs more work, I could use a hand on Saturdays. Flynn's bred six foals this year. He's filling up the ranch at this rate, and it's a lot of work, so an extra hand is always welcome."

"I'll talk to Ryan for you if you like. Don't know if I can get through to him, but he occasionally works at the Blue River too, so I'm sure he knows what to do. Or you can be sociable and ask him yourself."

Gable shrugged. "There's a reason you bring us groceries, Cal. It's so we don't need to be sociable." He chuckled. "You ask Ryan, and if he wants to make some extra money, just have him show up on Saturday."

Calley finished her coffee. "Let's put this food in the fridge, then."

She took hold of the box, but Gable pulled it out of her hands. "I'm capable enough to load my own kitchen." He smiled defiantly at her.

Calley raised her hands in defeat and sat down again, obviously eyeing Gable as he moved around the room. "You know, this isn't a bad view. I'm starting to see the attraction of letting you do all the work. Doesn't happen very often I get to see a prime ass like yours strutting around."

Gable turned to face her and narrowed his eyes. "If I didn't know any better, I'd say you were flirting with me, Calley."

"Maybe I am," she said mock seriously. "I figured, Flynn gets to see this every day, and I don't get to eye anything this nice anymore."

"Bill still not back?"

Now it was Calley's turn to shrug and feign disinterest. "Don't think he's coming back this time, darling. I pushed him so hard I pushed him away."

"I would love to say he'll turn around if you give him time, but it's more likely that, if three years and a divorce isn't enough, he's just being as stubborn as a mule, and he'll never see eye to eye with you."

Calley sighed. "He told me enough times that it mattered to him that he's not the father of our kids, and I just figured he'd see them and change his mind."

At that moment, the front door flew open, and Flynn burst inside with three kids hanging all over him. He was clearly reveling in the attention, but wasn't too disturbed by the fact that the two youngest immediately left his side once they spotted Gable. Within moments, they were both sitting on Gable's lap, Andy with his thumb in his mouth.

"Hey," Gable remarked, wiping the hair from the boy's face. "Aren't you getting a little old to be sucking your thumb?"

Andy shrugged and settled closer to Gable.

"He's tired," Calley said. "I can keep Vick up most afternoons, but Andy needs his nap or he gets really cranky."

Gable looked up at Flynn, who was staring at him. "What?" he asked.

"It's like seeing a miniature version of you, Gabe."

Gable looked at Flynn and felt himself go all warm inside. He knew how much Flynn wanted kids of his own and how he'd always said that Gable's kids were just as good. Then Gable turned his gaze to Calley, who looked loving and understanding, and he felt his throat grow tight. When he looked at Andy, he was sound asleep, and Vicky was softly caressing her brother's straight, sandy blond hair. When she spotted Gable looking at her, she smiled and started caressing Gable's beard.

"We can put them to bed here if you want, Cal," Gable said in a soft voice. "You know Andy hates it if you wake him up."

Calley nodded. "Sure, I'll pick them up after my rounds."

"Noah really liked the foals," Flynn added. "You can leave him here too. I'll put him to work with me. I'm sure he'll love it."

"Can I?" Noah asked, looking expectantly at Calley. "I promise I'll be good."

Calley smiled at him. "Are you sure? I'm not staying here with you. And I'm not coming back until late afternoon."

Noah nodded fervently. "Want to go see the little horses again."

"Are you sure, Flynn?"

"Of course I am. Wouldn't have offered it otherwise."

Calley got up and kissed Flynn on the cheek, then turned to Gable and did the same to him. "Take care of our babies, okay?"

Gable nodded and watched her leave. Through the open door, he could see Ryan sitting on the porch steps, but he got up as soon as Calley approached. "We'll leave the little ones here so they don't need to sit in the truck all the time."

Ryan looked like he was going to say something but then didn't.

"Who's up for going back to the little horses?" Flynn said to Noah, who seemed a lot less happy now Calley was gone. Flynn spread out his arms, and Noah smiled. "I am." He looked warily at Calley's disappearing truck, though.

"Come on, sport," Flynn urged him on. "With Gable babysitting the little ones, us men need to pick up the slack!"

Noah smiled broadly, skipping to where Flynn was waiting for him to walk to the stables.

LATER that day, when Flynn returned to the ranch house, it was quiet, so he held his finger against his lips to ask Noah to be quiet as well. They carefully tiptoed upstairs, and Flynn took Noah's hand before opening their bedroom door. Gable was asleep on the bed, both kids next to him, equally lost to the world, and a quilt draped over the three of them.

"Looks like Gable needed a nap too," Flynn whispered.

"Yeah," Noah sniggered. "Gable looks older than me, and I don't need a nap anymore."

Flynn smiled at him. "Well, he's had lots of fun with the horses today, and he probably had to give a good example to the little ones."

Noah nodded as he looked at Flynn. "I'm hungry."

"Let's go see if we have some cookies then, okay?"

ABOUT two hours later, Flynn returned upstairs without Noah. He was surprised it was still quiet in that part of the house and peered into his bedroom. Gable and the children were still asleep. This time Vicky was half on top of the quilt, her arm around Gable's neck and little fingers entangled in Gable's beard. Flynn couldn't help but smile. He walked inside and sat down on the bed opposite the children. When neither of them moved, he ran his hands through Gable's hair.

Gable startled, and Flynn shushed him. "Hello, sleeping beauty."

"Mmmh, what time is it?"

"About four."

"Four?" Gable said, opening his eyes wider. He looked at the two sleeping kids. "Vicky wouldn't go to sleep if I didn't get on the bed with them. Andy was out like a light even before we came upstairs."

"I should have taken a picture of you," Flynn said, kissing Gable's hair. "I could have sat here looking at the three of you all day long."

"Damn. Where's Noah?"

"Downstairs with Calley and Ryan. We mucked out the nursing stables. He kept wanting to go into the stalls with the little ones, but I was afraid the mares would get territorial, so I didn't let him. We had a good time, though."

"Let's wake these kids up, hey? Otherwise Calley'll curse me if she can't get them to bed tonight."

By the time they were walking down the stairs, Flynn carrying Vicky and Gable with Andy in his arms, both kids were yawning and only barely awake.

Calley smiled amusedly at the sight of the men and the little ones. "If I hadn't heard all these stories about playing with the foals from Noah, I would have guessed the four of you had slept the afternoon away."

"He did," Flynn quipped, pointing at Gable after he'd put Vicky down. Although Noah had gone shy again and was keeping to Calley's side, Flynn playfully ruffled his hair. "Me and this one worked." He winked at Noah.

"Well, I'm glad you had fun," Calley said, taking Andy from Gable. "Thanks, guys," she whispered as she gathered her kids and walked out. They never saw Ryan.

MUCH later that night, Flynn woke up from Gable's tossing and turning.

"And here I thought the twins were going to be the ones having a hard time sleeping," Flynn whispered, turning in Gable's direction.

"Sorry," Gable murmured.

Flynn moved even closer and kissed Gable's neck. "Don't be." He put his hand on Gable's stomach and felt the short hairs tickling his fingers. "I could make you a bit more tired?" he suggested.

Gable didn't answer.

"Or we can just lie here and talk a bit."

Flynn knew about Gable's silent, brooding side and had learned over the years when to shut up and when to drag him out of it. This didn't feel like the shut-up kind. "You enjoyed that, didn't you? Your nap with the kids."

"Yeah," Gable replied, barely audibly. "Vicky, of course, wasn't sleepy, but I wanted to give Andy the rest he needed. You know what he's like when he wakes up without his sister, right? So I figured I had to bribe her into lying down and being really quiet, so we played this game to see who could make the least noise. Of course I won, but by the time I was ready to proclaim victory, her eyes were drooping, and I figured if I just kept quiet for a moment longer, she'd be sound asleep. Next thing I remember is you waking me up."

"You looked adorable, kids draped all over you," Flynn said, smiling ear to ear. "Admit it, you're starting to enjoy this parenting thing more and more, aren't you?"

"Well, they're a bit older now, and you can talk to them and they talk back. They can tell you what they want. I hated the guessing."

Flynn chuckled. "Yeah, but now they talk back to you."

"Yeah, I suppose." Gable was silent for several minutes, and they just stayed like that, in each other's arms. "I'm glad Calley's so easy about leaving them with us, though. It's nice that they know us and trust us."

"You like the cuddles," Flynn said, poking Gable in the ribs. "You big teddy bear."

A giggle escaped Gable's mouth, and Gable kissed Flynn to stop it. "You know I'm your teddy bear. Does this mean you like the beard too?" He chuckled as they continued cuddling.

"You know I do." He rubbed his face against Gable's beard to show him. "You never knew you'd like this so much, did you?" Flynn suddenly said.

"What?"

"This. Just you and me kissing and cuddling without it having to result in sex."

Gable shrugged. "There was a time when this was all we could do. Then it was a frustration. Don't get me wrong. I love the sex. I'm just not in the mood right now. You know I love you, but—"

Flynn kissed him again. "Of course I know you love me. I never needed sex to believe that."

Gable snuggled even closer, his nose in Flynn's hair as he inhaled deeply. "I think I can sleep now."

—9—

"I THOUGHT they fed you guys at the ranch?" Calley commented as Cooper put down four oranges and a cantaloupe next to a bottle of red wine.

"They do, but I'm going out riding tomorrow and I'm taking a picnic."

Calley smiled at him. "Going out alone?"

Cooper smiled back. Like most of the women Cooper interacted with, Calley was too nosy for her own good. "I don't think that's any of your business, young lady." When he really looked at her, he thought she looked tired and worn out. They weren't close friends, but he'd seen her at least once a month in the past three or four years, and when she'd just had her twins, she'd sometimes looked a little haggard, but never like this, with dark circles around her eyes making her skin look even paler than usual. "Everything okay with you, Calley?"

She perked up. "Yeah, fine. Shop's been a little busy, that's all. And with Leah gone, I have the added burden of training another shop assistant. In fact, I don't suppose you know anyone? This last one just won't do."

"Sorry," Cooper replied. "If you need a hand around here sometimes, I can spare an hour or two. Lugging all the crates must be hard."

"I have Ryan for the lugging."

"He's not leaving with Leah?"

"Leah left the state because her husband found work elsewhere. Ryan and Noah are wards of the state, so they need to stay here. The boys also don't want to leave, so we're looking into alternatives. For now, they're moving into my house, but only because I know their social worker. It's temporary."

"Good," Cooper said. "I'm sure something will pop up." He looked at the back of the shop when he heard a crash and a loud curse. Calley made her way over there, and Cooper followed.

"I didn't do anything! The crate broke!" Ryan defended himself among dozens of red apples.

Calley put her hand on his shoulder, although he was easily a head taller. "Don't worry about it."

"But the apples will be bruised."

"We'll just put them on sale. That way they'll sell faster," Calley said matter-of-factly as she bent down to start picking up the apples.

"I'll take ten pounds. They'll be gone in no time at the ranch," Cooper said, helping Calley out. As he bent down, he came face to face with Ryan, and Cooper was surprised how familiar Ryan looked. He'd never allowed himself to really look at Ryan, and Ryan didn't generally invite people to do so either, since he had a heavy bang that usually obscured most of his face. Now this was tucked behind his ear, and Cooper looked into eyes that triggered a memory he quickly pushed away.

Ryan lowered his head, and the hair fell into his face again, shutting out any conversational possibility.

After helping to arrange the apples, Cooper paid for his fruit and carried a small bag with his oranges and cantaloupe to the truck, along with a crate containing the apples. He drove toward the ranch, but decided on a little more alone time before starting his afternoon work, so he drove closer to the mountains and a vista point that overlooked most of the Blue River Ranch and Blackwater, Gable's ranch, beyond that. This was his private little spot. From the cigarette butts and discarded liquor bottles, he figured the local youths had discovered it too, but they mostly came at night.

Cooper took out an orange and started peeling it as he let his eyes rest on the beautiful sight of horses the size of pins grazing in the distance. It was peaceful here. He was sure he had fifteen, maybe twenty minutes he could kill before he had to drive off again.

Cooper's orange was almost finished when a sheriff's car stopped next to his truck. Cooper eyed it sideways and saw Kelly exiting the car. When Kelly recognized him, his stern, professional look evolved into a smile.

"I was going to ask you to move along," Kelly said, pointing at the sign that said "No loitering," "but I guess I can waive that for a little while."

"Wouldn't want preferential treatment, officer," Cooper replied half seriously.

"I'm not giving you one. I always talk to the people standing here. Rarely give them a ticket."

"You gave me your smile," Cooper rebutted, realizing he was flirting with Kelly, something he'd promised himself he wouldn't do, so he straightened his face again.

"That's part of the public service," Kelly said, leaning on the side of the truck. "I need people to like me so they'll vote for me. So, Mr. Nelson, what brings you here? It's a little out of your way, isn't it?"

"That's how you charm people?" Cooper said with mockery all over his face. "You'll have to work on that."

Kelly turned toward Cooper, invading his personal space. He leaned down a bit, so their faces were at the same level, and Cooper thought Kelly was going to kiss him. Then Kelly retreated, as if he'd changed his mind.

Cooper smiled, trying to hide his disappointment. "It's a good thing this is a remote location and not a lot of people come here, officer, because you damn near kissed me, and how would that have looked to your voters?"

Kelly swallowed hard, his Adam's apple bobbing. "I'm sorry."

"No need to apologize." Cooper knew he should have pulled Kelly closer to him and really kissed him, but that would break his resolve of not seducing Kelly because of Nina.

"You're a hard man to resist, Coop," Kelly murmured.

"You're not too shabby yourself, Deputy Freed," Cooper replied just as quietly. He wanted to keep Kelly here a while longer. If he couldn't have him close, he still wanted him near. "Hey, listen. I'm going to take one of the new horses for a ride tomorrow. If you want, you can join me. There're plenty of new horses to handle. I bought some fruit at Calley's, and I can make sandwiches at the crew house to take for a picnic. If you can leave Nina for a few hours, that is."

"Okay."

"Don't know if you've ridden much lately, but you were always a better rider than me anyway, so I'm sure it's like riding a bike. It'll come back to you." Cooper knew he was rambling, but he wanted Kelly to come with him so they'd have some time together, just the two of them. He couldn't stand the thought of Kelly living in the same town and having to avoid him all the time. He'd have to find a way to strike up a friendship and nothing more. He looked at Kelly briefly, to see him patiently waiting until he'd stop talking. He was smiling too. "What?" Kelly didn't respond. "Did you say you'd come?"

Kelly nodded. "What time do you want me there?"

"What time can you leave?"

Kelly shrugged. "I'd have to square it with Teo, but if he has nothing planned, I can help Nina in the evenings both today and tomorrow, and I can have tomorrow morning off."

"How about seven thirty?" Cooper suggested.

"You bring the food, I'll bring the drinks. And maybe something sweet." Kelly looked at Cooper in a way that went straight to Cooper's groin. "Teo bakes," he elaborated. "I run every morning to keep in shape. Otherwise, I'd be built like our good sheriff in no time."

"Rotund?" Cooper asked, although it wasn't really necessary.

Kelly rubbed his belly, which was no doubt washboard shaped. "Yup. He's not just good to Nina. He's good to me too."

Cooper opened his mouth, wanting to jokingly ask about all the ways Teo was good to Kelly, but he decided it would give away too much of his own insecurities. He was jealous, it was true, but he had no right to be. Too much water had flowed under the bridge. Besides, he was the one who had left. It wasn't like he'd given Kelly a lot of choice fifteen years earlier.

Kelly pushed himself away from Cooper's truck and sauntered over to his own car. Cooper was glad he was sitting down, because his groin was straining against the zipper of his Wranglers.

Opening his car door, Kelly turned to Cooper. "I'll see you in the morning."

THE next morning, Cooper got up at five because he couldn't sleep. He did some chores, mucked out a few stables, and then returned to the crew house for a quick shower and to make some sandwiches. He was back at the stable by the time he heard a truck stop. It was way past seven thirty, and Cooper's nerves were getting the better of him.

"It's about time," he said gruffly as he heard boots on the stable floor.

"You were expecting Kelly?"

Cooper looked up after realizing the voice was Tim's, not Kelly's. "Yeah, I was. We were going out riding."

"He called to ask me to come over here and tell you something came up."

"Something came up? Swell."

"Coop, don't be too hard on him. He'll make a fine sheriff, but it does mean he pretty much needs to keep himself available 24/7."

"So it was work, then?" Cooper felt himself calm down a bit. Tim was right. Kelly was doing what he always wanted to do, and that came with certain sacrifices.

"He said to say it has nothing to do with Nina and not to worry. He also said he'd stop by the crew house later."

Cooper grabbed a saddle from the rack. "I might not be there. I promised Hunter I'd give the new horses some people time."

"Rory and I will help you, if you give me half an hour to go get him."

Cooper looked at Tim. The last thing he needed was to hang out with the lovebirds on his free Sunday. "No, thanks. I'm good on my own." Cooper walked into the stall to saddle the horse, leaving Tim outside to fend for himself. *Damn Kelly for getting his expectations up.*

"I can help if you like. I always need to help Rory with the saddling too—"

"Just leave me alone," Cooper hissed, cutting Tim off.

"I'm sorry."

Cooper let out a breath before slowly lowering the saddle onto the horse's back. Tim didn't deserve to be snapped at. He was the kindest, most patient man Cooper knew. If anyone deserved some slack, it was him. Cooper turned around without totally raising his gaze. He didn't need to, since he was taller than Tim. He didn't dare look him in the eye, though. "No, I'm sorry. I'm the one who needs to apologize. If you and Rory want to come along, you can. I guess Rory could use the riding practice too. And he's probably ridden all these horses at Gable's, anyway."

Tim smiled. "Okay, I'll go get him."

With that Tim walked out of the stable, and Cooper turned back to the horse he was saddling. Idly, he wondered if it was at all possible to get Tim angry.

—10—

KELLY couldn't keep his mind on the job. It kept drifting to Cooper and the promise of a horseback ride and a picnic and the fact this would have been their first sort-of-date, and he'd needed to cancel.

The truth was, he was working, and he couldn't explain what he was doing to Cooper, since he hoped to keep everything off the record. On top of that, since Cooper didn't own a cell phone, he couldn't tell him directly, so he could only guess what had gotten lost in translation. He'd elected to call Tim, since he was sure Tim wouldn't pass judgment, but even so, he would have preferred letting Cooper down face to face.

Now he was playing mediator in a case he hoped wouldn't need too much paperwork.

"What were you thinking, Ryan?" Calley asked her foster son.

Ryan barely looked up into Calley's exasperated face.

"You never even stole a candy bar from the shop in all those years you helped me out, and now you do this?"

Ryan still didn't answer. As far as Kelly had gathered, this was normal behavior for him, but he wanted answers almost as much as Calley clearly did.

"Ryan, why?" Calley asked in a much more soothing voice. "I can't buy you a motorcycle, but if you really wanted to ride one, we could have asked Grant. I'm sure he would have let you ride his on the ranch."

"I don't care about the motorcycle," Ryan grumbled.

"Then why did you take it?"

"I borrowed it."

Calley shook her head. "You know right from wrong, Ryan. What you did wasn't borrowing. You stole it."

"I put it back!"

Calley tried to put her hand on Ryan's arm, but he pulled away violently. She slumped down in her chair, but only for a moment, as if she wasn't about to give up. "Just talk to me, Ryan. I want to know why you did it so it won't happen again. When we agreed you and Noah were going to live with me, you agreed to stay out of trouble for me just like you did for Leah. Do you miss Leah that much?"

Ryan shrugged.

"I miss her too, honey, but just talk to me about her, then. Don't go around doing foolish things, just because you were bored or wanted to rebel."

"I wasn't bored."

"Then what? You can tell me. Remember when you used to come hang around the shop when you had a hard time with Leah?"

Kelly looked at the interaction between Calley and Ryan and couldn't help thinking he'd always wanted a family too. He'd never held anything against Nina, never had hard feelings toward her for the genetic curse that left their son so frail he barely made it through birth, but by God, even during the hard times—and these were hard times for Calley and Ryan—he wanted to be a father. And he had no doubt he'd be a good one too. Maybe that was why he'd always denied that part of himself that liked men. Maybe he felt he couldn't have his cake and eat it too if he followed those feelings. Even during the blissful times at college practically living with Cooper, he'd always figured it was a phase that he'd grow out of, and then he'd meet a girl and marry her and father a brood. Only being married to that girl now told him it wasn't just a phase. The problem was that his object of desire wasn't the fathering type, now even less than in college. He couldn't imagine Cooper sacrificing the solitude he seemed to like so much for the 24/7 responsibility that parenthood required.

Kelly looked at Calley and Ryan sitting together. Although she'd more than once expressed her need for communication, Ryan wasn't talking, but there was a quiet understanding between them as Ryan stared at the floor in front of his feet and Calley sat next to him with a resigned look on her face. He hated to break up the scene.

"We're going to have to make peace with Mr. Simmons over this, Ryan."

Ryan looked up at Kelly for a brief moment and then resumed staring at the floor.

"Will he press charges? I don't think there's any damage to the bike, right?" Calley asked.

"I think it would be wise for you and Ryan to follow me to Mr. Simmons's house to apologize. And then we can only hope." *For no paperwork,* Kelly thought but didn't vocalize. Of course, what was important was trying to prevent Simmons from pressing charges. Ryan was already a ward of the state, and if he got into legal trouble, he might lose his home with Calley.

"No," Ryan said in a firmer voice than he'd used before. "I'm not going to his house."

"Ryan," Calley said firmly, "if you do something wrong, you need to apologize." She didn't get angry, and Kelly admired her for it. He wanted to shake the kid and get him to tell them what really happened, because Kelly's intuition told him there was more going on than a teenager "borrowing" a motorcycle.

"He's the one that has some apologizing to do first," Ryan murmured, pulling his feet up on the chair he was sitting in. Calley swatted at his knees, so he lowered his shoes off the chair, but he kept hugging himself, and Kelly felt dread raising his neck hairs.

"Ryan, I can't make you go to him, but it would help your case." Kelly tried to keep his voice as steady as Calley's and to his surprise succeeded quite well. When Ryan didn't react, he turned to his foster mom. "Calley, can we talk in the other room, please?"

Calley looked at Ryan, infinite concern written all over her face, before following Kelly out of the room. She closed the door behind her and walked into the kitchen. "Coffee?"

"No thanks," Kelly said. "Gives me heartburn."

"I have great tea for that."

"Sounds good," Kelly replied, wanting to set Calley at ease. He waited silently until she was done boiling the water and adding it to a pot with a silver tea egg containing the loose tea. He thought it was very fancy for a town so far from a big city.

"I think there's more going on than just the bike," Kelly said, testing the waters. "How does Ryan know Mr. Simmons?"

Calley didn't look at him. Instead she kept herself busy getting cups and cookies out of the cupboard. "Ryan delivers groceries to him twice a week. I'd deliver them myself, but Ryan gets tipped well, and I wouldn't want to deny him the extra cash. It's not like I'm loaded, and he doesn't mind working for his money. He's done that for as long as I've known him, and he never complains." She looked up at Kelly when she handed him his mug of fragrantly spicy tea. "Besides, Ryan likes going to see Kaye Simmons. He volunteers to take his stuff over there every time. I never had any reason to believe anything strange was happening there."

Kelly could tell from the change in her expression that her mind was working too. "Why don't we try one more time to get Ryan to come with us, and if he doesn't, you and I should pay a cordial visit to Mr. Simmons to talk to him. You might need to apologize in Ryan's name to calm the waters."

Calley nodded, and all of a sudden she seemed tired. "Ryan's a good kid, Kelly."

"I know he is."

"I just wish he'd talk to me occasionally. I have his best interest at heart."

"I think he knows that. If he didn't, he wouldn't have asked to be allowed to live with you."

"He did it for Noah," Calley explained after taking a sip from her tea. "I never had any illusions I could keep Ryan here after his eighteenth birthday, but Noah and I really hit it off from day one. Even when he was still living at Leah's, he'd have sleepovers here. He loves the twins, and he's a really affectionate child. Leah, with all her other kids and foster children, had to divide her time much more than I did. Noah was a no-brainer."

"And Ryan?"

"Ryan's been working at the shop before and after school since he was twelve. He's a hard worker, and I respect him immensely for it. Not a lot of kids his age work that hard without complaining, but Ryan just doesn't talk much. Before last night, he'd never been any bother, so I gladly agreed to keep the brothers together."

"Do you know about their past? Their parents?"

"A little. Ryan's dad died when his mother was pregnant with Noah. After Noah's birth, she lost it. She couldn't deal with the kids, and they were taken away from her. I don't know if she's still alive, but they don't have any contact with her. Leah always promised she'd look into it if the boys ever asked, and I extended that promise, but they don't."

"Must be tough, especially on Ryan," Kelly mused.

Calley nodded. "Let's get this visit to Kaye Simmons's house over with, okay?"

—11—

AFTER their ride, Cooper, with the help of Tim and Rory, put the horses into the meadow close by the barn. Despite his misgivings about riding out with "the lovebirds," both Tim and Rory had kept it neutral, and Cooper had found he'd been able to relax enough to enjoy it even without the solitude. He'd shared the picnic he'd arranged for him and Kelly with the other two, and this had made his disappointment wane a bit.

"Anything else we can help you with, Coop?" Rory asked, standing next to Tim.

Cooper directed his gaze at the two men and found they looked good together. Tim was beaming, as usual, but even Rory looked relaxed and happy, a far cry from what he'd looked like a year ago. Even the difference from two weeks earlier, when Rory had had his altercation with John Delco, was remarkable. Being a free man clearly did Rory a world of good.

"I'm good," Cooper replied. "You lovebirds can go home now." He grinned at no one in particular when he thought of the cabin the guys lived in and that he'd helped make it habitable again. Up until three weeks ago, he'd never been envious of that, but now he wished he had a place of his own too. Not a mansion like Hunter and Grant's ranch house had turned into, but a cabin like Tim and Rory's would be nice, Cooper thought.

"See you in the morning, Coop," Tim said by way of good-bye, leaving Cooper on his own with the horses in the stalls. He was clearing out the last of the tack and saddles when movement caught his eye. He stopped in his tracks and listened.

"I thought they'd never leave."

Kelly.

"What are you doing here?" Cooper asked, trying to keep the vitriol out of his voice but not totally succeeding.

"I'm sorry I was a no-show this morning."

"Tim told me something came up," Cooper replied, grunting as he picked the heavy saddle off the floor and put it on the rack, making extra effort to dust it off just so he wouldn't need to look at Kelly.

"There was an emergency at work, and they specifically asked for me."

Kelly's voice was soft and apologetic, and Cooper was running out of things to do, so he stopped resisting and turned toward him. Kelly was wearing a tan woolen sweater that looked entirely too hot for the gorgeous fall weather they'd been having, and his lips were tense. He decided to soften his stance a bit. "Did you manage to get it resolved?"

"I think so. At least the emergency. I think there's more behind it, but nobody wants to tell me anything, least of all the people involved, so all I can do is keep my eyes open and hope it doesn't happen again."

Cooper looked at him, trying to keep his grin in check. "I have absolutely no idea what you're talking about. Want to go to the house with me and grab some dinner?"

"I thought the crew was on its own on Sunday?"

"Doesn't mean we starve," Cooper said, smiling full on now. "I cook, remember?"

"How could I forget?"

"You need to tell Nina?"

Kelly shook his head. "I called her when the job was finished. Teo's looking after her. Besides, she was tired, so she'll be going to bed early."

"Good," Cooper answered and then cursed himself in his thoughts for the eager response.

THEY walked to the crew house, the sun already low on the horizon.

"Days are growing shorter," Kelly remarked.

"They have been for a while now. Since the beginning of summer, actually."

Kelly snorted. "Wiseass."

"Hey, you're the country boy," Cooper replied with a grin. He liked the more relaxed atmosphere, and the fact his day had turned out nice despite the earlier disappointment helped in that respect too. He just had to keep the lust that boiled up every time he laid eyes on Kelly at bay.

When they walked into the crew house, the noise was coming from the TV room, where most of the guys were parked on the sofas, some with sandwiches, others with beer. The dining room and kitchen were empty. Cooper started clearing up some of the mess the other guys left and then took out a bag of assorted vegetables and a roasted chicken. He turned to take a pot out, poured in rice, then added water before putting it on to boil.

"Stir-fry chicken good for you?"

"Sure," Kelly said.

Cooper opened the fridge to avoid Kelly's smile. "Beer?"

"No, thanks."

Cooper turned back to face him. "Given up alcohol?"

"Not totally, but I'm tired, and if you liquor me up, I won't be responsible for the consequences."

Cooper grinned from ear to ear. "In that case, let me get my bottle of whiskey."

Kelly shook his head, but he returned Cooper's smile. "Better not, Coop. I'm just here to make up for this morning. I'll need to leave after dinner."

"Fair enough," Cooper replied, trying not to show his disappointment.

"This reminds me of law school," Kelly said.

Cooper tried not to be too distracted by Kelly's proximity, but he couldn't help himself. He wanted Kelly to hug him from behind like he used to when they were practically living together, but he knew he wouldn't. Instead, he contented himself with feeling Kelly's arm brush against his and the occasional warmth of his breath when he leaned closer to inspect Cooper's pots. "So is the run up to the election going well?" Cooper asked to change the subject.

"Who knows," Kelly said. "People are nice to my face, and they're getting to know me, but you never know how people will vote."

"So you jump at any chance to make an impression on people? Like this morning?"

"This morning it was Calley Haines."

"Why did Calley call the sheriff's office?" When he looked at Kelly, he saw him warring with his feelings. "Right, you can't tell me. I understand."

Kelly left his side, and Cooper heard the door to the TV room close before he returned.

"This stays between us, okay?"

Cooper nodded.

"How well do you know Kaye Simmons?"

Cooper shrugged. "Not well. He's a teacher. I think he has one of Grant's kids in his class, or he did last year. I heard Grant and Hunter talk about him one time, but that's about how far my knowledge goes."

"He accused Ryan of stealing his motorcycle this morning. Ryan says he 'borrowed' it and brought it back unharmed. I went over there with Calley, and we saw the bike. Like Ryan said, it was standing in his garage without as much as a scratch on it. When Calley promised Simmons it would never happen again, he was quick to agree not to press charges. I thought we did a good job resolving the situation, but I can't stop thinking there's more to it."

"What did Ryan say?"

"It's what he didn't say."

"I'm surprised he said anything at all. Usually he just looks at you as if you're a moron and walks away."

Kelly sighed as he turned around and casually leaned his tall frame against the counter. Cooper could see his mind whirling. "Ryan didn't want to go over to Simmons's house with us. Said Simmons had to apologize first before he would apologize to him. He wouldn't say what it was about."

"Simmons is a single man? In his early thirties, right?"

"Late twenties, I suppose, yeah."

"Gay?"

Kelly threw Cooper an exasperated look. "Gee, Coop, I didn't ask. Maybe you find it easy to ask people about their sexual orientation, but I don't."

"I don't either," Cooper admitted. "But did he seem gay to you?"

Kelly chuckled. "You had to kiss me silly before I realized *you* were. And according to Nina, you're the most obviously gay man she's ever met. My gaydar hasn't exactly improved over the years, Coop."

Cooper didn't reply right away. Instead, he tossed the stir-fry vegetables into the hot pan and shook the pan to cook them. They were done fairly quickly, and Cooper killed the flame underneath them.

"This is just a theory, of course, but what if Simmons made a pass at Ryan and Ryan fled. Maybe they were looking at Simmons's motorcycle, and the pass consisted of Simmons seducing Ryan with a ride on the bike in return for some 'favors.' And maybe Ryan said yes, because he really wanted to ride the bike, and then changed his mind while he was out riding alone and then told Simmons about it when he returned. Maybe accusing Ryan of stealing is Simmons's way of getting back at Ryan for walking out on their agreement."

Kelly smiled and shook his head. "You have some imagination."

"Did I ever tell you how I lost my virginity?"

Kelly shook his head again.

"I was fifteen, and our new neighbor was in his early twenties. I couldn't look at him without springing a boner, so I pursued him mercilessly. It took me months to break through his barriers. He kept telling me he wasn't gay and that I had to run home to momma, but I wouldn't take no for an answer."

"You were always too confident for your own good."

"Usually I'd argue with you over that," Cooper said with a smirk. "In this instance, you were right. After I finally made him cave in, he admitted he was scared of being indicted for statutory rape. Said the fact I was the one to pursue him wouldn't matter. He was a law student, so he knew."

"He the reason why you wanted to be a lawyer?"

Cooper shrugged. "Possibly. That and all the big-ass billboards around the city with all those fat, rich lawyers on them."

"So where is he now?"

"No idea," Cooper said. "He moved away, and I never heard from him again."

"So you're saying Ryan seduced Simmons, and Simmons is afraid of the law, meaning me, finding out, so he's covering his ass?"

"That, or something happened like I said, or I could be totally wrong, and Simmons may just be very forgiving of Ryan stealing his bike because he brought it back. All those teachers have God complexes anyway, and they think they can save a poor foster kid."

"Ryan doesn't seem the kind to seduce anyone, anyway."

Cooper shrugged. "Let's eat."

—12—

STUFFED to the gills, Kelly sat back on the none-too-comfortable kitchen chair opposite Cooper. The simple stir-fry Cooper had made for him tasted like gourmet cooking and was better than anything he'd ever had made by his family's cook, Teo, and any restaurant chef he'd ever met put together. A little voice inside him said this was because it was made for him with love, but he quickly discarded that idea. No, Cooper was simply a very good cook. He'd proven that time and again in his little excuse for a kitchen at the apartment Kelly had pretty much lived in for most of the year they'd been at school together and where Cooper would make him the most amazing meals every night because he couldn't afford to take him to the restaurants littered all around the campus. Kelly never missed being taken out, because nothing could top Cooper's food. Even now, fifteen years later, Cooper had lost none of his golden touch. And on top of that, being here with Cooper was comfortable and easy. Even easier than Kelly remembered.

"I really need to go, Coop. I need to get up early tomorrow so Teo can sleep in. He's been on duty all day long. And after that I need to work."

"So Teo doesn't sleep in your bed, then?"

Where did that come from? "Of course not. How did you get that idea?"

"Something Nina said."

"What did she say?" *Damn, Nina.*

"Something about how Teo didn't just take good care of her, but you too. I figured Teo was her nurse and your toy boy."

Kelly almost choked on the wine he'd been drinking ever so slowly all evening long. "Damn, Coop. You should know me better than that."

Cooper hadn't shown as much restraint as Kelly and had cracked open a second bottle of wine near the end of dinner. That bottle was all but finished too. "Come on, Kelly, I wasn't your first man, so I can't believe I was your last. Nor did I expect you to remain faithful to me. God knows, I wasn't either."

"I married Nina," Kelly said as flatly as he could.

"You aren't meant for a woman any more than I am, Kells."

Kelly swallowed to keep himself from lashing out. Even after all these years, his instinct was still to deny. He knew he'd be lying, though. He'd realized long ago that what Cooper had just said was the truth. He loved Nina. Hiding behind her was easy, and she'd always facilitated it, but she'd never made his blood run faster. Even the few quick, nameless encounters with men he'd had after Cooper left him and the one not-so-nameless tryst with the guy he'd apprehended during a drug raid at a gay bar had stirred more lust in him than Nina ever could. But the only guy who'd ever come close to being everything for him—love and lust combined—was Cooper. Could he divulge to Cooper that Nina had given him permission to pursue him?

"Nina loves me. She said I should—" At that moment Kelly's phone rang, and he recognized the ringtone he'd assigned to his dispatch desk. "I need to get this." As he moved away from the table, he saw Cooper starting to clear it.

"Kelly? Jennifer here. I just called an ambulance for Calley Haines."

"What happened?"

"I'm not sure. It was her foster son on the phone. He was frantic. He didn't make a lot of sense."

"I'll go see what happened. I'll keep you posted." He ended the call and saw Cooper looking at him. "Calley Haines is in trouble. I'm going over there."

"She's alone with the kids. You might need help."

"Okay," Kelly replied, knowing Cooper made sense. He turned to look into Cooper's compassionate eyes, both to see into those aqua blues and to gauge whether he wasn't too drunk to come along. "Good idea."

On the way into town, Kelly was playing all the possible scenarios in his head. Did Ryan do something to his foster mother? Did anything happen to any of the kids? Why didn't Calley call? He knew he'd have to stop doing that because it was wasted energy. They wouldn't know what really happened until they got there, and then the solutions would come automatically. He just had to keep his cool.

As soon as they rounded the corner and the shop with the small house attached came into view, they saw the flashing lights of the ambulance. Some of the neighbors had gathered outside, but they fortunately kept their distance. One EMT was getting equipment out of the back of the ambulance. Kelly parked his car next to it and got out.

"I'm Deputy Freed, of the sheriff's department. My dispatch called this in. I'm a friend of the family's."

"It's the mother. We're getting ready to take her to the hospital. Can you arrange for someone to look after the children? Alert the father?"

Kelly nodded. He knew his place in these situations, but he didn't want to tell the EMT there was no father to call. Instead, he hoped he'd be able to talk to Calley and ask her what she wanted to happen to the kids.

On the way in, they encountered the gurney with Calley already strapped on it. While the EMTs were gathering the rest of their equipment, Kelly tried to talk to her. "Calley, where do you want me to take the kids?"

She didn't respond, just looked confused and lost.

"Calley, please. Try to focus. Do you have any family or friends who can take care of the kids for a while?"

She murmured something.

"We need to take her, sir," the EMT Kelly had talked to earlier said with some urgency in his voice.

"Okay," Kelly agreed, taking a step back so they could pass. He looked at Cooper and saw him standing in the hallway as well.

"I'll go see if the kids are upstairs," Cooper said. "You try to talk to Ryan and figure out what happened."

Kelly nodded. "I asked her where to take the kids, and she murmured something I didn't understand."

"Gable and Flynn," Cooper said calmly. "We need to take the twins to Gable and Flynn, and with a little luck they'll be able to put up Noah as well. I'll take Ryan with me to the Blue River. They know him there, and they can give him a bed for the night in the main house."

Kelly was impressed that Cooper knew what to do. He'd had no idea Cooper knew Calley and her kids so well. He didn't have time to dwell, though. Cooper made his way upstairs, and he needed to go in search of Ryan, who had made the call to the sheriff's office.

He found the kid on the couch in the living room, knees pulled up against his chest and his shoes on the couch. Kelly's first instinct was to tell him to put his feet on the floor, but the kid didn't seem very receptive, as he was staring at the rug in front of him. Kelly decided to tread lightly.

"Thanks for calling us, Ryan. They're taking care of her now."

Ryan didn't respond or even indicate he heard what Kelly had said. When Kelly touched his knee, he jerked away.

"Can you tell me what happened?"

Again no answer.

"Cooper is upstairs getting the little ones so we can take them to Gable and Flynn's. Is that okay?"

This time Ryan looked at Kelly. His hair was in his face and his mouth was a thin line. "That pervert needs to stay away from the kids."

"Cooper?" Kelly asked, feeling his throat go dry.

"Yes, Cooper Nelson. He can't be trusted with the little ones. They don't know how to defend themselves."

Kelly tried to keep his cool. "I can assure you the little ones are safe with Cooper. He and Calley are friends. He knows she wants us to take them to Gable and Flynn's."

"I suppose that's okay. She always leaves them there. But not Noah. I'll take care of Noah."

Kelly moved a little closer, and Ryan pulled back, so Kelly resumed his earlier position on the ottoman in front of the couch. "Cooper suggested you could stay in the main house of the Blue River. But it's probably easier for Noah to stay with the twins. I think the women at the Blue River have their hands full already, right?"

"I suppose," Ryan shrugged. "As long as you don't leave Noah with Cooper."

Kelly didn't get a chance to ask Ryan why he didn't want Cooper near Noah, because at that moment Cooper walked in carrying a very sleepy bundled-up child. Holding his other hand was a larger boy Kelly figured was Noah, and Noah was holding the hand of a little girl with tear tracks on her cheeks. She wasn't crying anymore, though.

"I think we should get these three across town as quick as we can so they can go back to sleep," Cooper said softly.

Kelly looked at Ryan, who remained seated while eying Cooper with such a hostile look it chilled Kelly's heart. He knew they had to get moving, though. "I'll call Gable's to tell them we're coming. Ryan, do you have a key to the house so we can lock it up?"

Ryan nodded and got up from the couch. He gave Cooper a wide berth as he walked to the hallway to grab his coat. After putting it on, he unearthed the keys from his coat pocket.

"Okay, I think we're good to go."

They put the kids in the back of the car with Ryan and drove in the direction of Gable's ranch.

"Did you call Gable?" Cooper asked.

Kelly rubbed his face, trying to get his mind to kick into gear. The great food and the wine he'd had—luckily no more than probably a glass and a half over the course of the evening—were getting to him. He dug into his pants for his cell phone and handed it to Cooper. "The number is under Blackwater."

"And I'm supposed to know how to work this?"

Kelly chuckled, grabbed the phone, and after clicking a few buttons, handed it back to Cooper. "Press the green button. You do remember how to talk to someone on the phone, right?"

"Bastard," Cooper hissed. His smile reappeared almost immediately, though.

While Cooper called, Kelly looked at the kids in his rearview mirror. Ryan seemed indifferent to the children. The smallest boy was crying, and Noah was trying to soothe him. The girl was staring out in front of her, seemingly half asleep. Kelly wanted to park the car at the side of the road to soothe the crier but figured it would be better to just get them all to Gable's ranch.

"They're expecting us," Cooper said as he shut the phone. "Gable had lots of questions and seemed very worried, but I told him we didn't have any answers yet either. He's okay to let Noah stay there."

"I'll call the Blue River when we're at Gable's," Kelly said, hoping to inject a thank-you in his tone of voice. They turned into the driveway to the Blackwater Ranch and saw the porch lights were on.

—13—

AS SOON as the car stopped, Flynn leapt down from the porch and opened the back door. Andy was crying, so he grabbed hold of him first. "It's okay, honey. Flynn's here. You're safe." The child held on to Flynn for dear life and kept hiccupping as Flynn helped Noah get out of the car as well. Gable went round the other side to pick up Vicky, Andy's twin.

"Any news on Calley?" Gable asked.

Kelly shook his head. "They took her to Mercy. Our priority was getting all the minors taken care of. We'll take Ryan to the Blue River."

Gable looked at Flynn, and Flynn nodded. "No need to wake that house up as well at this hour. Ryan can sleep here on the couch for tonight, and we'll take him over there after school tomorrow. If that's okay with you, Ryan?"

Ryan didn't seem too sure, but he nodded anyway.

"Come on inside," Gable suggested. "Coffee's brewing. You can have a cup while we settle the little ones in for the night, and then I'm driving to Mercy to see to Calley."

While Gable and Flynn went upstairs with the three youngest children, Kelly stayed downstairs with Cooper. Ryan sat down on the couch that would probably be his bed for the night.

"Do you want a glass of water, Ryan?" Kelly asked. He didn't exactly feel comfortable in Gable's kitchen, but since Gable had offered them coffee but hadn't poured it for them, Kelly figured he'd been given permission to make himself at home.

Ryan shook his head without looking at Kelly.

"Coffee?" Kelly offered to Cooper.

"Yeah, I better. The wine's making me sleepy," Cooper answered, going to the right cupboard as if he owned the place and taking out two mugs. Kelly's raised eyebrows obviously demanded an explanation. "I help out here sometimes, and the guys don't stand on ceremony. They're good with you going into their fridge or taking out a mug to pour yourself a cup of joe. And Gable did offer." Cooper poured a mug and handed it to Kelly.

"Not for me, thanks. Gives me heartburn."

Cooper pursed his mouth. "I remember when you used to run on this stuff."

"Not for the last ten years or so." Kelly took a glass from the still-open cupboard and tapped water from the kitchen faucet. "I stick to water and herbal tea now."

"Fancy, Mr. Sheriff," Cooper said with a chuckle. He took a swig from his mug and murmured something that sounded appreciative.

At that moment Gable came down the stairs. "Mercy, you said?" Kelly nodded. "The little ones are tucked into bed, and Flynn will take care of Ryan. Thanks, guys."

"We'll go with you to Mercy," Kelly said. "I need to find out what happened to Calley for my records, since Ryan called the sheriff's office for help. Besides, they might not give you any information since you're not family."

To Kelly's surprise, Gable smiled. "Calley and I have each other's power of attorney. Legal and medical." He held up official-looking papers. "I might need to prove a few things, but if she's seriously sick, they need my signature."

"You can ride with us," Kelly suggested.

"If it's all the same to you, I'll take my own truck in case I need to stay longer than you need for your information, Kelly."

"We'll see you there, then."

Kelly saw Gable look at him, then Cooper, and then back to him before walking to his truck and driving off.

"What was that all about?" Kelly asked Cooper when they got in his car.

"Gable was wondering what I was doing there," Cooper replied with a smug look on his face. "He knows I helped with Rory's case, and that's our connection as far as he knows, but this thing with Calley is unrelated. He doesn't know you're gay, so he doesn't know there's more between us than the fact I helped you with Rory."

"It's not like we're having this sordid affair," Kelly said, not sure what Cooper was aiming at.

"No, but he doesn't know we have a history."

"Mmh." Kelly thought Gable had put two and two together. He didn't like the feeling that he was possibly found out. Was he that obvious? He knew he had to stop looking at Cooper all the time, but he couldn't help himself. Despite all his misgivings and his need to hide the feelings he had for Cooper, Cooper still had a big influence on what occupied Kelly's mind. And the thoughts were anything but chaste.

They drove through the night, occasionally spotting Gable's truck lights ahead of them, but otherwise on deserted roads. Since Cooper wasn't talking and Kelly didn't know what to say, Kelly had too much time to think. He hoped Calley would be okay and that her kids could stay with Gable and Flynn, because he didn't feel like calling child services to come take them away. Didn't small towns take care of their own? He'd try to find other ways for the kids to be safe before putting them in the system, even temporarily. Maybe it would even be better to call their father than to put them in a foster home. He wouldn't need to make the decision, but he could make sure all possibilities were explored before taking more drastic measures.

In any case, he was worrying about things he could do very little about. His mind jumped to the Serenity Prayer and something about knowing which things he could change and which he couldn't. Before they knew how Calley was doing, he wouldn't know if he needed to change anything for her, so it was no use mulling it over.

"Exit!" Cooper shouted, as if it wasn't the first time he'd said it.

Kelly yanked his steering wheel to the right, and the car swerved, only just making the off ramp. Cooper's shoulder bumped against his just before the car chose the middle of the road and drove straight again.

"Where were you?" Cooper asked in an accusatory tone. "If I hadn't drunk all that wine, I'd tell you to pull to the curb and let me take over."

"Sorry," Kelly said. "Was thinking."

"About me?" This time Cooper sounded like he was teasing.

Kelly didn't dare look at him, but he felt warmth in his belly anyway. "Yeah, something like that."

"You can park there," Cooper pointed at the emergency parking, which was empty, right by the entrance of the ER.

"Naah, someone might need it."

"There are three spaces just sitting there. It's the middle of the night. And it's not like you're going to write yourself a ticket, Deputy."

This time Kelly did look at Cooper. "Just because I can doesn't mean I have to. There are plenty of spaces here, and it's just a few yards more. Neither of us are old enough to not be able to walk that distance."

They got out of the car, and as Kelly engaged the central locking, Cooper muttered "Goody two-shoes" under his breath. Kelly couldn't stop himself smiling. If anything, it showed there was still some of the old, defiant Cooper underneath that thin veneer of indifference. He followed Cooper into the emergency room and spoke to the triage nurse. It didn't look too busy.

"My name is Deputy Kelly Freed of Fremont County. Calley Haines was brought in here a while ago after a call to our switchboard. Is there anyone who can give me some information about her?"

The triage nurse looked at him over her glasses. "She already has a visitor."

"I know. We called him. He's her next of kin. I just need information on how long she'll be here, because I might need to make arrangements for her children."

Again, Kelly got an annoyed look from her. "Sit down there." She pointed over his shoulder at the waiting area, which held a couple of old drunks, a mother with three screaming children, and a man clutching his bleeding hand, which was wrapped in a towel. Kelly also saw Cooper sitting in a corner. He was patting the seat next to him.

"You'll ask a doctor to come talk to us?"

"As soon as he goes to get a much-needed cup of coffee." It was clear that she wasn't going to make him hurry.

Kelly nodded at her. He knew he had to pick his battles, and he wasn't going to win this one, so he went to sit down next to Cooper.

"You know, if she has to stay in the hospital, I'm going to have to call Bill," Kelly said, flopping down next to the ranch hand.

"Ah, don't do that. The kids are fine at Gable's. Flynn's a mother hen. They love him to bits, and they have a healthy respect for Gable. There's no better place for those kids if they need to be away from Calley."

"But Bill is their father."

Cooper gave Kelly the same look the triage nurse had just given him. "Bill is their father in name only. The kids don't know him, Kelly, so just leave them be."

"But I have a legal obligation. You of all people should understand that."

Cooper sighed deeply. "You obviously don't know the whole story."

"No, I don't."

"Calley and Bill Haines had been trying for kids for as long as I knew them. First I heard of it, I was still a lawyer. Calley had asked me some questions about adopting a child, but Bill didn't want to raise someone else's kid. I told her she'd have to get a divorce if she wanted to do it without Bill's say."

Kelly nodded.

"So with me being disbarred, I kind of lost track of her until the whole commotion about Grant leaving Gable in the lurch after being injured happened. I didn't find out the finer details until much later, but at the time, one of the rumors that was circulating was that Grant had had an affair with Calley and that he was the father of the child she'd lost somewhere midway during her pregnancy."

"So she had another kid before her twins?"

"Yes and no. She lost the baby before it was old enough to take its first breath. She was devastated, and Bill was nowhere to be found.

He didn't show up until she was already home from the hospital. Luckily, Gable took care of her then, just like she took care of him after his accident. Now the strange thing was, they remained close friends, even though, according to the grapevine, Gable got wind of his lover's affair with Calley and threw Grant out just before he had the accident that eventually cost him his leg. So I don't believe it's true, but we never found out why Grant left Gable in the first place." Cooper looked at Kelly. "The rumors died down pretty quickly. This isn't the sort of town that's comfortable talking behind people's backs about a single man's love life. I'm sure there are still people in town who prefer to believe that Flynn just works at Gable's."

Kelly chuckled. "The same with Grant at Hunter's, I'm sure."

"I understand them not wanting to kindle the fire."

Kelly nodded in agreement. It was confirmation for why he could never start his relationship with Cooper again, despite knowing why he came to Idaho in the first place.

"Anyway, Calley and Bill got back together after the dust settled, and Calley finally got her wish. She got pregnant, but Bill stopped coming home near the end of her pregnancy, and she had her twins alone."

Kelly threw Cooper a compassionate stare.

"Okay, not entirely alone. Bill showed up at the maternity ward to stake his claim, but Calley told me much later that Bill wasn't the biological father." Cooper waited for effect. "According to her, Gable is."

"Wow. So that's why she drops the twins off at their house when she's really busy or when she needs to go out of town. I figured they were good friends, but I never realized Gable was actually their dad."

"And why you can't call Bill Haines to come and pick up his kids. You can't do that to Calley, or Gable and Flynn, for that matter."

Kelly nodded. "As long as Gable and Flynn are fine taking care of them and nobody stirs the pot, I can keep the wolves at bay. Bill Haines is a well-known figure around here, though. If someone tells him about Calley being sick and he stakes his claim again, I could be in trouble."

"This is the right thing to do, Kells."

Kelly smiled. When did Cooper start wanting to do the *right* thing? The changes in him weren't all bad, it seemed.

"However this turns out for Calley, she's going to need to put her affairs in order," Kelly said, trying to get his mind back on track.

"I told her after the kids were born that she needed to make Gable legal guardian of the twins, only it's not so easy with Bill being the official father. He's on the birth certificate, since they were legally married at the time of the birth."

"Calley needs to have a blood test done on the kids to determine paternity," Kelly suggested.

"That's what I told her."

Kelly wrinkled his forehead. "The trouble is, even if the blood test is in Gable's favor, getting this settled will involve a judge's decision, and unless Bill voluntarily relinquishes his rights, I don't see a single judge awarding custody to a gay couple over the legal father. Even if one of that couple is the biological parent."

"That's what I told her too. It's in her best interest to get Bill to sign away his rights, only Bill isn't known to be the most congenial fellow. He's going to make life hard for Calley, simply because his pride was wounded when she had her affair with Grant."

"Did he remarry?"

Cooper shook his head. "He lives with a woman who has two kids."

Kelly sat up straight. "Why don't I try to dig up some dirt on Mr. Haines? Off the record."

Cooper narrowed his eyes at Kelly. "Why, Deputy Freed. Are you talking about crossing the line?"

"I like Calley. And I like Gable and Flynn too. If Calley wants Gable to have the kids, the law shouldn't stop her."

"We need to keep it legal."

"Oh, I will. I'm the sheriff. I need to walk the line."

"You're not the sheriff yet," Cooper quipped. "And you can't boast about it to the press."

Kelly threw Cooper a mock mean look about his first comment and then answered his second. "Of course not. Like I said, we'll keep it off the record. If all goes well, nobody needs to know about my involvement. You can take all the credit." Kelly smiled like the cat that got the cream.

"You're enjoying this, aren't you?"

"Guys like Bill Haines get away with murder. One of the reasons I wanted to go into law enforcement was that I could stop them."

Cooper smiled. "I wish I could be that naïve again."

"I'm not naïve. Just idealistic."

Cooper grabbed Kelly's hand and squeezed it.

Kelly squeezed back and felt the calluses rub over his softer skin. Then he noticed one of the children looking at him, and he let go of Cooper's hand. Cooper didn't protest.

—14—

GABLE stood just inside the curtain looking at Calley, pale and sleeping as she lay on the gurney. He fidgeted, not knowing what to do with his hands now he didn't have the rim of his hat to play with. He stopped when he caught himself, thinking how he'd taken on the habit from Flynn, although it had always mildly annoyed him in his partner.

Calley stirred, opening sleepy eyes and looking around. Gable froze, afraid his presence had awakened her.

"Gabe darling," she said in that low voice that always surprised Gable because it didn't seem to fit her frail-looking body. She beckoned him closer. "You're a sight for sore eyes. I was afraid Bill would show up like he did when I had the twins."

"It's just me."

"It's never just you," Calley said with a soft smile as she held out her hand and Gable took it. "You're the only welcome face next to my hospital bed."

Her hand felt cold, so he tried to warm it by enveloping it with both his hands. "So, you're okay then?"

She nodded. "The doctor is running tests. I fell down the stairs. I got dizzy."

"You work too hard," Gable replied, still rubbing her hand. "Between the shop and your kids...." He didn't finish his sentence. She knew he worried about her a lot.

"I love being a mother, Gabe. I have a purpose in life because of them. Not just Andy and Vicky, but Ryan and Noah too. They both need a mother, probably more than the twins do."

"The twins need a mother too. One who takes care of herself. It's all they have, Cal."

"They have you and Flynn too."

Gable saw Calley's free hand move to her belly. It was an unusual gesture for her, and Gable had only seen it when she was first pregnant with the twins. He looked up at her face for confirmation.

"There was one fertilized egg left, Gabe. I figured it wouldn't take, but I couldn't just let it sit there. You just have to look at the twins to see we make beautiful babies together. And you know what? It worked. I'm pregnant again. Our last baby."

Gable swallowed. "You didn't tell me."

"You always said it was a gift. That I could do with it as I pleased."

Her face was a mix of worry and fear. Gable couldn't, in all honesty, be mad at her. She was right. It was a gift. A big one, but still a gift, and he'd always agreed with her that he would never lay any claims to the results of that gift. This included not having any say over what she did with the remaining embryos after she had the twins. He just never expected to love the children as much as he did. Or see Flynn's whole face light up when they came for a visit and climbed all over him. Although his worry for Calley overshadowed his joy, he knew telling Flynn that Calley was pregnant again would make his better half giddy with happiness.

"And the baby's fine?"

"They think so, but they're still waiting for a few results."

"And what made you faint?"

She shrugged. "I just felt dizzy. I was tired. You remember my first trimester with the twins. I could barely stay on my feet."

Gable nodded. He was still too worried to be happy for her. "How are you going to manage the shop with five kids and Leah gone?"

She looked at him compassionately. Gable thought she was the one who should get that look, not him. "This is why I'm being so difficult about a new shop assistant. I want somebody who can manage the shop for me, not just follow my orders. I want to have more time for the mommying, and in between I can do the books and take care of the orders and do the deliveries. I'll manage, Gabe."

Gable caressed her hand and along her arm and then put his hand on her burgeoning belly, where he let it rest. He put his head down next to hers. "Promise me you'll take care of yourself, Calley. If not for you then for the babies. They need you. This one and the ones already walking around."

"Is Flynn looking after our little ones?"

Gable looked up at her. "Even the big one. Ryan's asleep on our couch. The other three are tucked in upstairs."

"Were they very upset?"

"At first, but you know Flynn. He works his magic, and then they look at him as if he hung the moon and the stars."

She reached up and caressed Gable's beard. "He's a god in your eyes too. Why wouldn't they see the same thing in him?"

Although Calley had always been his biggest supporter, it was still strange for Gable to hear someone talk so openly about his love for Flynn. He felt it, all right, every single moment of the day. Flynn had saved him from himself and from a life that was essentially lonely and only filled with hard work. They'd built up a life together, with a flourishing ranch and the occasional visit from the kids. Kids he'd only considered giving Calley because Flynn had a strong wish to be a father. That same wish had resulted in Flynn turning Blackwater into a horse breeding ranch, where it was only a training facility before. All that and more Gable gladly did for his man.

Gable's thoughts were interrupted by a petite Asian woman entering. She wore scrubs and a white coat.

"Mr. and Mrs. Haines, I'm glad to have you here together," she said without a hint of an accent.

"I'm not Mr. Haines," Gable interrupted. "I'm Gable Sutton."

She looked at him suspiciously.

"He can stay for whatever you need to tell me," Calley added, squeezing Gable's hand to acknowledge their bond.

The petite woman looked at her chart. "There is no indication that something is wrong with the baby, Mrs. Haines. The fall didn't start any contractions, and there is no bleeding. The ultrasound showed normal mobility."

Gable heard Calley sigh contentedly. Less than an hour ago, he hadn't known Calley was pregnant again, but the good news about the baby made him feel more at ease now too.

"However," the doctor continued, "during the exam, I noticed you had swollen glands under your left armpit. And you have a small lump in the upper outer quadrant of your breast, which is a common place for breast cancer nodules. We will need to examine that further as soon as possible."

"Breast cancer?" Calley stammered at the same time Gable was thinking it. "But I'm pregnant."

"This does complicate things," the doctor admitted. "But it is not unheard of. There are treatments available, especially since you are past your first trimester. But let's not jump the gun. We need to do more tests. The lump may be benign, and the symptoms we see may have other explanations."

The doctor continued with a barrage of questions for Calley, but all Gable could think of was that there was something seriously wrong with the mother of his children, and although their relationship had never extended beyond a friendship that had been almost symbiotic at times, he couldn't bear to lose her.

"Gable, please let go of my hand."

Gable looked up into Calley's calm face and then realized, by the willpower he needed to invoke to actually let go of her hand, that he'd been squeezing it way too hard. "I… I'm sorry." She was doing it again. She showed him her most compassionate expression when the one needing the compassion was her, not him. He wanted to shout, be angry at the world and at fate dealing them a rough hand, but he couldn't. Calley's quiet acquiescence nipped that in the bud. Instead he tried to stay focused, holding her hand much more gently and keeping himself under control by remembering how patient and calm she'd been when he was sick and in need of help.

He was simply going to have to be the one to help her through this.

—15—

"SO HOW did you get disbarred?" Kelly handed Cooper the can of Coke he'd gotten from a vending machine as they'd exited the ER in search of some fresh air.

"Long story," Cooper replied, plopping down on a bench just next to the walkway.

"I have time." Kelly sat down next to him.

Cooper sighed. "I'm not kidding."

"Neither am I." Kelly leaned back and entwined his hands as they lay on his stomach. "I'm just curious."

Cooper chuckled nervously. "I was deemed unfit to practice law in the state of Idaho."

"That I could have figured out without asking you, Coop, since it's pretty much the definition of disbarment. It doesn't happen all that often, though, so I want to know what happened to a guy who was a legal star and could do no wrong."

"I slept with a married assistant DA."

"See, that wasn't so difficult," Kelly replied with the same even tone he'd used to ask the question. "So they disbarred you for an affair?"

"Martin was slated to become the next district attorney. He was married and had kids. His wife was old money, and her father was a retired judge who'd made it to the Supreme Court. Not to mention, Marty and I were always pitted against each other in my cases. It was a conflict of interest, but it wasn't like I could ask for a different assistant DA every time Marty showed up in court. And he could only make excuses for so many cases."

"You were together for a long time, then?"

"Five years."

Kelly whistled. "That's longer than you and I were together." He looked intently at the older man. "Did you love him?"

Cooper swallowed hard. "I suppose I did."

"You suppose?"

"It took some sneaking around. Mostly Martin coming to my house when I lived just outside of town. Actually, even if nobody ever found out about us sleeping together, the fact we spent time together at all outside of the courthouse was enough to get both of us in trouble."

"He must have loved you too," Kelly stated, trying to keep his voice in check. He knew just how Martin must have felt. And that included the being married to a woman but pining for a man bit. He knew way too much about that aspect too. Even now, sitting next to Cooper on the bench in near public, he still felt the pull. It didn't matter that Cooper was only a shadow of his former self, and he'd lost his almost regal comportment and proud, straight back long ago. Kelly could still see the man he fell in love with so many years ago, even underneath the lines in his face and the graying temples.

"So what happened when all hell broke loose?" Kelly asked.

"A newspaper photographer managed to take a picture of us in flagrante. We'd celebrated Marty's victory in a big case a little too hastily in the johns at the courthouse. It was one of those things. They ask you when you knew your life was going to change. Well, it was that moment I saw the camera's flash. Martin tried to stop the man, but he wouldn't hand over the pictures. He tried to go the legal way and stop publication of the article, but it didn't work. Freedom of speech, etcetera. Marty went home and left his car running in his closed garage. His wife found him later that night, but it was too late."

"He killed himself?"

Cooper nodded. "Yeah." He got up and stared over at the half-empty parking lot. "It's a long time ago. We sometimes talked about what would happen if anyone found out. I knew he couldn't live with that. He loved his kids. He always said that was the only good thing about marriage." Cooper stayed silent for what felt like forever. Then he started walking away.

"I miss you, Coop," Kelly said quietly, praying Cooper wouldn't hear it. His prayers weren't answered when Cooper turned around.

"Should have thought of that before you chose her over me, Kells."

There wasn't much vitriol in Cooper's words. In fact, Kelly thought he sounded resigned. He got up from his seat and saw Cooper retrace the few steps he'd taken away from him. Before he could react, Cooper pressed his lips against Kelly's and then pulled back, eyes squeezed shut and his lips thin, tense lines. He placed his hand over his mouth and then walked away, leaving Kelly to wonder what had just happened. After watching Cooper walk across the parking lot toward the road, Kelly licked his lips, hoping to find a taste of Cooper there, but he couldn't.

He'd gotten enough information from the ice-cold triage nurse and knew Calley needed to stay in the hospital for more tests, so he figured he might as well go home to sleep. But first he needed to find Cooper and drive him back to the Blue River Ranch.

He caught up with Cooper just before the main road, where he was trying to hitch a ride. They didn't speak after Cooper got into his car and only said good-bye when Kelly dropped him off at the crew house.

The flame was reawakened, though. During his shower the next morning, Kelly jacked off to images of Cooper like he remembered him: wanton, always horny, always sexual, whether they were alone or in "polite" company or just with their friends. Innuendo was simply the way Cooper spoke whenever Kelly was around. And probably when he wasn't too. He had the most wicked smile and loved to tease, but Kelly could always see the love in his eyes. Cooper could never hide that. The only time Cooper seemed serious was during mock court, when he stole the show with his eloquence, knowledge, and quick, dry wit. Where was that man now? Had Marty's death knocked it out of him? Kelly hoped he'd get a chance to ask one day.

And he hoped it was right after he'd apologized for the worst decision in his life. For Kelly knew the exact moment his life had changed as well. It was when he'd asked Nina to marry him. It was spur of the moment, but the direct result of having been turned down for a job by a guy who knew him from law school and who couldn't give "a job with such big moral responsibility" to a "fruit." It wasn't that he didn't love Nina, but she knew which side his bread was buttered on, and after realizing Cooper was going to want to fly solo after passing the bar, Nina was a close enough second. She loved him, in a no-nonsense, no frills sort of way. She was a woman who knew what she wanted and wouldn't let something like Kelly's pining for Cooper stop her. Not that she didn't respect it. She'd never made a pass at Kelly until she knew Cooper was as good as out of the picture, but once that came around, she'd pounced on him like a tiger. And Kelly had used his head, not his heart, to decide he wanted to stay with Nina. She was a career woman, and Kelly figured she wouldn't demand too much of him when it came to affection and love. She didn't, not even after they were married. Like when he and Cooper were still together, she was his buddy, his friend. They laughed a lot and had fun. Occasionally, she satisfied his need for human warmth and affection, and he figured he did the same for her. They worked well together too, and she allowed Kelly to pursue a career in law enforcement while she became an assistant DA. It wasn't until Kelly's eye started wandering again that he realized how trapped he was.

And then it was too late.

—16—

GABLE returned home just before dawn. He took his boots off downstairs, remembering just in time to stay quiet because they had a houseguest on the living room couch. He threw a quick look at the sleeping Ryan, assuring himself the kid was fine, before tiptoeing upstairs. The door to the kids' room was open, so he looked inside there as well. Vicky and Andy were sharing a bed, as always, despite the fact they'd fitted a bunk bed into the small bedroom even before they were ready for a big bed. Gable tucked them in, both kids completely oblivious. Noah was in the top bunk, and Gable spotted the reflection of what little light was illuminating the hall in his eyes.

"Go back to sleep, buddy."

Noah lay down, but his eyes remained open.

"Everything will be okay," Gable said, running his hand through Noah's hair. "Ryan's downstairs and the twins are asleep, so you need to stay quiet for a little while longer as well. Can you do that?"

Noah nodded, not totally convincingly, but Gable had no choice but to accept it. He wished Flynn was here, since he was so much better with the kids, but didn't want to wake his partner up for something so trivial. He didn't stop rubbing Noah's hair until the youngster closed his eyes.

Feeling dead tired after a night with no sleep, Gable entered his bedroom. He knew he'd have to get up again in an hour, but just wanted to lie next to Flynn for the time being. Sitting down with some care in the hope of not waking Flynn up, Gable started unbuttoning his shirt before pulling his pants off. He took care to roll the sock over his stump down before popping it out of his prosthetic leg and rubbing it to make sure all the skin was intact. It had become habit, although he clearly remembered the times when the only one who could stomach taking care of it was Flynn.

Gable didn't jump when he felt Flynn's arms snake around his thin waist. "Calley okay?"

"She's pretty sick," Gable whispered. "We'll need to take care of the kids a little longer than just tonight." A slightly stubbly kiss landed on his shoulder as he felt the warmth of Flynn against his back.

"I'm not one to complain about that."

"I know," Gable answered with a smile directed only to himself. He never ceased to enjoy the care Flynn bestowed on him or the kids, and he'd never once regretted agreeing to father Calley's brood, simply because it had made Flynn so happy to have the youngsters around. Gable considered himself to be like his own father, a little quiet and distant, but reliable and sturdy, and now understood where that came from. The difference was that Gable had grown up without a warm mother figure, and he was glad Vicky and Andy had Calley for a mother and Flynn for a mother hen. Flynn would spend every waking hour with the little ones when they were at their house, and it didn't really matter to Gable that he missed out on some attention from Flynn, because they never stayed for long. Gable was content to watch how Flynn kept the kids busy while continuing with his own work, whether that was mucking out horse stalls or fixing dinner.

Gable was literally pulled out of his thoughts by Flynn. "Crawl under the covers. This is too cold."

"It's almost time to get up again," Gable murmured as he snuggled closer to Flynn.

"Not for you," Flynn answered in a sleep-drunk drawl. "You've been at the hospital all night. I'll get up with the kids. You sleep."

Gable didn't want to. He didn't want to leave Flynn to deal with four worried kids when he had some of the answers to their questions, but felt himself drift off anyway. When he woke, he was alone in bed, and he heard voices downstairs. One of them was Flynn shushing the kids to be quiet.

He dressed quickly and made his way downstairs, where he found Flynn coming in from the porch with Andy on his arm and Vicky close by.

"Hey, sleepyhead." Flynn came over to kiss him good morning. "Tim just picked up Ryan and Noah. He's driving them to school along with the Krause brood. I figured we could keep these two here until we know more about when Calley's coming home."

Gable nodded as he saw the breakfast table in disarray but the kids dressed and jumping with energy.

"Can we go out and play, Flynn?" Vicky asked.

Flynn smiled at them. "Only on the porch. And wear your coats. It's cold outside." Flynn helped them button up and put on their boots before sending them outside and closing the door behind them.

When he returned, he looked at Gable intently. "So how is Calley?"

Gable bit his lip, wondering how long he could wait to say the *P* word. "She fell down the stairs. She said she was dizzy."

"Dizzy?"

Gable nodded.

"And how come she was dizzy?"

Gable figured he couldn't keep a secret from Flynn anyway, whether it was an important or a trivial one, and this one wasn't trivial by any means. "Good news or bad news?"

"Good," Flynn answered.

"She's pregnant."

Flynn's mouth opened, but no words came out. At the same time, his face lit up as if someone had flicked on a light switch. "Pregnant? She has a boyfriend? Is that why she's leaving the kids here more often?"

Gable had been shaking his head since Flynn brought up the boyfriend, but Flynn didn't seem to notice. "No boyfriend. There was one more fertilized egg, and it caught, apparently."

Flynn's smile grew even wider, if that were possible. "You mean it's ours? Yours, I mean? We can babysit it like we can with Vicky and Andy?"

"It's not born yet, honey," Gable said in a soothing voice.

"How far along is she? When will it be here?"

"Just under four months, so another five to go."

Flynn shook his head. "You don't look happy. There's something wrong with it, isn't there. That's why you had bad news too. You know I don't care, right? If there was something wrong with the baby. It's yours. I'll love it even if it isn't perfect. You know that, right?"

Gable took a step forward and enveloped Flynn in his arms. He needed the comfort. Part of him didn't want to give Flynn the bad news, because nothing was one hundred percent certain yet, and he knew how much Flynn worried, but he had to share this. "They think Calley has breast cancer."

"But she's pregnant!"

"They're doing more tests to be sure, but the doctor says they can treat her and it won't harm the baby." Gable said it so quietly he wondered if Flynn had heard him. Flynn's lack of response, other than to hold him tightly, seemed to corroborate that.

Then Flynn pulled away and took Gable's head in his hands. "We'll take care of her. We'll take the kids in and rally the guys to build an extension to the house so we can make room for Ryan and add a downstairs bedroom for Calley and she can stay with us. We can't let her live in town alone when she's going through chemo and radiation and whatever else she'll need to do to beat this." He pulled Gable closer and kissed him fiercely. "We can do this."

Gable knew part of Flynn's reaction was because of Lee, Flynn's first real boyfriend, who had died of cancer while Lee's mother refused to let Flynn near him. Another part of it was Flynn being a mother hen and wanting control over the care situation. Gable was grateful for both, because he wanted to do the same things for Calley.

"Let's play it by ear, okay? The diagnosis hasn't been confirmed yet. They're doing more tests today."

Flynn smiled at being let down gently. "We can build the extension anyway. Two kids in a bunk bed isn't bad, but once they grow up they'll need more space, and we'll have to accommodate five occasionally. Wait until they're teenagers and they no longer want to share a room."

Gable smiled and kissed Flynn back, a lot more gently than Flynn had done earlier. "I suppose we can ask the guys to lend a hand for that."

—17—

DURING the next week, Cooper purposely stayed away from Kelly. He'd broken his own rule. He'd kissed Kelly, and all hell had broken loose in his head. He knew from their earlier encounters that Kelly wanted to start up their relationship again, but he'd held off, telling himself Nina came first, and he refused to be responsible for her losing her husband now that she needed him most. To hell with what he wanted, and to hell with what Kelly wanted too. That wasn't important. They'd lived without each other for fifteen years and could certainly continue to do so for the foreseeable future. At least that's what he told himself whenever his attention drew to Kelly while he was working.

At night, alone in bed, he sometimes indulged in his own fantasies. Bringing up the lake cabin and the bunk bed fueled many a wanking session. He thought he'd be safe if he kept his fantasies confined to his own bedroom, but he couldn't stop thinking about Kelly, even while he was working.

On Friday, Grant stuck his head into the barn where Cooper was fixing a hinge on a stall door.

"You almost done?"

Cooper nodded. "Yeah. Do you have another job for me to do?"

Grant smiled. "Kind of. It's voluntary."

Cooper raised an eyebrow.

"Calley's running behind with her deliveries, and she asked me whether I could spare you."

"She asked for me?"

"Yeah," Grant answered casually. "You'd be doing her a big favor."

"Sure enough, boss."

Grant chuckled. "Shouldn't set you back more than a few hours, and since you're done here anyway…." Grant didn't wait for an answer, and Cooper knew he didn't need to give one. He'd gladly help Calley out.

TOWN was its usual busy self for the last day before the weekend. Cooper hoped he wouldn't run into Kelly, but other than that he walked along the shops like he always did, head held low, Stetson deep over his eyes, and not making eye contact with anyone.

Calley's shop was busy, so Cooper waited for a while. Calley wasn't around, and a new girl was manning the register. She was young but friendly and looked like she knew what she was doing. She looked a little Goth, with black hair and thick, dark eyeliner, and for a moment Cooper wondered if she knew Max from the clothing store up the road. He had an idea these two would get along famously.

"May I help you?" she asked.

Cooper looked up at her from under his hat. "Is Calley in?"

For a moment, the girl froze, her smile disappearing from her face, and Cooper wondered what had happened. He was the only one in the store, though, until the doorbell chimed and a few other people entered. When he looked back at the girl behind the register, she had composed herself. "Anything I can get you, sir? Yes, you were looking for Calley. Are you the guy who is going to do the grocery run? She's in the back. She can give you the instructions."

Cooper tipped his hat at her and walked through the store to find Calley.

TEN minutes later, he was on his way with a truck full of produce and other groceries, and a list of all the other places he needed to go. To his surprise, one of his stops was Kaye Simmons, the guy who'd accused Ryan of stealing his motorcycle. Cooper decided it was time to do a little investigating and put on his game face. He knew it had to match his appearance, so he didn't exactly ring the doorbell sporting his million-watt smile as if he was still the slick lawyer he used to be, but he wasn't going to let on that he knew what had transpired.

The man who opened the door, ear to his cell phone, was a short, compact-built, ash-blond guy who looked about twenty at most. Cooper knew he had to be older, since he'd been a teacher at the local middle school for a few years. He smiled at Cooper when he saw the contents of the box and gestured at the garage door next to the entrance. A few moments later, it opened, and Cooper spotted a beautifully maintained Moto Guzzi motorcycle. Cooper could see why Simmons had made such a fuss. If it had been Cooper's bike, he would have been particular about it too.

"Nice bike," Cooper remarked casually.

"Thank you," Simmons replied, tucking his cell phone into his jeans. "It takes a lot of work, not to mention a nice chunk of change, to maintain, but with all the country lanes to drive on around here, it's more fun than a car."

"I can see that," Cooper said, admiring the motorcycle a bit more before following Simmons into the kitchen. Cooper put the delivery slip next to the box, but Simmons didn't move to sign it.

"How is Calley doing?" he asked.

Cooper thought he looked nervous. "She's better. Getting there."

Simmons started unpacking the box and, with his head in the fridge, asked, "And Ryan?"

Cooper had wondered if Simmons would dare mention Ryan's name. He figured he had more to gain by staying mum. After all, Kelly had made him promised not to tell anyone, and Cooper was sure the whole incident had been clouded over nicely. "He's working hard, poor kid. But he doesn't complain."

"He's a good worker," Simmons replied, this time facing Cooper but not looking him in the eye as he picked more groceries out of the box. "He used to deliver here, but I guess he's too busy now."

Although Cooper had imagined this guy to be somewhat of a sleaze, he seemed genuinely concerned. From his experience dealing with scumbags, he knew looks could be deceiving, but Cooper had always had a sixth sense about people, and this one told him he wasn't a bad guy. He'd give him the benefit of the doubt. "I'm sure once the dust settles, he'll be back for the grocery run. I'm sure he misses the tips."

Kaye Simmons looked up, startled. "Of course. How terrible of me." He picked his wallet out of his back pocket and took out a few bills. "Thank you."

Cooper looked at the bills and smiled. Ryan was indeed making good tips, and Simmons didn't seem to have any problems giving the same money to other delivery boys. He pursed his lips. "That's not why I said it. I'm doing the deliveries as a favor to Calley, not for the tips. I have another job, so you can keep this." He pushed the bills back in Kaye Simmons's direction.

Kaye looked at the money. "It wouldn't feel right. Where I come from, you tip the person who does something for you. I made my way through college working for tips."

Cooper looked at Kaye. He didn't seem devious or malign. He was inclined to file him with the good people. So he took the money. "I'll put this in Ryan's till."

"Don't tell him it comes from me," Kaye was quick to add.

"I'm sure he'd appreciate it, since he's losing out on tips now," Cooper replied. He was fishing, hoping to draw Simmons out of his cage.

"He's mad at me. We had a… difference of opinion about… something."

Cooper nodded, not saying anything. Damn, he was still good at this! He tried not to gloat and simply give Simmons the chance to confess.

"He admired my motorcycle, like you did, many times. He kept looking at it whenever he passed it in the garage. I let him sit on it one day, showed him how to start it. I knew he wanted to take it for a spin, but you see, this is my baby. I scrimped and saved for it while working off my student loans. I bought it old and fixed it up. I was scared something would happen to it, but Ryan kept asking, and one day I told him he could take it round the block. He took forever to come back, though, so I called the sheriff's office. I swear I was only worried that something had happened to Ryan."

Cooper stayed calm while Kaye clearly got worked up about the whole thing. Kaye's speech didn't feel rehearsed, and Cooper didn't get the idea that Kaye was lying. Maybe he wasn't telling the whole story, but what he was telling seemed to ring true.

"I'd be worried about an inexperienced kid riding my bike too," Cooper replied. "I'm sure the sheriff saw it your way." Playing the sympathy card came easy for an ex-shark of a lawyer like Cooper.

"It was his deputy. But yeah, he got me to drop the charges. I guess I overreacted. But Ryan hasn't been around here since he brought the bike back."

Cooper raised his hand, with the money still in it. "Ryan has a box under the register where we put his tips. I'll just add it to them. He won't know it comes from you."

Kaye smiled. "Thanks. I appreciate it."

As Cooper turned to leave, Kaye spoke again. "I have a few of Calley's boxes here. Ryan... didn't take them last time. I was hoping... never mind."

Cooper was hoping too. That Kaye would divulge some more, for instance, but he figured if he wanted to pretend to be innocent, he couldn't push. He had to appear oblivious. Maybe he could get a second chance when he did Calley's grocery run the next week. "I'll take them off your hands. Calley can always use more boxes," he said casually.

On the way to his other deliveries, Cooper kept mulling over the conversation he'd had with Kaye Simmons and wondered if Ryan would let him come close enough to ask him a few things as well. The problem was that he was the wrong person to talk to him. Ryan had issues with Cooper, and they were best dealt with staying as far away from him as possible.

As Cooper turned up the dirt road toward the Blackwater Ranch, he decided to throw Gable a lure and see if he was willing to try and coax something out of Ryan. He had only the deliveries for Gable and for the Blue River left in his truck, so he had some time.

Just as he stopped the truck, Gable came walking over to the homestead. "You're late." There was no malice in his voice.

"Had to finish my real job first."

"Calley told me about asking Grant for a hand. Come on inside."

After Cooper put down the box, Gable immediately started unpacking it. "Want a cup of coffee?"

"Sure," Cooper replied. "I'll get it. You too?"

Gable nodded.

Cooper decided to get right to the point, like Gable always did. He was sure the man would appreciate it. "So how's Ryan working out here?"

"He's good. Hard worker. Doesn't talk back. Reminds me a bit of Rory when he first arrived here." When the box was empty, he dropped it on the floor and sat down opposite Cooper to drink his coffee. "Which makes me worry a bit, but then it's probably not my business, so I don't pry."

"Why does it make you worry?"

"Rory had a few skeletons in his closet. Flynn actually worries more than I do. I believe everyone carries a cross, and if it becomes too heavy, we automatically find out where we need to help alleviate the burden. But Flynn wants to help before it becomes too much, so he worries. And tells me about it. What can I do? Nothing, so I don't worry until I absolutely have to."

"Well, I worry too," Cooper admitted.

Gable snorted. "You and Flynn." He shook his head. "Never took you for a mother hen, Coop."

"There's a lot you don't know about me."

"Just don't poke Ryan too much, okay? He's not your biggest fan, with everything he's been through in his life. Your boyfriend would probably have a better chance at that."

Cooper felt the coffee he was drinking go down the wrong way. "What?" he sputtered.

"Your deputy friend. Kelly Freed. Ryan likes him better. He could probably talk to him. Ryan respects the uniform."

"He's not my boyfriend, Gabe. He's married."

"Mmh." Gable nodded, taking a sip from his mug as if he was brushing Cooper's statement off.

Cooper knew Gable was right, of course. If anyone had a shot at talking to Ryan it was Kelly. He'd scored points with Ryan before, which meant Cooper needed to talk to Kelly about the conversation he'd had with Kaye Simmons. He got up from the table. "Thanks for the coffee. I have two more errands to run."

"Thanks for bringing around our food," Gable said, escorting him outside.

ONCE he was driving again, Cooper was determined to talk to Kelly about Ryan. Instead of taking the next dirt road home, he drove the truck across town to the remote road that lead to Kelly's house. As usual, he was greeted by Teo.

"Mr. Nelson, what brings you here?"

"I'd like to talk to Kelly, if that's possible."

Teo smiled accommodatingly. "He's not home yet, I'm afraid, but Nina will kill me if I don't invite you in. She's out back. You can wait for him there."

Cooper hesitated for a moment. He didn't know if he was ready to spend time alone with Nina and figured that after Kelly arrived, he wouldn't be able to speak to him alone either. Teo's slightly impatient look made the decision for him. "I don't suppose you know how long he'll be?"

Teo shook his head.

"Fine. I guess I can wait for ten minutes or so."

Cooper walked around the wraparound porch and heard Nina's clear voice at the back. He waited just before the corner to listen to her speak.

"Maybe the case isn't as open and shut as you imagined. *Full Stop. New Line.* Go over the new text again and add the corrections mentioned in the amendment. Send it back to me, and I'll read it again. *New Line.* Talk to you soon, *Comma. New Line.* Nina."

He took a step forward. She was sitting facing the yard, laptop computer in front of her and slim earphones with speech mic on her head. Cooper didn't think she'd heard him.

"*E-mail To* Jeffrey Pike. *Correct* Jeffrey." She sighed, then grumbled. "Bloody speech program. Blast! *Delete Three Last Words.* For crying out loud! *Go To Sleep.*"

Cooper couldn't resist chuckling, and a small change in the way she held her head signaled she knew he was there. He took a few steps forward until he was in her range of vision. The deep lines across her forehead lifted as she smiled at him. "Cooper, darling. So good to see you! What brings you here?"

"I thought I'd come here to hear you curse. And in true Nina fashion, you keep it clean."

"I can't stand all this technology. I wish I could live without it, but I can't."

Cooper lifted his hands in defeat. "Don't look at me. I don't even own a cell phone."

She continued smiling. "Yeah, Kelly told me. It drives him crazy that he can't reach you. Act surprised if he buys you one for your birthday."

"Not much use," Cooper replied, "I'd probably lose it in a haystack somewhere."

"You do a lot of fooling around in haystacks these days?"

Cooper chuckled. "I muck out stables for living. Not that it's any of your business, but there's not that many guys to fool around with at the ranch."

Cooper sat next to her and caressed her hand for a moment, hoping it would take her mind off his personal life. He knew it would take more than that. "I have some information for Kelly. Something for a case he was called out to last week and that didn't amount to anything. I guess it's not that important."

Nina narrowed her eyes. "Last week? Ryan something? And a local teacher. About a motorcycle that did or didn't get stolen?"

Cooper smiled, feeling himself relax a bit. "You can draw blood from a stone, Nina Alexander."

"It's not that hard. Kelly tells me everything. I don't get out much, don't have the burden of actually knowing these people, and

Kelly is very good at presenting only the facts. Something he learned from you in school, if I recall."

"Yes," he agreed. "I told him he could never be a good lawman if he kept letting the facts be clouded by his emotions. Judges' decisions can only be made regarding the facts."

"Which is why you, Cooper, were such a deft hand at playing with a jury's emotions!" She smiled broadly, her eyes twinkling.

"Well, you were always good at drawing strange conclusions. What did you think about the motorcycle case?"

"Sounds like there might be more to the relationship between Ryan and that teacher."

"Something inappropriate?"

Nina cocked her head. "Depends on your definition."

"Try: within the confines of the law."

"Yes," Nina answered casually. "According to the law, it would be inappropriate for an adult to have a relationship with a minor. Because, according to the law, said minor cannot consent. Of course we both know some minors are very capable of consenting. Still, we need to protect the minor."

"He's not allowed to make deliveries to the teacher's house anymore, and he's kept busy inside the shop, where the teacher rarely, if ever, comes."

"And how about school?"

"The high school is separated from the middle school where the teacher works."

"And is Ryan happy?"

"He's a Goth teenager. They don't come in 'happy' these days. Only in 'emo' it seems."

Nina laughed again, and Cooper was reminded of how much he enjoyed her laugh. She was still smiling as she continued. "Now let's talk about someone else's happiness."

"Oh?" Cooper replied, feigning innocence.

"Yours and Kelly's." The smile was gone from her face, and Cooper simply wanted to run, but he couldn't do that to her. He was snared into her web, though, and he remembered very clearly why she was called the killer queen.

"After our first time reconnecting, I told Kelly to pursue you. I literally gave him permission."

"Why?" Cooper asked flatly, knowing what was coming.

"Because he needs you almost as much as you need him."

"You're his wife, for heaven's sake."

"And bad me, should I be ashamed of what I'm offering you? Well, I'm not. He and I have never been husband and wife, other than by law. We've been friends, very close friends, luckily, but I knew when I married him that I could never give him what he needed other than respectability and acceptance by his peers. Well, he got that."

Nina's face was tense with determination, but that was about all the emotion she was showing. At the same time, Cooper felt the emotion well up inside him. She was still on their side, still rooting for them from the corner. He could have his cake and eat it too. He could have Kelly and still make sure Nina was taken care of. If only he could get over himself. If only he could set aside the promise he'd made when Martin killed himself.

"Nina, he's still your husband. What you said doesn't change anything."

Her face softened. "He was rejected by you, Coop. He's not going to make the first move. He's too scared of being rejected again. He'd rather live not knowing than knowing for sure you don't want him. And I know you still want him. I can almost smell it on you. I can see it in the way you look at him." This time there *was* emotion in her face. And it was love. Love for Kelly and maybe even love for him.

"He's still your husband," Cooper repeated.

"And he'll continue to perform his husbandly duties, such as they were up to now. He'll still make sure I'm taken care of. He'll still love me as much as before. Who knows, maybe he'll love me even more once he finds you again."

Nina's face twitched slightly, and almost without conscious thought, Cooper wiped a tear from her cheek with his bare hand. She turned into it, and he pulled off her headphones so he could envelop her head in his arms, rocking her ever so gently while she cried. Cooper kept it dry, but his throat felt swollen and his eyes itched. Nina didn't cry for very long. She wasn't the woman to dwell on her own misery.

They sat together until Teo came out.

"Everything okay?"

Nina nodded, and Cooper let go of her.

"Kelly called to say we should eat. He's stuck in the office." He turned to Cooper. "Are you staying for dinner, Mr. Nelson?"

Cooper shook his head. "I need to deliver one more batch of groceries. I better go home. Besides, I kept you from work." He put down the headphones he was still holding, then nodded and turned around to walk off the porch to his truck.

—18—

AS KELLY sat in his car in front of the Blue River Ranch crew house, he was constantly wavering between extremes. He knew if he walked in to find Cooper, there would be no way back. His body ached for Cooper's touch like it was nobody's business, and although he'd driven there telling himself that if he indulged himself just once, he'd get it out of his system, he knew that wouldn't be the case. That one short kiss Cooper had bestowed on him had made that clear. Ever since that night, Kelly couldn't even keep his mind on his job. One time wouldn't be enough, just like one kiss hadn't been enough.

He'd already gotten out of the car once, only to get in again. It was crazy. He didn't even know which of the many rooms in the house was Cooper's, since he'd only been inside the communal areas. Sitting back inside, he was drumming his fingers on the dashboard, moving from leaning forward to sagging back against his seat as he wavered between going inside and starting the car up to drive away.

What did he have to lose by walking inside?

Try everything he'd worked for before he came to Idaho. This wasn't a big city full of liberal thinkers. This was a rural area in a red state where same-sex relationships were spit upon and people were fired for less than being gay. And he was running for public office. He'd never get elected, and this was the closest he'd ever gotten to the law enforcement job he'd dreamed of since he was old enough to think about what he wanted to be when he grew up. He'd have to hide who he was, hide his love for Cooper, and not just now, but forever. Hadn't Cooper said he didn't want to be anyone's dirty little secret anymore, or was this something Kelly had put into his own mind?

Then again, hiding who he truly was had become second nature to Kelly. He'd even hidden it from himself. After college he'd barely looked at another man, had only indulged himself with a little taste here or there, and stopped altogether when he realized it gave him no satisfaction. He'd simply compartmentalized the urges, put all those attractions to men in a big box and hid it at the back of his wardrobe along with all the memories of the one time in his life he'd felt truly fulfilled. That year with Cooper. Those memories hadn't resurfaced until Cooper walked back into his life again.

Kelly hit the steering wheel with the side of his fist and got out, locking the doors with the little gizmo attached to his key. To hell with consequences. He wanted Cooper's tall, sinewy body under his hands, and if Cooper rejected him, then Kelly would go home and lick his wounds, but not before he tried. It was his father who'd taught him that not succeeding was one thing, but you had to try at least once. Kelly smiled at the thought that his old dad surely hadn't meant it to apply to this particular situation, but he was going to apply it anyway. He was going to walk up to Cooper and tell him he wanted him. Right there and right now. To hell with romance or delicate sensibilities. They were men. Raw, lustful, horny men.

Kelly took big strides toward the crew house and gained entrance by swinging open the back door Cooper had used when they were there before. The hallway was dark and quiet, and in the distance Kelly heard cascading water that stopped abruptly. He didn't stop walking, though, determined to find Cooper and show him why he was here. He looked around to find his bearings and stopped in his tracks when he saw Cooper coming out of the shower block, jeans barely hanging on to his hips and a towel hung over his shoulders.

"A little late for a social visit, isn't it?" Cooper said in his familiar, overly confident drawl.

Kelly felt his confidence evaporate. Cooper had always been lean, but manual labor had certainly done nice things to his body. Seeing the sparse-but-certainly-there chest hair taper off into a treasure trail down to the almost-visible pubic hair that was flirting with the rim of Cooper's jeans made Kelly's own jeans grow even tighter than they were before. He swallowed the excess saliva in his mouth as Cooper cocked his head.

"Official business, then, Deputy Freed?"

Kelly shook his head in one quick jab. "I'm… I missed you at the house. I… I'm here for you. To see you."

Cooper's arrogant gaze softened some. "Let's take this somewhere more private, then." He didn't wait for Kelly's answer, but turned to the hallway stairs and started walking up them without looking to see if Kelly was following.

Despite his determination abandoning him, Kelly couldn't *not* follow Cooper up the stairs. He was here now, and Cooper clearly wasn't turning him away. He knew from experience the only way Cooper was not going to have his way with him was if Kelly walked back to his car and drove off. His internal compass was pointing up the stairs, though, and putting one foot in front of the other, he followed.

When Kelly turned into the only room where the door was still open, he saw Cooper putting on a T-shirt and felt a pang of disappointment.

"Close the door, will you? Do you want a drink?"

Kelly did as he was asked and stood waiting, too unsure what to do to move from his spot near the door. Cooper took out two tumblers and a bottle of Jameson. "I don't drink," Kelly said with a clear croak in his voice.

"Sounds like you could use some, though. Just to oil that voice of yours." Cooper took a few steps closer, until Kelly could smell his soap.

"No hard liquor," Kelly said, sounding marginally less rough. "The occasional beer or glass of wine, maybe, if the occasion calls for it."

"That's why it's occasional," Cooper replied with the teasing smile that always made Kelly go weak at the knees. This time was no different. Kelly tried to hold his ground by stretching his back. It made him feel taller but achieved little else. He was a bigger guy than Cooper, broader, heavier, more muscled even, but Cooper had always been the stronger one. Cooper had always been the one in charge of their relationship, from their first crushing kiss in the men's room of the law library to their last bout of lovemaking before Cooper left. Cooper was even in charge if he was the one biting the pillow and being plowed into the mattress by Kelly, and Kelly knew it. Even fifteen years later, Kelly was still waiting for Cooper to make the first move.

Only this time, Cooper was teasing but not following through. Cooper was hovering around Kelly's personal space but never quite breaching it: inviting him to drink and then withdrawing the glass, brushing past him on the way to the small washbasin to fill the other tumbler with water, stepping closer to offer him the glass. Kelly had the urge to pull Cooper closer and tell him to stop the teasing but couldn't make his limbs move. He wanted to crush his lips against Cooper's the way Cooper had done after their last talk, but he didn't dare. What was he afraid of? He didn't think Cooper would reject his advances. And if he ever wanted to assert that he'd changed, that working in law enforcement had made him grow from the shy puppy dog he was in college to a grown man, in charge of his own life and capable of taking the upper hand, now was the time. So why didn't he, then?

Kelly took the glass of water from Cooper and watched him sit down on the edge of his bed.

Cooper saluted him with his glass, filled with about half an inch of Jameson, which he downed in one gulp before setting it on the nightstand. Then he patted the bed. "Sit. You're making me nervous standing there."

Kelly hesitated. It felt very intimate to sit on the bed and reminded him very much of their first time together.

"I won't bite. Unless you specifically ask me to."

Kelly smiled, more because he was nervous than because he thought Cooper was funny. That line was Cooper's favorite way to break the ice. He said it to anyone and everyone. Kelly had even heard Cooper use it in mock court, and he was sure it could be found in certain court transcripts from Cooper's real cases as well.

"I bet you say that to all the guys," Kelly replied in an effort to lighten his own mood.

Cooper flashed his perfect row of teeth and broke his incessant stare. "Not lately."

Kelly detected something he thought he'd never see again. Cooper was lowering his guard. Cooper was letting Kelly see behind the near-arrogant façade he always wore in public. Fifteen years ago, it had taken a long time for Kelly to get a glimpse of the real Cooper, and now he was getting it almost right off the bat. Then again, when he'd walked into Cooper that first time in town, he had almost not recognized him because Cooper was intentionally trying to blend into the crowd, something the old Cooper would never have done. Maybe more changes had occurred in the last fifteen years?

With some apprehension, Kelly slowly sat down on the bed, making sure they didn't touch.

"Will you just relax a bit, Kells?" Cooper asked, nudging Kelly with his elbow before returning to his own space.

"It's hard," Kelly said softly.

"I saw that when you were standing up," Cooper teased. "Should be easier now you're sitting."

"Not really," Kelly replied. He was starting to feel a bit more at ease now it was apparent Cooper wasn't going to jump him. He didn't know why, because he actually wanted Cooper to make the first move.

"So why *did* you come here tonight?"

Kelly shrugged. Was he brave enough to tell Cooper the truth? "I… I blocked all thoughts of you pretty successfully for the last twelve years or so. I can't anymore… for some reason."

To Kelly's surprise, Cooper didn't immediately reply. In fact they sat together in silence for what felt like long minutes and just stared at the floor in front of their feet. Kelly had expected some witty reply from Cooper, stating that it was natural that Kelly couldn't stop thinking about him because he was so irresistible, but it didn't happen.

Instead, Cooper cleared his throat. "I almost did more than kiss you in front of that hospital, Kelly. I had to walk away, or I would have done some very inappropriate things to you."

"Why didn't you?"

"We were practically in public. Any car could have driven up that parking lot, and the driver could have seen our next sheriff kissing a man." Cooper chuckled. "I know we never used to mind an audience—"

"*You* never minded an audience. I was always scared we'd get caught."

"But you were always good to go anyway." Cooper chuckled, and Kelly wondered if he was nervous. Cooper nervous? This was unheard of.

"I wished for you to turn around. I wanted to get up and chase after you. That night I dreamed I did and we fucked against the car."

"Al fresco? You naughty man."

Kelly caught Cooper eyeing him sideways, a contented smile plastered all over his face, and he moved a little closer, hoping Cooper would kiss him. When he didn't, he sighed. "You made me naughty. You and your constant innuendo. You and fucking in the law library after our fellow students left. You and your determination to show me it was good whichever way we did it."

"You were a very good student. I loved tutoring you."

"So kiss me, then."

Cooper didn't kiss him. Instead, he rubbed his nose against Kelly's. "Remember that bunk bed in that cabin on your parents' estate?"

"Fuck, Cooper, how could I not?" All of a sudden, Kelly's cock was pushing harder against the zipper of his jeans, and the images came flooding back.

"You were so receptive, so turned on. You came, what? Five times?"

"Four or five. I stopped counting."

"In less than an hour. Every time I touched you. Every time I rubbed you or pinched your nipples you'd moan, and I just had to hover over you and you'd shoot. Five. Fucking. Times."

"I was young. And I loved you."

Cooper snorted. "You were so turned on anyone could have gotten you off."

"No, Cooper." Kelly shook his head. "Not just anyone. You. It was always you."

Cooper smiled at him as if he didn't believe it, but Kelly kept looking at him, waiting for the coin to drop. Slowly, realization seemed to invade Cooper's mind. His smile waned.

"Those things don't happen, Kells. You like men, not just one man. Gays aren't just gay for one man."

Kelly bit the inside of his cheek, trying to come up with a way to explain it to Cooper. "Before you, I fooled around a bit. A few hand jobs, one blow job, and I was on the receiving end of that one. Before you, there was also a girl. She didn't do it for me. I knew that. But she was what my parents wanted for me."

"Your parents—"

Kelly cut Cooper off by holding up his hand. "It's what society wanted from me, and although I knew I liked boys, not girls, I was raised to know it wasn't right. So I tried to do it right. In their eyes."

"By marrying Nina."

"Will you just let me finish?" Kelly said, exasperation in his voice and written all over his face.

Cooper nodded and bit his lips.

"I'm sorry I wasn't as gay as you right off the bat, Coop." Kelly saw Cooper start to say something and then stop, which he was grateful for. "Okay, I was as gay as you, but I didn't feel as free to express it. At the time, I believed it was a phase and I would grow out of it, and then I met you, and that all went out the window. You made me believe that it was actually possible. That I could actually have a relationship with a man and that it would make me happy."

"And then I left." Now it was Cooper's time to raise his hand to stop Kelly talking. "I know you told me to stop interrupting." He lowered his hand again and gestured to give the floor back to Kelly.

"Yes, you left. Without an explanation." Kelly felt a little calmer now, and he paused for Cooper to explain himself, but Cooper stayed uncharacteristically silent. Maybe it wasn't so out of character for the new Cooper. "I was naïve. I thought that what we had was forever."

Cooper scooted back and turned so he could sit with his back against the headboard of the bed, facing Kelly. His knees were pulled up and his bare feet on the covers, just far enough back so they didn't touch Kelly's thigh.

Kelly didn't look at Cooper, feeling both the distance Cooper had created and his piercing stare. The earlier sexual tension between them had changed to something more hostile, and Kelly didn't like it, but this talk had been a long time coming, and Kelly hoped they'd come out of it with at least some closure.

"I got a great offer, Kelly," Cooper said after a long silence. His voice sounded a lot softer and less bitter than Kelly had predicted. "You had two more years of school ahead of you. Your grades were a lot worse than I thought they would be, so I knew I was distracting you."

"You weren't distracting me, Coop."

"Yes, I was. And you need good grades in law school. There it's not just a matter of finishing. You need to finish first or second. Even for a law enforcement career, Kells."

"Next you're going to tell me you left me for me."

Cooper bit the side of his finger and stared without looking at Kelly. "No. That's what I told myself at the time, but no, I didn't leave you for that. I left because I thought it was the best thing to do at the time. It was a great offer, and I... I thought it would be easier to go to a firm that didn't know me and just took me on because of my grades. I figured I could make a name for myself, and then it wouldn't matter that I was gay. I thought we could just keep in touch, and if it was really more than infatuation, we could pick up the relationship again after you finished school."

"I would have stayed in touch if I'd known where you were." Kelly had felt bitter and angry, but he'd managed to *not* put that in his voice. Instead he sounded like a little kid, whiny and afraid. It was in the silence after his statement that Kelly realized this was how he felt now. He was scared of losing Cooper again, but at the same time, he wasn't sure if this Cooper was still the man he'd fallen so desperately in love with. Occasionally, he saw glimpses of the overly confident man who could talk his way out of any situation, of the gregarious, flamboyant lawyer who had left him behind at school, but most of the time, the Cooper he saw now was a quiet, brooding man who no longer had all the answers.

Kelly finally dared to look at Cooper again and met his eyes. There was no defiance in there and no apology. Instead, Kelly saw something he hadn't expected. He saw unconditional love. And maybe a little regret.

Cooper slid his feet forward and wiggled his toes underneath Kelly's thigh. Kelly couldn't help smiling. Cooper's long, slender feet had been begging to be touched all the while they'd been sitting there, but Kelly hadn't dared. Now feeling those bony extremities wiggling underneath him provided the only connection between them. Kelly put his hand on Cooper's leg but didn't know how to proceed from there.

"I talked to Nina," Cooper said, his seductive smile still on his face.

"Oh?" Kelly felt the tension return, so he looked at the place where his hand touched Cooper's leg.

"I'm sure if she'd had the use of her arms, she would have wrapped you up with a big red bow."

"What do you mean?" Kelly asked, although the conversation he'd had with her about Cooper a few weeks earlier gave him a pretty good idea.

"She handed you to me on a plate, Kells."

When Kelly looked at Cooper again, Cooper was no longer smiling. Instead, he was looking at his hands resting in his lap, waiting for Kelly to make a move. But hadn't he just made that move, coming here without being invited? "She told me."

"And is that why you're here now?"

Kelly shook his head. "She didn't tell me today. She told me weeks ago. I just... I don't know why I didn't come then, but I had a hundred reasons why I couldn't."

"And now?"

"I can't concentrate on my work."

"So you're here because of work?"

"Dammit, Cooper, stop doing that!" Kelly shouted.

"What?"

"Messing with me. I'm not that stupid little kid from law school anymore."

"You could have fooled me."

Frustration was getting the better of Kelly. Cooper was being an ass, just like he'd always been an ass in law school. Only then Kelly was so blinded by love, he hadn't really noticed how Cooper got off on getting under Kelly's skin and teasing him, only to back off at the last minute. He'd been acting just like that since Kelly had walked into Cooper's room He was still being an arrogant SOB, and Kelly couldn't take it anymore. He put the tumbler of water down on the floor before getting up from the bed and turned to face Cooper. With his left hand, he grabbed the leg that was closest to him and yanked it, making Cooper slip down the bed until he was almost flat on his back. Kelly lifted his knee onto the bed and planted it between Cooper's legs before putting one hand on either side of Cooper and leaning over him. He waited only a moment to see the look of surprise on Cooper's face before he leaned down and kissed Cooper hard.

To his relief, Cooper kissed him back almost immediately. Cooper reached for Kelly's head and grabbed it so he'd stay put.

Not that Kelly was going anywhere. Cooper's mouth tasted of Jameson, and he smelled soapy clean yet manly, which was no surprise since he'd seen him walk out of the shower. As Kelly dared to lower his body over Cooper's, another thing became apparent.

Cooper was hard inside his jeans.

—19—

WHAT Cooper had feared most about getting reacquainted with Kelly had arrived sooner than he'd expected. While Kelly had walked into the crew house highly strung and nervous, his state had morphed into disappointment in less than half an hour.

Cooper had been pleasantly surprised that he could still get Kelly riled up, even to the point where Kelly had taken the initiative to kiss him. It had gotten out of hand way too quickly, as Kelly had started grinding against Cooper to the point where Cooper had feared they were just going to get each other off like a couple of randy teenagers, and Kelly would then realize what had happened and would run off, embarrassed, just like their first time together. And Cooper was too old for that nonsense. He'd lived without for long enough to realize that a quick frotting session wouldn't be worth it for him.

And yes, he still had the habit of overthinking and rationalizing everything. It's what had made him a great lawyer and what had kept him out of most troubles he'd encountered in his lifetime.

So he'd pushed Kelly away, and now Kelly was lying next to him on his bed, staring at the ceiling.

Cooper knew he was no prize. He was only a distant remnant of the man he'd been when Kelly, in all his youthful enthusiasm, had followed him around law school like a lovesick puppy. He couldn't blame Kelly for feeling let down. Not after spending fifteen years pining for a man who no longer existed. This was why Cooper hadn't put the moves on Kelly despite Kelly practically offering himself on a silver plate. Not to mention Nina applying all her skills to push them toward each other.

It wasn't for lack of want. Over the course of the last weeks, he'd had a hard time banning Kelly from his thoughts. The fact that Kelly sought him out, asking for his help on a number of occasions and then making excuses to come back to the ranch just to say thank you, didn't help matters. Although he'd blocked himself from all sorts of advances for the last few years, the looks Kelly had given him hadn't escaped him. In any sort of official capacity, Kelly was very different from the kid he'd fallen for in law school. In uniform Kelly was in command, and his formidable presence, with a crew cut and a clean-shaven face on top of a tall, bulky frame, gave him the perfect balance between being authoritarian and approachable. In private, Kelly was still insecure and reluctant to make the first move, to the point of being submissive.

In school, Cooper had naturally taken the upper hand. There he was older, more experienced, and basically a lot more in your face than Kelly could ever be. Now the tables had turned. Cooper was just a ranch hand, invisible, inconspicuous, and Kelly would soon be the town sheriff, a man of quite some power in their neck of the woods. Yet Kelly was still looking at Cooper to instigate things. Or was that just Cooper's wishful thinking?

"So why did you really come here tonight, Kelly?" Cooper asked softly after Kelly's breathing had become almost unnoticeable next to him.

Kelly moved his arm a little so his sleeve was brushing against Cooper's arm. The warmth emanating from Kelly spread farther up Cooper's body.

Cooper had been turned on since mentioning the memory of their very sensual encounter in the cabin, and he'd moved away from Kelly just to keep himself from pulling the younger man into his arms and bending him to his will. That's what the old Cooper would have done in ten seconds flat. But he wasn't the old Cooper anymore. His arousal had been overwhelmingly clear when Kelly had let his weight come down on Cooper, though.

"I told you."

"You can't stop thinking about me," Cooper repeated, hearing some of his old mocking tone seeping into his voice.

Kelly reluctantly nodded.

"Is it sex you want?"

"No!" Kelly was quick to answer, resulting in Cooper looking at him sideways.

"Yes," Kelly continued more subduedly. "But not *just* sex. I didn't wait fifteen years for a romp in the proverbial hay."

Cooper couldn't help turning even more in Kelly's direction, telegraphing he still didn't believe Kelly.

"If I want just sex, I can go to a gay bar and get laid."

"You're not in Boston anymore, Kells. You know any gay bars around here?"

"As a matter of fact, I do," Kelly said with clear confidence, puffing up his already nicely chiseled chest. "But I don't want some anonymous encounter. I tried those after you left, and they weren't exactly… satisfying."

Cooper enjoyed seeing the confidence return to Kelly's features. It made him want to see how far he could go. He turned to his side, resting his head on his hand. "So you came here wanting to get laid. Because you know what you can expect from me?" Cooper moved a little closer to Kelly, invading his personal space. In fact, he could whisper in his ear. "Because you know I'll let you fuck me or do anything else you want, and it will be good either way?"

Kelly pulled back and turned his head so he could look Cooper in the eye. Kelly's breathing had become more deliberate, which hadn't escaped Cooper's attention. For just a moment, Cooper let his eyes wander to Kelly's groin, and he smiled as he saw the bulge he'd clearly felt earlier still there. Kelly was still aroused, and even more so than when he stood at Cooper's door earlier.

Cooper moved so close his scruff was almost touching Kelly's no longer so cleanly shaven jaw. "So what do you want, then?"

"I… I don't know."

Cooper pursed his lips. "Guests get to choose. My only stipulation is we need to keep the noise down. I don't want to let the whole house enjoy your moaning."

Kelly swallowed, and although Cooper liked Kelly's earlier rise in confidence, he had to admit that seeing the big guy go insecure again also had its perks.

They continued breathing the same air. "Tell me what you want and I'll give it to you. Tell me nothing, and nothing is what you'll get."

"Kiss me again," Kelly croaked.

Cooper pushed his face against Kelly's, their lips crushing together as Kelly put his hand on the back of Cooper's head and pulled him on top of him. Their tongues started battling again as Cooper pushed his leg between Kelly's and his groin against the bulge in Kelly's jeans, mimicking the way Kelly had seduced him earlier. Their movements instantly became frantic, as if it all had to be over in a New York minute. Kelly was pulling up Cooper's T-shirt and running his hands over Cooper's long sides while Cooper tried to pull the shirt from Kelly's jeans. They broke the kiss so Kelly could undo his belt and they could pull the shirt free together. Cooper took a few moments to enjoy the sight of an almost six-pack covered in downy hair, but allowed himself to be pulled back into a kiss that made his toes curl.

The loosened belt gave him access to the top button, and Cooper managed to pop it with his left hand. It certainly paid to be ambidextrous. He was going to get a good look at Kelly, even if taking their time, like he'd wanted to, didn't seem an option.

"Your jeans are too loose."

Kelly grunted. "I lost weight. Don't wear these all that often. Uniform."

Cooper unzipped Kelly's pants and inserted his hand over the tented gray boxer briefs underneath. "Uniform's nice too. Shows off that bubble butt of yours."

Kelly grunted and grabbed Cooper's ass, pulling them closer together again and forcing Cooper to let go of Kelly's cotton-covered cock. He had plenty of skin to cover, though, and the grinding had its own merits. Cooper threw his head back as Kelly latched on to his neck. He couldn't help smiling at the familiar feeling of Kelly's body under his hands. It was like fifteen years disappeared and they were back in Cooper's tiny law school apartment on his rickety bed. And just like fifteen years earlier, they were too rushed, too turned on, and way too impatient to make it last.

"Easy, Kells," Cooper said in an attempt to make Kelly calm down. Kelly didn't listen, though. He kept sucking at the skin over

Cooper's pulse point, and Cooper knew he was going to be marked. It turned him on even more, and he couldn't resist moaning.

"Keep it down, Coop," Kelly murmured against his skin.

Cooper had his eyes closed. "What?" he only just managed.

"Shhh, you're making a lot of noise. What if the other guys hear you?"

"What if...." Cooper pulled back as if he was stung, pushing at Kelly. The words sank in, and suddenly he saw the whole thing play out. Kelly wanted him for the sex, but there was no way he'd ever be able to be open and honest about who he loved. He was becoming Kelly's dirty little secret. He pushed at Kelly again, but realized he wasn't strong enough to push the lawman's bulky frame off him completely. Then Kelly raised himself up, resting on his outstretched arms as he looked down on Cooper, and Cooper saw his chance to roll to his side, giving Kelly no other option than to drop down on the bed next to Cooper.

"What's wrong?"

"What's wrong?" Cooper said, redirecting the question with eyebrows raised. "How about your motives for coming here?" He practically jumped out of bed, pulling up his unbuttoned pants and fastening them again after tucking in his shirt.

"My m—" Kelly stopped midword. "I wanted you. I want you. Present tense. I realized that today, although I suppose I've known that for weeks, but I just never saw I could actually have you until today."

Cooper determinedly shook his head, his lips pursed. "I'm not going there again. I'm not being some other man's dirty little secret. It killed Marty and caused irreparable damage to too many other people."

"What are you saying? That what we're doing here could be detrimental to my life? I'm not going to kill myself, Cooper. Even if you tell me now you never want to see me again, I'm not going to off myself over it."

"I'm not talking about not wanting you. What if the good folks of this town found out their sheriff liked to fuck guys? You think they'd elect a man like that? You're never going to risk being seen with me, because they might think you like taking it up the butt from that queer over at the Blue River. And then what, Kelly? All your dreams out the window because of one indiscretion?" Cooper shook his head. "I won't be the cause of that. This needs to end here."

"Cooper, please." Kelly was begging unashamedly. "Tell me what you want. I'll do anything for you. You know that."

Cooper's face softened, and his anger was replaced by pain. He leaned down, resting his hands on Kelly's knees. "There's no way, Kells. Nobody's going to buy it. You're a young guy with a sick wife, which is a great sympathy card if you play it right and make it clear that her condition doesn't in any way interfere with your ability to be on standby practically 24/7. But if they find out you're sleeping around behind her back, your reputation goes down the drain. And no amount of explaining how you two have a marriage of understanding and you only stayed with her out of a sense of duty is ever going to make them forget you fucked around behind your dying wife's back. I won't even need to argue that it was a man you slept with." Cooper pushed himself off Kelly's knees, hissing. He'd gotten carried away, and he didn't like that feeling. He wasn't a lawyer anymore. He couldn't "argue" Kelly's case. It was a lost cause, anyway.

Kelly's face showed he understood. The pain visible made it clear to Cooper he'd hit home. He wasn't happy with it, but he didn't know whether he could live through getting this intimate with Kelly again and walking away a second time. Better to end it before it really got started.

Kelly stood up and straightened his clothes. "I better leave."

"Yeah, you better."

—20—

BACK outside the crew house, Kelly got into his car. He sat there for a little while, going over what had just happened. Cooper had rejected him. That felt pretty bad, but the worst part of it was that he was right. They didn't have a future, no matter how much Kelly wanted this. The town would never forgive him. And he was so close to getting his dream. Well, as long as he neglected that other dream, the one about reconnecting with the man he loved. Then again, he'd done just that for the last fifteen years.

Kelly started the car and drove off. He knew he'd have to come back to the crew house tomorrow to entice Cooper into helping him out with the Calley situation, but first he needed a good night's sleep. And maybe a little stress release in the shower.

Turning into his driveway, Kelly tried to forget for a moment that he might have done irreparable damage to his friendship with Cooper. There was nothing he could do now. Cooper didn't have a cell phone, and it was almost midnight, so it wasn't like he could call Tim and ask him to bring Cooper a message. Besides, how was he going to convey his feelings without divulging what had just happened? No, Kelly knew he'd have to speak to Cooper about it face to face. Tomorrow. Tonight the damage was done, and if Cooper was mad at him, he'd only make him more mad by trying to sort it out now. Cooper had done the right thing and ended any possibility of them rekindling their relationship, and Kelly knew that, given enough time, he'd be grateful for it. Right now he felt gutted, though. He couldn't let it hurt too much. He'd bide his time and wait for the pain to ease. At least he'd tried. His dad would be pleased.

With that thought in mind, he parked his car and snuck into the house. He carefully walked down the hall, purposely avoiding the planks that creaked, and peered into Nina's bedroom out of habit. She was in bed, her CPAP machine helping her breathe at night and providing the only sound in the room, which, like the rest of the house, was quiet.

He was still getting undressed when her buzzer went off. He didn't hurry but didn't stall either. It was more likely that she'd just spotted him looking in but hadn't been able to call him over in the short time he'd been there than that she was in any sort of trouble. He didn't walk so carefully, though. The buzzer would have woken Teo as well, and with that the whole house would be up.

"Everything okay, Nee?" Kelly asked, wiping her hair from her forehead before taking off her breathing mask.

"I'm fine, just wanted to talk to you," she replied before Teo walked in.

"Need any help, Kelly?" Teo asked.

Kelly looked at Teo, remembering how Cooper had thought that Teo was his toy boy. It made him smile. "Everything's fine. You can go back to bed. Sorry for waking you up."

Teo shrugged. "'S okay. I was still reading. Good night."

Kelly waited for Teo to leave to turn back to Nina. "So what did you want to tell me?"

"Crawl into bed with me?"

"Nina," Kelly cautioned.

"Don't make me beg for it, Kells. I just need to be held from time to time for more than just washing or dressing, and you look like you could use it too, so I figured...." She didn't finish her sentence, but Kelly knew what she meant. As usual, she was right. "I know I'm not the person you want to be close to right now, but then I've never been able to replace him, anyway."

Kelly closed the door, indicating to Teo to stay out, and walked around the bed before taking out the placement pillow that kept Nina on her side for a portion of the night. He crawled into the vacated space and snuggled closer to her, careful not to hurt her with any rough movements. She was right. He needed the closeness of his friend right now.

"You were with Cooper tonight."

It wasn't a question, and Kelly wondered how she knew, because he'd done what he always did and had simply phoned home that he would be working late. It had only been a half lie, since he'd actually had to reply to a call, but he was done by eight and had then made the decision he was going to go to Cooper's.

"I had to sort a few things out."

"And did you?"

Kelly sighed. "I might have made things worse."

"Atta boy."

Kelly was confused about her reply. "Meaning?"

"I knew it would only be a matter of time before the two of you ended up in bed together again. It just happened a lot sooner than I predicted."

There was no use trying to cover it up. Nina always knew. Kelly had often wondered if it was at all possible to blindside her. He didn't even want to try. "But I screwed it up anyway."

"How?"

"I… said something I shouldn't have. And he…."

She didn't stop his torture by interrupting him or even trying to finish the sentence for him. The long moments of silence seemed to drag on forever.

"I doubt Cooper would turn you away for saying something wrong, Kells," Nina said eventually. "It was that good, hey?"

"Nee." Kelly grunted in frustration. He hated talking about this with Nina. It was no different now than it had been fifteen years earlier in law school. On the other hand, she was a master at putting things in perspective. If a person existed he could discuss this with, it would be her. "All right. You win. We kissed. And groped a little. It wasn't perfect or stellar, just…. He made me see what I was missing." He rested his head against the back of hers, clamoring for comfort, wishing she could turn around and give him a big bear hug like she did fifteen years ago after he'd finally admitted to another living soul that he wanted Cooper in his bed.

Instead, she sighed. "Life isn't fair, is it?"

It flipped Kelly out of his funk. Nina was right. Life wasn't fair. Nina was the prime example of that. All of a sudden, his man problems seemed trite and unimportant. He'd figure out a way to live with his feelings and, if Cooper still wanted to give him the time of day, find a way to live with Cooper's feelings too. Who knows, maybe they could meet each other halfway. And he'd continue to be the best sheriff he could be. His passion for his job and the fact he put these people first had to mean something. He had to believe that if he just did the right thing, something as inconsequential as the fact he loved a man wouldn't matter. He just couldn't come out and say it. For Nina's sake. They might understand he was gay, but they'd never forgive him for taking on a lover while he had a sick wife at home. They'd never understand she had given him permission. Or that they'd entered a marriage of convenience, albeit a very loving one.

Lulled by his fatigue and the warmth of Nina's proximity, Kelly found himself drifting off.

"Kelly?"

He inhaled audibly, shaking himself awake.

"Tuck me back in, give me my mask so I can breathe, and then take a shower."

"I smell?" Kelly asked, still struggling to get through the cloud he had for a brain.

"I can smell Cooper all over you. Brings back memories of better times, but still…."

"Okay," Kelly conceded, getting out of bed and replacing the pillow before walking toward the door.

"Kelly? Oxygen?"

Kelly returned, shaking his head at his own denseness. He organized Nina's CPAP machine without saying another word and then whispered a good night before walking into the corridor to take a shower.

—21—

COOPER was sitting alone in the kitchen of the crew house, bent over some of his old law books, when footsteps caught his attention. Usually he didn't look up, since guys were always coming and going in the evening, but these steps stopped right in front of the kitchen table.

"Deputy Freed. What brings you here?" he said, closing the book before looking up.

Kelly was still in uniform, turning his hat in his nervous hands. "I came to…. Can we go somewhere more private?"

Cooper surveyed his surroundings. The door to the TV room was ajar, and they could hear faint noises of some movie playing, but there didn't seem to be a lot of guys watching it. "Unless you want to bend me over the table, I think we're safe."

Kelly didn't smile at Cooper's obvious taunt.

"Lighten up, Deputy. I'm not carrying a grudge."

"Stop calling me that. I didn't think I was anything other than Kelly to you."

"You're in uniform," Cooper started, smiling broadly at Kelly. He hadn't been entirely truthful about not carrying a grudge. He'd felt rejected and used after Kelly had made it clear their relationship would never see the light of day, and they hadn't talked since, so he was still feeling like he needed to give him a hard time. Kelly's demeanor, slumped over and submissive, which looked a little strange on such a broad man, made Cooper soften, though. "It's not that I don't like your uniform, but it always makes me want to call you Deputy." He gestured at the bench on the other side of the worn table. "Sit. You're too tall to look up to all the time from where I'm sitting."

Kelly sat down, his hat next to him on the table and his elbows resting on the worn wood. He was still making himself smaller than he was, and Cooper almost instinctively sat up straighter. He stacked his books and tried to make it seem accidental when his knuckles brushed over Kelly's folded hands. It wasn't, though. Their interaction, now almost twenty-four hours ago, had lit a furnace in him that was hard to suppress. Despite being the rational one and ending it, Cooper still craved Kelly.

"So what are you looking for in your old law books?" Kelly asked casually.

"Family law. Child custody."

"For Gable?"

"For everyone. Temporary and permanent," Cooper replied. "Calley needs to put everything in order. Ideally, this would mean she needs to get custody away from Bill and set Gable up as legal guardian for her twins, maybe even Flynn as a second legal guardian."

"That may be pushing it a bit."

Cooper looked up at Kelly. "We don't need to establish Gable and Flynn's relationship for that. If we let the courts decide, it's never going to happen, but if Bill no longer has legal guardianship, Calley can decide on her own who becomes the children's guardian or guardians, plural, in case of her death."

"And what about Noah and Ryan?"

"That's another matter," Cooper said with a sigh. "They're wards of the state. If anything should happen to Calley, they revert to the state, and it's the state's responsibility to find them another family. The problem there is that they might do it even before Calley's eventual death, when they feel they're too much of a burden for Calley to carry if she's sick."

"Let's hope she's not too sick to care for them, then. I don't look forward to calling child services for those kids. They seem perfectly happy the way they are now."

Cooper agreed, but he knew it would be an uphill battle. He didn't think Kelly had come here to talk about what Cooper did in his spare time. He just had to ask. "So, what brings you here?" He tried to sound lighthearted but was not feeling it. In fact, he dreaded the answer, but he also hated the insecurity.

"I'm sorry about the other night," Kelly replied softly.

"What?" Cooper asked. He'd heard what Kelly said, but wanted to make sure.

"I'm sorry… about what happened last night," Kelly repeated, this time in an almost normal voice. "I didn't mean to say what I said. I wanted—" Kelly looked around as if he was still worried people would overhear. "—to stay and—"

"It's better this way," Cooper interrupted. Kelly's answer wasn't what he'd expected. He'd predicted that Kelly would have excuses, all sorts of good reasons to tell Cooper he'd made a mistake coming in the first place, that he hadn't really wanted to be there, but Kelly had all but admitted his only mistake was wanting him.

"My whole world caved in last night, Coop."

Cooper looked at him, forehead in a deep frown. Kelly looked like a little kid who was about to start crying. Cooper wanted to grab him by his lapels and shake him. Or maybe he wanted to hug him. Instead he got up from the table and went to the kitchen counter to pour himself some coffee. Behind his back, he heard Kelly get up, and for a moment he thought Kelly was going to walk out.

"I'm serious, Cooper."

Uh-oh, full name.

"For the first time since I got back, I realized that I still wanted you. I still loved you."

Cooper resisted turning around to see Kelly's expression. He looked at the wall in front of him instead.

"But I can't ask you to go back in the closet for me."

"I don't fit in the closet anymore, Kelly," Cooper said. "Nobody in this godforsaken town will ever let me forget I'm the queer."

"And I don't want you to either. But I'm scared of losing you again, and I'm willing to throw everything out of the window for it."

"Meaning?"

"I'd give up the sheriff's position."

This time Cooper did turn around. "Don't be stupid."

"I'm not… stupid."

"This is all you ever wanted to be. Not a big crime fighter. Not the kind of sheriff on the front page of the local newspaper. Not the one catching the big crooks. You wanted to be the kind of small-town sheriff from the fifties who was adored by the whole town and who solved problems, not crimes. The guy everyone could turn to. It's a romantic idea, not very in tune with reality, but then you never were."

"Cooper?" Kelly lamented.

"These days you need to be tough with people, not a pussy, Kells. These days they respect guns, not… Andy Griffith."

When Cooper turned around, Kelly was slumped over on the bench, elbows resting on the table and his hands brushing over his fair hair. Cooper sat down next to him, his knees creaking as he did so. "Friends will have to do, Kells. I'm not letting you throw away all of your dreams because of me."

"One of those dreams was being with the man I loved, Cooper."

Kelly wasn't crying, but his eyes were bloodshot, so Cooper knew if he said the wrong thing, Kelly was going to turn to mush. Cooper bit his lip before replying. "We have work to do in this town. And it will take both our talents. It's better than nothing, right? You can be Andy Griffith and rescue the people who need rescuing, and I'll bend over my books and pretend to be a lawyer again. I'll work in the shadows, and you can bow to the applause."

Kelly didn't react.

"We can make this work, Kelly."

Kelly let his hand drop, seeming to casually brush against Cooper's thigh. Cooper knew there was nothing casual about the touch, though. He grabbed Kelly's hand to stop him going any further and then saw the pain in Kelly's face. He leaned closer and kissed the hair behind Kelly's ear. "I'll never stop loving you," he whispered. "But I've ruined enough lives already. I'm not about to ruin yours and Nina's." He knew using Nina was lame, but he was also pretty sure it was a better argument in Kelly's mind than Cooper not wanting to ruin his career. "We can't do this to Nina, Kells."

"Nina's okay with it. You know that."

Kelly's voice was that of a whiny ten-year-old, not a well-into-his-thirties built-like-a-brick-shithouse officer of the law. Cooper understood what he meant but couldn't be persuaded to change his mind. He put his hand on the back of Kelly's neck and got up from the bench. "She still thinks she can take on the world, but if the town crucifies you, she'll go crazy for feeling so helpless to support you. I don't want to put her in that situation." *Or you*, Cooper wanted to add, but Kelly had already said he'd give up everything for him, and Cooper knew he couldn't live with the regrets that would certainly follow sooner or rather.

Kelly seemed to understand, as he straightened his back while Cooper walked around the table again.

"Now how about Gable and Calley's kids? I think we should get them to have the paternity test done and then find a way for Bill to relinquish his rights to those kids."

Kelly perked up at the change of subject. "I think I should go talk to that social worker who placed Noah and Ryan with Calley and ask her some informal questions about what we need to get Gable temporary custody of the kids until Calley gets better."

"Great idea," Cooper replied, happy to see Kelly's eyes light up. "I can tell Gable one thing. He's going to have to put that rifle of his in a locked cabinet."

Kelly nodded, a faint smile on his face. "I remember Rory knew exactly where to find it not too long ago."

—22—

AS GABLE sat down on the icy porch next to Ryan, he tried not to grunt too much as his muscles protested their unusual position. Ryan had helped him around the ranch that afternoon, and he was now waiting for Flynn to drive him back into town so he could do his chores at Calley's shop. Gable had seen Ryan sporting a shiner, but hadn't talked to him about it before. He figured he couldn't let it slide, though, so he looked to the side to signal to Ryan he'd seen the black-and-blue shadow on his face, despite the curtain of hair blocking it.

"Don't suppose you want to talk about it?"

Ryan didn't react, so Gable handed him the steaming mug of coffee he'd brought out with him. Ryan didn't take it. Instead he eyed it with the kind of suspicion Gable had long grown accustomed to. He wanted Ryan to warm himself, though, because he was shivering inside his too-thin coat.

"It's a clean mug, and I haven't drunk from it. You look like you need it more than me."

Ryan took it from Gable and looked at it.

"It's got sugar. Nothing else."

Gable smiled just a little as Ryan drank, holding the mug with both hands.

"So. Kids at school give you a hard time?"

The mug of coffee was empty by the time Ryan nodded.

"Did you start the fight?"

Ryan shrugged.

"Don't tell your social worker I told you this, but I'm not going to give you a hard time about it. For all I know, you had every right to slug him."

"He called Calley a...."

Gable looked at Ryan with his eyebrows raised.

"A whore."

"Because she's pregnant?"

"He asked me whether I knocked her up."

Gable cocked his head. "He was asking for it, then?"

Ryan shrugged again.

"Don't tell your social worker this either, but you've got to learn to duck when he returns the gesture, Ry."

To Gable's surprise, Ryan was trying hard to suppress a smile.

"I ducked, but then he told me I couldn't possibly knock Calley up because a queer couldn't do that. I guess I hesitated one moment too long."

"You need ice to put on that?"

Ryan shook his head and tucked his hair behind his ear. "It's too late. It happened this morning."

"So that's why you're sitting out here in the cold, hey?"

"You think I'm stupid for sitting out here."

It wasn't a question, but Gable answered it anyway. "I sit out here all the time. It's a good place to think. I usually wait for spring to set in, though. I'm not a big fan of my ass freezing to the steps."

"It's not *that* cold."

By now Ryan was full-on smiling, and Gable looked out at the barn in an attempt not to look smug.

"Were you ever beaten up for being queer?"

Gable was a little surprised by the question but tried not to show it. "Nobody knew when I was at school."

Ryan nodded in understanding.

Gable took in a sharp breath. "I was beaten on the street once. In Boise. I made a pass at a guy, and he didn't take it very well. He got his friends to 'teach me a lesson.'" Gable wasn't fishing for sympathy, so he wasn't disappointed when he didn't get any from the teenager. He was content having gotten a few words out of him, which was quite a feat. "So are you okay living here for the time being?"

Ryan nodded.

"I know the couch isn't a bed and you need your privacy, but we're adding a few rooms to the house for that." When Ryan didn't react, Gable continued. "Calley's going to have it rough for a while, with the treatment she needs and the baby on the way, so I offered to have her stay here with the kids, and that includes you. On school days, we'll drive you into town so you can help Sadie out in the shop in the morning like you did Calley, and then you can walk to school. That okay?"

"Who's taking Noah to school?"

Gable figured the unspoken answer was "yes." "Whoever is driving the Krause kids will be picking him up first. Are you still okay working at Calley's? You getting along with Sadie?"

"Sadie's good. Sadie's...."

Gable looked over at Ryan when he didn't finish. Ryan was rubbing his boot back and forth over the porch step to clear away the snow. "Sadie's what?"

"Sadie's my sister."

"She is? I didn't know you had a sister. Calley never told me."

"Calley knows. She hired her so we'd get reacquainted."

Gable nodded. "She hired Sadie because she trusts her to run the shop when she's not there. Maybe she thinks she'll do a good job on account of you and Noah."

Ryan shrugged, indicating he either didn't know or didn't care.

"Well, as long as you two get along, that's okay then. Between the two of you and Cooper running the deliveries, Calley can take the rest she needs."

"I wish someone else could do the deliveries. I asked Calley, but she said Cooper volunteered so she can't fire him."

"Cooper's one of the good guys, Ryan."

Ryan didn't answer, and Gable didn't push. He just sat next to Ryan until Flynn walked outside.

"We leaving, Ryan?"

Ryan got up and followed Flynn to the truck without looking back.

WHEN Flynn returned from town, Gable was still sitting on the steps of the porch. "Need help getting up, old man?" Flynn asked with obvious glee in his voice.

Gable didn't answer, so Flynn sat down next to him. He put his hand on Gable's knee and rubbed it.

"Did you know that Sadie was Ryan's sister?"

Flynn shrugged and nodded. "Calley told me."

"And you didn't think this was interesting enough information to share with me?"

"I figured with you and Calley being peas in a pod like you are, she would have told you too."

Gable glared at his partner.

"So she didn't. I'm sorry."

Gable took a deep breath, knowing he could pretend to be mad at Flynn, but he wouldn't last past breakfast. "I didn't even know he had a sister. I thought it was just him and Noah. What is she like?"

"Young, quirky. A bit like Maxie from the clothes store."

"Goth?"

"I believe they call it emo these days. Anyway, like Max, she's not broody or down, but rather, lively and upbeat, which is why she gets away with pitch-black hair, tons of eyeliner, and tattoos in visible places. Come to think of it, they'd make a great couple."

"Max and Sadie?"

Flynn shrugged and smiled. "At least Max is into girls. Don't know about Sadie."

Gable smiled back at Flynn, feeling his earlier angry mood dissipate. "I'm sure they can figure it out for themselves, Flynn. They must run into each other all the time."

"Well, if either of them is anything like you, they'd need a major shove in the right direction."

Gable entwined his fingers with Flynn's, and Flynn leaned against him, allowing Gable to share his heat. "I'm still glad you were so insistent. So is the house extension coming along?"

Flynn nodded. "Wood's ordered. I invited Grant and Hunter to come by to go over the plans with us so everyone knows what to do next weekend."

Gable looked out over the driveway and up to the barn where the ground was glistening with frost. "I hope we don't get more snow before the foundation is laid."

"We won't," Flynn replied.

"It's going to be a big change to have Calley with us," Gable continued with some trepidation.

"I know," Flynn said, squeezing Gable's arm again. "It'll be good."

Gable wasn't so sure, but at least Flynn was on his side.

—23—

COOPER finished his grocery run and drove up into the mountains. It was a cold but clear night, and he wanted to clear his head before going back down to the ranch to turn in for the night. The vista point was deserted, which wasn't a surprise given that it was a school night, and sitting there too long, even inside a heated car, was considered self-flagellation, even if it was a great place for high school boys to make out with their girlfriends.

As he got out of the truck, tucking his warm coat around himself, he felt the craving for a smoke, although he'd given that up many years ago because Martin didn't like it. The craving always came back in quiet moments like these, when he wanted to have something to do with his hands. He chuckled as he realized it was just like craving a certain man under his fingers when he was lying alone in bed at night.

The sound of car tires on the gravel didn't make him look around as he leaned against the front of the truck. Footsteps did, simply as a precaution. Cooper's smile grew even wider when he recognized Kelly, still in uniform.

"Not loitering, Sheriff," Cooper said, hands raised and tongue firmly planted in cheek.

"Thought it was your truck."

"So what brings you here?"

"Got a call just down the road for a domestic disturbance, but they were already making up when I got there."

"Good for you. And them," Cooper said with his gaze now directed at the dark lands below. He didn't want to look at Kelly, afraid it would give away his earlier thoughts of how much he wanted him. "So you're on your way home, then?"

"Working day is over."

"And then some," Cooper added, looking sideways at Kelly, who had joined him leaning against the hood of the truck.

"There comes a point where it doesn't matter how late I am, because the only one still up is Teo."

"And that time is—" Cooper looked at his watch. "—ten?"

Kelly chuckled. "Thereabouts. Nina needs her rest. She's usually down by nine or nine thirty."

Silence fell between them as Cooper found himself thinking he could live with Kelly working late, since this is what he'd wanted to do since he was a kid. Then he shook his head, dispelling the thought he'd probably never get to test.

Kelly was anxiously looking around and almost ducked when a car passed on the otherwise deserted road behind them.

"So you just stopped to talk?" Cooper asked, trying to get the conversation going again.

"I recognized the truck, and… yeah, I suppose I did." He smiled as if he'd been caught.

"Maybe standing around leaning against my truck while you're in uniform isn't the best idea."

The smile disappeared from Kelly's face.

"Get inside," Cooper said softly. He turned around and crossed in front of Kelly as he got into the driver side of the truck. Kelly hesitated for a moment and then got in on the passenger side.

After he closed the door, he looked at Cooper. "People will still recognize my car."

Cooper leaned over him, unearthed a folder, and gave it to Kelly. "Registration?" Cooper said in response to Kelly's questioning look. "You can say you were checking my papers."

"We're not supposed to get into the suspect's car."

"It's cold, and you know me," Cooper suggested. "You trust me."

"I shouldn't," Kelly replied, but Cooper thought he was smiling, although this was definitely debatable.

Cooper took the folder from Kelly again and was leaning toward the glove compartment to put it away when he felt a hesitant hand on his shoulder. When he looked up, he couldn't read Kelly's face. He didn't look all that shy, more expectant, or maybe hopeful. Cooper's eyes drifted to Kelly's mouth, and suddenly he knew he needed to kiss him. "Don't shoot me, okay, Sheriff?" He didn't give Kelly the chance to answer and pressed his lips against Kelly's. It was a chaste kiss, with closed lips and no tongue, but that changed when Kelly's hand moved from Cooper's shoulder to the back of his head and he started kissing Cooper back. The folder, which hadn't quite made it back to its rightful place, dropped to the floor of the truck, but there wasn't even the start of a thought in Cooper's mind to pick it up. He was going to enjoy their mutual moment of weakness for as long as it lasted.

Cooper finally pulled away when he felt Kelly loosen his grip. "I thought you didn't drink coffee anymore?"

"I don't," Kelly replied, chuckling. "But the couple involved in the domestic disturbance felt guilty for calling me over for no reason, and she wouldn't hear no. It's going to give me heartburn."

Cooper smiled as he sat back on his side of the bench. He regretted the distance between them almost as much as the silence that had fallen.

Kelly inhaled deliberately, as if he wanted to say something, but he only got it out in the second try. "I don't want to get caught here, Coop. And I know that feeds right back into the whole 'I don't want to be your dirty little secret' thing, but I can't help that."

"So come back to the ranch with me, then," Cooper replied quickly so he couldn't change his mind.

Kelly threw him a helpless look, and Cooper felt his stomach sink. He knew he was going to regret it, but he'd already regretted making their break so final. Maybe he just had to throw caution to the wind and deal with his wounded heart later.

"Drop the car off at the station, and I'll pick you up there. I'll even drive you back afterward. That way you won't get caught."

Kelly grabbed Cooper's hand, his eyes rigidly pointed down. "It won't change that... thing. I can't burst out of the closet, Coop."

"I know," Cooper said, trying to keep his voice from jumping. "I know," he repeated, more for himself than for Kelly's benefit.

Kelly nodded curtly before getting out of the truck and taking big strides toward his car.

Cooper started the truck and followed Kelly's car into town, where he drove to the back of the sheriff's office and waited for Kelly to come outside. They didn't speak as they drove to the Blue River Ranch, but Cooper felt the tension rise the closer they got. He didn't know what to expect but hoped it wouldn't be aborted like last time. At least now he knew it wouldn't mean Kelly was moving in with him the next week. He had to admit he was at the point where he could take being Kelly's bit on the side if it meant Kelly's dream could still come true.

When he arrived at the crew house, a few trucks were parked outside, and one of them clearly had occupants, judging by the fact it was moving. Cooper chuckled, and with a clear "Right!" he drove past the parked trucks to the back of the house. "View's better here, anyway." Not that it mattered, since it was dark outside, but Cooper figured they'd have a better opportunity to get out without being spotted.

"Stay here for a moment," Kelly asked, grabbing Cooper's hand as he started to get out. He pulled Cooper closer and kissed him again.

Cooper enjoyed Kelly's take-charge attitude and easily gave in. It was a reversal of the way they'd interacted fifteen years ago, but Cooper didn't mind one bit. He moved a little closer to Kelly so the steering wheel wasn't in the way quite so much and pulled Kelly on top, reveling in the feel of the bulky frame bearing down on him. He inserted his hands underneath Kelly's heavy winter coat, knowing the thin fabric of his uniform wouldn't prevent him from feeling Kelly's muscles.

Their kissing intensified as Kelly started grinding against Cooper, and his arousal was unmistakable. Cooper grabbed his ass to intensify the friction. He felt the ache in his groin as well. The temptation to take care of it right there was definitely present, but they weren't teenagers anymore. Cooper had a room upstairs, and they'd be a lot more comfortable there.

"Kells," he groaned. "Kelly, stop for a moment."

When Kelly looked up, he was flustered, his lips swollen. "Don't want to."

"Come upstairs with me. The corridor will be empty. My room is warm, and it has a bed."

"I know," Kelly replied with a smile. "I've been up there, remember?"

"So?" Cooper asked, feeling uncharacteristically unsure.

"I can't stay all night."

Cooper nodded. "I told you I'd drive you back later. Just come up for an hour. Tops."

"Is that all I get?"

It took Cooper a few moments to realize Kelly was teasing. "You get as long as we need. And then we're getting dressed again and I'm driving you back into town so you can take your car home."

"Yeah, the car gets homesick, otherwise."

Cooper mock growled at Kelly for the lame joke but was pretty happy to see that his warped sense of humor was returning. They could do this. If he was honest with himself, he could be Kelly's dirty little secret and not mind that much. After all, they had Nina's permission, and that's what made it different from the Martin situation. And they could be careful so Kelly wasn't outed. It wouldn't be so different for Cooper. He could just be his grumpy self in public.

Cooper looked around the corridor as they made their move upstairs. He stopped maybe twice, but Kelly bumped into him every time, eager not to lose contact. Once inside the door, Kelly was all over him again. For a moment, Cooper feared a repeat of the first time Kelly had come to his room, but the scorching kisses they were sharing soon put a stop to that. They didn't stop the flood of memories assaulting him, though. He'd missed this so much, tasting Kelly, feeling Kelly's hands finding their way underneath his clothes, sensing the sheer weight of Kelly's bulk. Cooper was trying to get Kelly out of the uniform that looked great on him but didn't feel so nice to the touch. His winter coat was already on the floor, his gun belt on top of it, and Cooper was trying to get Kelly's shirt out of the tight tan trousers when Kelly put his big, warm hand over the bulge in Cooper's jeans. "Fuck,"

Cooper muttered, trying to continue kissing the owner of the hand. He needed all the breath he could spare, though. Kelly was grinding against him, full body, and it was turning Cooper on to no end.

Suddenly, Kelly stopped and looked at him.

"What's wrong?"

Kelly leaned his forehead against Cooper's. "You wanted me to come upstairs so we'd be more comfortable, and here we are making out against a door."

"I like the unstoppable force you've become. Besides, I was about to cream my pants. Who was I to stop you?"

Kelly leaned in to kiss Cooper, and this time it was a long, deep, languid kiss that made Cooper's toes curl. What had ever possessed him to turn Kelly away on the mere technicality that they could never be open about their love for each other?

By the time they were moving to the bed, Cooper's checked shirt was unbuttoned and hung from his shoulders. Kelly was still fully dressed, although his tan shirt wasn't neatly tucked into his pants anymore. Kelly grabbed the side of Cooper's shirt and pulled him along as he sat on the bed. He started kissing down Cooper's lightly furred chest, holding him in place with his hands on Cooper's hips. When Cooper tried to create enough space between them to start working on Kelly's shirt, Kelly wrapped his arms around Cooper's waist.

"Tease."

"Indulge me," Kelly grunted. "You know how long it's been."

"Yeah, pretty much," Cooper replied. "In years, months, and possibly days."

"If you don't count our last time…."

"Let's not talk about that," Cooper said. His patience was growing thin, so he pushed Kelly down on the bed and crawled on top. "Why are you still dressed?"

Kelly grunted before flipping Cooper over onto his back. Cooper let him and waited for a moment to indicate that the ball was in Kelly's court. He wanted to get naked with Kelly, though.

Kelly rolled to the side so he could unbutton Cooper's pants. He was clearly feeling the urgency too, as he was trying to go too fast, and so it took twice as long as it usually would, but Cooper didn't help him, despite wanting to. He preferred trying to commit the image of Kelly's hands on him to memory. In the meantime, Kelly wasn't wasting any time pulling down Cooper's boxers. When he took Cooper's cock out, he looked up at Cooper.

"What?" Cooper asked, seeing Kelly's worried face. "I'm not twenty-five anymore. I need a little more stimulation these days."

"You were hard earlier. I felt it. Are you…?"

Cooper almost rolled his eyes, but instead opted to pull Kelly's face closer to him again. Nose to nose, Cooper picked out his most confident voice. "I can still get it up, sport. I may be out of practice, but trust me, it's like riding a bike."

Kelly leaned his forehead against Cooper's. "I sure hope so."

"Count on it."

"I hope so for me. It's been longer for me than for you."

Cooper pulled Kelly's face away from his and looked him in the eye. "I know." He smiled. "So what do you want to do?"

Kelly's expression remained shy, but his actions spoke of something different. He moved down Cooper's chest, and Cooper barely had time to grunt before Kelly took him in his mouth. The heat felt glorious, and Kelly clearly hadn't lost his technique during his dry years. Although after the initial frotting session Cooper had remained almost completely flaccid, he felt himself fill up so quickly he was glad he was lying down or he would have felt the room spin. He tried to look at what Kelly was doing—hungrily sucking and licking Cooper's quickly hardening cock while holding it by the base—but Cooper couldn't without feeling the end come near with crashing speed. So he dropped his head back to his bedcovers and tried to simply feel it, tried to savor it, because, just like Kelly, he'd missed this for many long years.

Soon enough, Cooper had to redirect his mind again, so he opened his eyes and reached out for Kelly, but he was too far away.

"Come here," Cooper asked with a much less steady voice than he'd aimed for.

Kelly didn't look up at him, but instead crawled closer, licking up Cooper's chest while pulling his jeans down.

Cooper had meant to ask Kelly to change positions so he could suck Kelly's cock, but Kelly had interpreted it differently. Not that Cooper was complaining about being able to kiss Kelly's delicious mouth again, especially not because he felt Kelly's strong hand circled around his cock and Kelly's erection rubbing up against his own.

Kelly's eyes were closed, his face tense and crunched up, his lips and tongue moving against Cooper's. He was moaning and, when he came up for much needed air occasionally, grunting, all the while thrusting violently into his hand and against Cooper. Although Cooper was quickly spiraling out of control as well, he wasn't surprised when Kelly stilled on top of him and then thrust again, this time gushing hot jizz over Cooper's cock and belly. Feeling Kelly come sent Cooper over as well, and when Kelly collapsed on top of him, Cooper wrapped him in his arms.

Again, Cooper felt this need to savor the moment. He had no idea how they were going to proceed, or whether this was going to get a repeat. He simply wanted to hold Kelly close just in case this was the last time he'd get to.

When Kelly pulled away, Cooper had to stop himself panicking that Kelly would leave. Instead, Kelly started unbuttoning his shirt. He looked down at the stains on his shirttails. "I'm going to have to drop this into the washing machine without Teo spotting it."

"You can wash it here if you like."

"No time. I can't stay that long." Kelly threw his shirt on the one chair in the room and stepped out of his pants.

Cooper wiggled out of his clothes before Kelly joined him in bed again. Kelly's naked skin against his made the heat rise again soon. This time they took it slow, with Kelly giving Cooper ample time to rediscover his body, which was definitely different from fifteen years ago but started feeling familiar again in no time.

"You need to leave, Kells," Cooper murmured about an hour later. He was still pressed against Kelly's body, savoring the warmth and the smell of salty, sweaty skin and sex. "Run downstairs for a quick shower, and I'll drive you back."

Kelly groaned and reached back for Cooper. He remained still, tightly holding onto Cooper's arm.

Cooper rested his cheek against Kelly's shoulder.

"You have an extra towel?" Kelly asked when he finally moved.

"Plenty."

They showered together, the house quiet after midnight, and were out of the door without as much as a kiss or a hug. Cooper dropped Kelly off near his car behind the sheriff's office, as if he'd given a drifter a casual lift on the highway, and drove back to the ranch to sleep so he'd be ready to get up in time to start his morning chores.

All through the morning, just about every casual movement he made, whether it was dragging along something heavy or lifting a saddle onto the saddle rack, reminded him of the fact that he'd used muscles he hadn't used in ages. Even when he started yawning around lunchtime, reminding him of the fact he'd barely slept at all, it made him smile.

And then Hunter came to get him, because there was an urgent call for him at the house.

—24—

COOPER ran into the corridor they'd directed him to and found Kelly sitting on the floor, his head resting in his hands.

"Kelly?"

Kelly looked up, his eyes bloodshot. From his expression, Cooper could tell Kelly wasn't overjoyed to see him.

"Jennifer called me."

"She shouldn't have." Kelly buried his face in his hands again.

"Is it Nina?"

Kelly didn't answer, so Cooper crouched next to him. "Something happened last night?"

Kelly nodded without looking up.

Damn. Cooper knew this was Kelly's worst nightmare, that something would happen while he wasn't there, and what made it worse was that he was the reason Kelly hadn't gone home last night.

"What happened, Kells?"

Kelly was shaking his head when a nurse stuck her head out of the room. "Mr. Freed? She can see you now."

Kelly jumped up like he'd been sitting in a nest of fire ants. He sniffed once and ran his hand over his face. "Come with me. Talk her out of this."

"What are you saying?"

"She might listen to you. God knows, she's not listening to me."

Cooper stopped Kelly from turning away from him. "I'll go with you if you tell me what's going on."

"She has a DNR in place. She's a lawyer. What did I expect, right?"

"Kells, you're talking gibberish."

"DNR. Do Not Resuscitate. No heroic measures. She has pneumonia, and in her condition, because she has no reserves, that means she needs to be put on a ventilator, but she refuses. She's told me numerous times that she's at a point where she's losing the will to live, that the benefits of staying alive are no longer outweighing the suffering. But since she can't move anymore, asking someone to give her pills is asking them to kill her, and they'd be implicated. So she wants to die of natural causes."

Cooper sighed. "She knew it was only a matter of time before she'd get sick."

Kelly nodded, and Cooper wanted to wrap him in his arms like he had for most of the night, but they were in a very public place, and although the nurses wouldn't talk to the press about Nina, they could easily let something slip if they caught their acting sheriff being hugged by the town queer.

Instead, Cooper gently touched Kelly's arm. "Let's go inside and see if we can ask her to hold on a little longer, hey?"

When they walked into the hospital room, Nina didn't even look up. She was lying still, on her side, laboring to breathe. Gone was the vivacious woman, replaced by a ghost of her former self, her hair mussed and her makeup removed. They'd even taken the bright-red nail polish off her fingers.

"She can't cough," Kelly whispered. "That's why it turns bad so quickly."

"She's been here before?"

Kelly nodded. "Just over a year ago, before we came here. She was on a ventilator for almost two months. It took them that long to wean her off it. She told me then she never wanted to go through that again."

Cooper touched his throat. He realized why Nina had the scar there.

"The part she hated even more than being confined to a hospital bed was that she couldn't talk."

Cooper chuckled, more from feeling out of his element than from the humor in what Kelly was saying. "I can imagine that would be the corker for her."

"She knows she might not get off the ventilator this time, and she's always made me promise not to put her on it again."

Cooper touched Kelly's arm again, because he felt it was the only way he could show his support. Kelly let him but didn't acknowledge the touch.

"She wants me to watch her die, Coop."

They were speaking in muffled tones, but Cooper kept looking at Nina to see whether she overheard them. She didn't give any indication, but then he knew from when they were in college she had the hearing of a bat. He wouldn't put it past her to be following the whole conversation, even in her precarious state, and never let on.

"Why don't we sit by her, hold her hand."

Kelly looked up at him as if he'd asked him to betray his country, or something else hideous.

"She needs your support, Kells, even if you don't agree with her decision."

"Well, I don't, and she knows it."

"Kelly." He sighed and dreaded making things more difficult, but he knew he had to give Kelly all the choices. "Her living will only goes so far. It indicates her choice, but legally, you, as her spouse, can easily overturn it. If you give them permission to intubate her, they will." This seemed to brighten Kelly up. "You'll also have to live with her wrath, Kelly." His face clouded over again. "All she's asking for is a certain quality of life. For her, that means being able to talk. She knows she's getting weaker. She's told me she fears losing her ability to swallow. Maybe what happened last night was an indication of that. Maybe you need to give her that much control and let her die comfortably."

Without warning, Kelly turned toward Cooper and pushed his entire bulky frame against him. Cooper was glad for the wall behind him, and all he could do was envelop Kelly in his arms and squeeze him. It felt good to hold him like that, even when Kelly started shaking and Cooper knew he was sobbing. While stroking Kelly's back, he looked at Nina and tried to imagine losing her. He still loved her to bits, but he could see she was suffering. It would be kinder to make sure she was comfortable and to let her die on her own terms. The longer they waited, the more her chance to choose was diminished. Purely selfishly, Cooper knew that, even if she didn't want to be, she was an obstacle to them getting together. He shook his head to quickly erase that thought from his mind. Last night proved they did just fine sneaking around.

Kelly was still holding him tight, but he was breathing more calmly now. It wasn't a surprise when Kelly pulled away, his face red and his eyes bleary. He wiped his hand over his face as he straightened his shoulders in an attempt to recompose himself.

"Better?"

Kelly nodded, then shrugged.

"Let's go sit by her."

There was only one chair, next to the wall, and Cooper pulled it closer to the bed. "Sit."

When Kelly did and took Nina's hand, Nina opened her eyes.

"Hey, gorgeous."

She smiled behind her oxygen mask.

"Your hair is a mess. Want me to brush it?"

She nodded almost imperceptibly, and Kelly got up from the seat to retrieve her brush and stand behind her.

Wanting to give Nina something familiar to look at, Cooper took his place in the chair. "Hey, Champ."

"Cooper," she mouthed.

"Don't waste your energy talking. We'll just sit here smiling at each other like long lost lovers." He rubbed his thumb over her emaciated hand and tried to convey his love for her. She closed her eyes as Kelly started brushing her short, dark hair. "That's right. Rest and let Kelly pamper you."

She tried to say more, without opening her eyes, and Cooper thought she said something along the lines of "Help Kelly."

"Help Kelly with what?" he tried.

"Letting go," she said, managing to raise her voice enough to be heard over the oxygen mask. Her eyes were still closed, so Cooper looked up at Kelly and saw he was crying again. His hand never stopped moving the brush, though.

Cooper knew that if he said anything more, he would only make it harder on Kelly, but he was acutely aware of what little time Nina potentially had left, so he didn't want to beat around the bush. "He loves you, Nee. He wants to keep you around as long as possible."

"He loves you too," she said soundlessly, "and I'm ready."

Now it was Cooper's turn to fight his emotions. He knew he couldn't look at Kelly, although he was sure he wondered what Nina had told him, because he stopped brushing.

"Let's give her some rest," Cooper said to Kelly, his eyes still focused on Nina. "Nee, we'll just be outside the room. We'll be back in a few minutes, okay?" Nina didn't acknowledge his words or the fact Cooper let go of her hand. He walked outside calmly and heard Kelly follow him. In the corridor, he sat down on the bench against the wall opposite Nina's room. He couldn't look at Kelly when he sat down next to him. He had to broach the difficult subject again, though. "She said she was ready."

"Yeah, but I'm not." Kelly's voice was soft but cracking, which gave away that he was still crying.

"Neither am I, Kells. I just found her again. She was my rock for years. My partner in crime. Leaving her behind was every bit as hard as leaving you."

"She was the only thing that kept me going. If it hadn't been for her, I'd have never gotten a law degree. Or a helicopter license or a shot at a sheriff's office." Kelly sat in silence, his arms resting on his thighs and his hands hanging loose between his knees. "Who am I going to bounce ideas off of? Who is going to tell me I need to get my shit together and not play Andy Griffith?"

Cooper wanted to tell Kelly he could always come talk to him, but he didn't. He knew what Kelly meant. "You can still talk to her. After fifteen years, I'm sure you can dream her answers."

Kelly let his head drop. "I'll never be ready to let her go, Cooper."

Cooper patted Kelly's shoulder in what he hoped looked like a show of support. He still wanted to pull Kelly into his arms, but he didn't think Kelly would let him, as exposed as they were in the busy corridors of an intensive care ward. "You probably won't be."

They went back inside to sit next to Nina's bed, and Nina opened her eyes every now and then, unable to muster more energy than to simply smile at whoever was sitting in her line of sight. Her breathing was becoming more labored by the hour, and it didn't go unnoticed. Late in the afternoon, her doctor asked to speak to Kelly outside the room. Cooper joined them because Kelly asked him to.

The man looked very worried as he sat down across from them in his office. "I'm going to cut to the chase. She's losing the battle. She doesn't have the muscle power to keep drawing breath because her lungs are filling up with mucus despite the antibiotics she's getting. If we don't intervene, she'll simply stop breathing."

"Intervene?" Kelly asked, as if he didn't know what the doctor meant.

"Intubate. Put a tube in her lungs to help her breathe," the doctor explained.

"She doesn't want that," Kelly said as if he was on autopilot.

"That's why we need you to sign a paper stating you agree with her living will."

Cooper sat up straight. "That's why she has a living will. So Kelly doesn't need to do this."

The doctor looked at Cooper as if he had no idea what Cooper was doing there and turned back to Kelly. "A living will is something that has limited legal strength. On more than one occasion, the relatives of a patient have sued us for following their relative's wishes, and on a few of those occasions, they've won. We need to make sure you agree with her."

"And if I don't sign?"

"Then we'll go against her wishes. To be frank, the chance you'll sue us is much greater than the chance she will." He slid the piece of paper in Kelly's direction.

Kelly looked at it without touching it. Cooper was sure he wouldn't sign it.

"You're asking me to kill her?"

"We won't kill her, Mr. Freed. We won't give her the treatment she needs to stay alive, but this is according to her wishes. I called her neurologist here and the one in Boston. They both concur that she knew what she was signing and knew the consequences, but that it was definitely her choice. She knows that as long as she can speak she has some control over what happens, despite being totally dependent on her caregivers. If we put her on a ventilator, she most likely won't come off it again, and she'll lose that control too."

Cooper let his knuckles brush over the side of Kelly's knee, hoping to convey some support without drawing the attention of the doctor. Only, it seemed he wasn't even drawing Kelly's attention.

Kelly was still staring at the paper when the doctor's buzzer went off. He got up and looked at it. "It's her. I need to go and intubate her."

The doctor didn't run, but the urgency in his step was recognizable. Cooper was torn between staying with Kelly and running after him to be with Nina. Kelly seemed to feel the same thing, because he got up from his seat and walked outside to the corridor, where it was surprisingly quiet.

The open door to Nina's room revealed a flurry of activity inside, though.

"On her back, in three. One, two, three." Cooper heard gloves being put on and the clanging of metal. "Scope?" the doctor called out. "Suction." A sickening sound came from the room, and Cooper looked to the side. Kelly was looking as pale as the off-white walls. "Seven or eight?" A woman's voice. "Seven French will do." The doctor again.

"Stop."

Cooper looked over at Kelly, who had uttered the word.

"She doesn't want this, Coop."

"I know, but you heard the doctor."

Kelly turned back into the doctor's office and took the paper and the pen next to it. He signed it and walked straight into Nina's room. "Stop. I signed the paper."

Cooper followed and saw Nina on her back, her chest exposed, a tube sticking out of her throat.

"She's coding, doctor."

They started chest compressions.

"Stop for a moment," the doctor ordered. He looked at the monitor, which showed a lot of squiggly lines Cooper didn't know how to read. They eased off as soon as the nurse stopped pushing into Nina. The doctor looked at Kelly, and Kelly nodded.

"Time of death: 5:32 p.m."

The doctor filled the syringe attached to the tube and carefully pulled it out of Nina's throat before wiping the fluid away from her mouth. Then he walked over to Kelly.

"Give us a few minutes to make her comfortable, and then you can see her again." He turned back to the nurses. "Stacey? Take good care of her." He walked over to Kelly and took the paper from him. "Thank you for clearing this up. I'm sorry you had to lose her, but I admire her for the courage to put it in writing."

"She's a lawyer," Kelly replied with a chuckle. "What did you expect?"

Cooper could see how Kelly was faking it a mile away. He hoped they'd make it through the first few days.

—25—

KELLY opened the door to his house. "Teo?" No answer. He turned to Cooper. "Thanks for bringing me home. I can take it from here." He bent down to pick up a towel that had been discarded as they'd loaded Nina into the ambulance.

"I'll help. Especially with Teo not being here, you could use an extra pair of hands." Cooper closed the door behind him and followed Kelly through to the living room.

Kelly shook his head, not looking at Cooper. The last thing he needed was Cooper hovering over him. He had to get on with life. He had a house to clear up and a sheriff's election to run. "Thanks, but we'll be fine. Teo was pretty shook up this morning. You could help by looking for him when you drive back through town. If you see him, tell him I could use his help." When Cooper didn't budge, Kelly walked back to the front door and took the handle. "Please, Coop. I need some time alone."

"Just promise me you won't do anything desperate."

Kelly chuckled humorlessly. "I lost Nina. That's all. It's not like I didn't see it coming. I'm not going to kill myself, Cooper." He opened the door, and at that instant, a flash hit him square in the face.

"Deputy Freed, our condolences. Could you tell us what happened?"

The only thing he felt at that moment, when it was still black in front of his eyes, was Cooper's hand on his shoulder. He shrugged it off instinctively and took a few steps forward onto the porch, where a middle-aged blonde reporter he recognized from the local Channel Ten news was standing with her cameraman and sound guy. She was joined there by a few newspaper reporters he'd had dealings with in the past.

Almost instantly, he knew he had to give them what they wanted and then politely ask them to leave so he could get on with his life. If he slipped up, he could kiss his election good-bye, and right now that was all that kept him going.

"This afternoon, my wife, Nina Alexander, died of complications from motor neuron disease. For fifteen years she's been my rock, and she was instrumental to getting me here and encouraging me to run for sheriff."

"Will you continue your campaign?" one of the male reporters asked.

"It was a dream for both of us, so I have no intention of stepping down," Kelly said decisively. He took a deep breath. "Now if you could please give me some privacy, I'd like to arrange her funeral without the whole county looking over my shoulder. If you leave me in peace right now, I'll give you the details of her funeral once they've been arranged."

Realizing this was all they were going to get, they slowly trooped off, and Kelly felt he could breathe a little easier. He waited for them to leave his property before he gave in to the urge to look behind him and see whether Cooper had been good enough to keep himself out of the picture. The last thing he needed was for Cooper to be standing by him in front of a news camera. It wouldn't take his opponent in the election long to figure out who Cooper was, and although he wasn't proud of it, he really didn't need to be associated with him right now.

To his relief, the porch behind him was empty and the door to the house had been closed. He decided to walk along the porch to the back instead of though the front door. Near the screen door at the back, he found a form huddled in a heavy blanket and recognized the mop of black hair.

"Teo?" He shook him, and Teo opened his eyes, squinting against the invasion of daylight. Almost immediately, a hand came out of the blanket to shield his face.

"Is she…?"

Kelly shook his head and then realized Teo had to hear him say it. "She died a couple of hours ago. I honored her request not to be put on a ventilator, but the infection was so bad she couldn't breathe on her own anymore. They made her comfortable in the end." The images of Nina on her back, naked, and nurses attempting to resuscitate her were etched in his mind, but he knew how hard Teo would take her passing so Kelly figured a little white lie would go a long way.

Teo nodded, his eyes mere slits. "She choked on her soup. She tried to cough, but couldn't. And then she was fine. At least she said she was. When I put her to bed, she looked like she was coming down with a cold, but she kept saying she was fine. I shouldn't have believed her. I should have called you then, but she wouldn't let me, Kelly."

"I know," Kelly said, trying desperately to soothe Teo. "You've taken such good care of us, both of us. It's not your fault. What are you doing out here? You could have frozen to death!"

"After they took her away, I went a little crazy."

"Crazy drunk?"

Teo nodded. "I stayed here in the house. Nobody saw me."

"You must be really thirsty, then. Let me get you some water."

Teo grabbed his hand. "I'm okay. Yeah, a little hungover, but... can we talk about what happened?"

Kelly sighed. He knew Teo was the kind of guy who liked to talk everything to death, and he wasn't sure he was ready for that treatment yet, but he figured he owed him, so he sank down on the porch next to Teo.

"She was ready, T. She knew it was happening, and she was calm. She was ready."

Teo was sobbing in his arms, and all Kelly could think of was that this is what it must be like to have a child. If his son had lived, he'd be consoling him too.

COOPER looked through the screen door at the back of the house and watched the interaction between Kelly and Teo. Kelly had sat in front of Teo, crouching down to talk to him, but he'd switched to sitting next to him and now had his arm around Teo's shoulders. Cooper had to admit he felt jealous. Kelly had always denied any involvement with

Teo, and part of him believed him, but he couldn't help feeling left out. Didn't Kelly realize he'd lost someone dear to him as well?

Cooper shook his head and turned away from the goings-on on the porch. He needed air. He had to get out of here. Kelly had made it clear he didn't want him here anyway.

By now the reporters were gone, so Cooper could walk to his truck unseen. On the way over, he wondered where he would go and felt incredibly lonely. What he and Kelly had shared the day before seemed like a distant memory, and what had felt like total bliss now felt like a letdown. Kelly had simply used him. What he'd feared hadn't even come to fruition. He wasn't going to be Kelly's dirty little secret. He wasn't even on Kelly's mind right now.

Driving along through town and passing Calley's shop, he realized he hadn't called her to say he couldn't do the deliveries. It wasn't like he had anyplace else to go, so he might as well do them now. When he walked in, Calley was behind the register. "Sadie not here?"

Calley gave him a faint smile. "She's getting your deliveries ready."

"And Ryan?"

"He's helping Grant and Gable move the wood for the extension to Gable's house."

"A worthy cause. So you're moving in with them?"

"Probably. I miss the kids, but I don't have the strength at night to take care of them anymore."

"I'm sure Flynn is taking that task to heart with gusto."

She nodded. "I'm glad they have two dads they trust."

"So how are you holding up?"

"Barely," she said with a laugh that betrayed how honest she was being. "But you look like you haven't slept either."

"I'm okay," Cooper replied, trying to keep his face looking neutral. Her doubtful expression showed him she wasn't buying it. "Nina died this afternoon."

"Oh, Coop," she said with such compassion he felt his eyes fill with tears. She rounded the counter and pulled him into her arms. "You'd only just found her again. What happened?"

He explained the circumstances. "She didn't want to live like that, and Kelly honored her wishes."

"Oh my God, that's right! Kelly too. And so soon before the elections."

"The press were already on his doorstep. He gave them a statement as if he'd prepared it all and then asked them to leave."

She smiled at him compassionately. "He's no longer the Kelly you knew in school, is he?"

"No, I guess he's not." He inhaled sharply. "I better get going if I want to bring people their food before it gets dark."

She ran her hand over his hair, not a mean feat since he was almost a head taller. "Don't bottle it all up, okay, Cooper? Share this with Kelly. Who knows? It might bring you closer."

Cooper gave her one more squeeze and then let her go. "He's got Teo to comfort him."

"That young man who took care of Nina? Is he…? I see."

Cooper didn't want to tell her they were only suspicions and he had no real proof. "Don't tell anyone anything, okay? It'll spoil his chances, and I think he'll make a great sheriff. Better than the alternative, in any case."

"Oh, I agree." She pretended to close a zipper over her mouth.

"I'll go…." He gestured over his shoulder at the back of the shop, watched her nod at him, and turned around without looking back.

"Sadie," he greeted Calley's shop girl as soon as he entered the storage space where the deliveries were usually waiting. Sadie pulled away from someone, and when she took a step back, Cooper saw it was Ryan. They both looked guilty as hell. He decided not to call them on it, but it didn't mean Cooper wasn't wondering what was going on. "Calley thought you were with Gable, picking out wood."

Ryan looked at him through his curtain of hair. "I was, but we were done, and Gable dropped me off here."

"So are the deliveries ready? Will you come with me so I can drop you off at Gable's?"

Ryan looked at Sadie and then back at Cooper. "They're not all done yet. They still need me here."

Cooper looked at Sadie. "Is there a delivery for Blackwater?" She nodded. "I'll come back to pick that up later and take Ryan with me then. Ryan, can you call the guys and tell them that I'll bring you?" He didn't look at either of the kids and simply checked the order sheets and the boxes he needed to take, picked up what he could carry, and took it to his truck.

On the way to his delivery addresses, he kept thinking about seeing Sadie and Ryan embracing and then pulling apart as soon as he entered. They clearly didn't want him to see what he'd seen, and this made him wonder what it was all about. Especially in light of the whole situation of Ryan and Kaye Simmons. Maybe he'd had it all wrong. Maybe Ryan really was straight, and Simmons had made a pass at Ryan, which, in that light, hadn't been very well received. Cooper didn't like jumping to conclusions, but if his assumptions were true, it did make Simmons a predator. And therefore a potential danger around the kids he was teaching. Damn, he wished he could drive over to Kelly's and throw some ideas around.

—26—

GRANT and Hunter were sitting around Gable's kitchen table discussing the plans for their house extension.

"It's a big job," Grant said, sitting back. "And you want it yesterday, right?"

Gable smiled broadly. "Calley needs a place to rest and be with her kids. Ryan desperately needs some privacy. The little ones are fine upstairs sharing the bunk bed, but if child services comes to call, they won't be happy seeing we only have two beds for three kids and one of them is a girl. It won't matter that we can barely keep the twins from sharing a bed."

"I see your problem," Grant admitted.

"So three bedrooms to start with?"

Flynn and Gable both nodded.

"I'll ask Cooper to bring our leftover wood around tomorrow so you can add that to the wood you ordered. How soon can you get the guys together for a good old-fashioned barn raising?"

"This weekend?" Flynn offered. "I ordered extra supplies from Calley, so we have plenty of food for hungry stomachs, but I can always ask for more."

"Sounds like a plan," Grant said, shaking on it with Gable. "I'll bring Rory along somewhere this week to put down the foundation. Shouldn't take more than a day or three. After that we need some muscle to put up the frame, and then the two of us with Flynn's help can put in the walls."

Hunter raised his hand. "I hate to burst your bubble, but Saturday is pretty close after Election Day, and a lot of guys will be hungover, first and foremost one strong hand."

"Spoilsport," Grant muttered under his breath before replying, "Our next sheriff?"

"I don't see Kelly spending all day here when he's newly elected," Hunter added.

"Mmmh," Grant agreed. "How about we promise to drive all the guys into town to go vote on Thursday if he comes and lends a hand on Saturday? I'm sure he'll welcome the extra votes."

"Let's not lean too heavily on him," Gable said solemnly. "He's burying a wife the week after."

"Right," Hunter replied. "Cooper said something about that. I never met her, though."

Gable looked at Hunter, his face still serious. "She was confined to their house. Her death wasn't unexpected, but it's still a blow. Cooper knew her too, from when he and Kelly were in college."

"Maybe we should ask Cooper to invite Kelly over?" Flynn suggested. "It could take his mind off the fact he has an empty house to go to." Flynn took Gable's hand under the table.

Gable looked at his companion and knew they were thinking the same thing: how glad they both were that Flynn was making Gable's house less empty. He squeezed Flynn's hand before letting go. "We could postpone, but I'd rather not. We've already had our first snow and if we wait longer it won't melt again until spring. Also, we might not get it finished over the weekend, and I really can't keep Calley from her kids much longer."

"And if we leave her in town, she wears herself out working, even if she says she doesn't," Flynn added.

Hunter put his hands flat on the table. "Well, you can count on us and Rory and Tim for sure. I'll ask Christy and Izzie to come over so you guys don't need to worry about feeding us." He pointed at Flynn. "We need you up that ladder and not behind the stove."

Flynn chuckled. "Sure thing."

After Hunter and Grant left, Gable sat back down next to Flynn. "We have our work cut out this week. We need to flatten the surface next to the house, take out some of the shrubs—"

"Move the outdoor shower," Flynn interrupted with a knowing smile.

"Definitely need to move that," Gable agreed, not hiding his glee either. "Although God knows when we'll be able to use it again."

Flynn smirked. "We can still shower outside in the summer. We just can't, you know...."

"I know," Gable replied with a mixture of regret and amusement. "They won't be here forever."

"I know," Flynn said, grabbing Gable's hand. "Let's check on the kids and then turn in. Busy day tomorrow. Doesn't mean we can't do in the privacy of our room what we used to do under the outside shower."

"As long as we do it quietly."

Flynn leaned across the corner of the table and kissed Gable. He lingered, and then Gable took hold of him so he couldn't pull away yet.

A muttered "Great" coming from the direction of the living room made them pull apart anyway.

"Sorry, Ryan," Gable said. "We thought you were asleep."

"I'm not a five-year-old," Ryan sneered.

"We know," Flynn answered. "With a little luck, you'll have a room of your own next week."

Ryan didn't answer. He walked into the kitchen without looking at the men, took a glass, filled it with water from the tap, and disappeared into the living room again.

Flynn sighed. "Will we ever get through to him?"

Gable shrugged. "Not before he's eighteen, I fear."

Flynn looked in the direction of the living room. "He's always so mad at the world."

"He's been through a lot," Gable mumbled in the same subdued way as Flynn had, hoping Ryan wouldn't overhear them. "We both know what it's like to lose a mother at a young age. We had fathers to take care of us. Ryan didn't have that either."

"And he's got Noah to look after as well," Flynn added.

—27—

KELLY was glad he could stay busy. The people in town seemed to understand that he tried to keep it "business as usual" and that he didn't go around shaking hands and smiling at everyone. In fact, people came up to him on the street to pat his shoulder and offer their condolences. Part of him just wanted to be left alone, but another part of him was glad he could still do his job and that it distracted him enough.

Coming home late at night was another thing altogether, though. Teo was there, of course, doting on him and making his favorite food and then warming it up as soon as Kelly came home. Kelly didn't have the heart to tell him he wasn't particularly hungry, so he ate just to please Teo, who seemed utterly lost. Kelly figured they both delved into work so they wouldn't break down, but Teo had to stay inside the house where all the memories were, despite the fact they'd only lived there for the better part of a year.

Kelly avoided Nina's room, although the door was open and he had to pass it on the way to his own bedroom. He'd ventured just one look, and had seen how spick-and-span it was, perfectly cleaned and organized by Teo, all her clothes tucked away and the equipment neatly stored. Even the bed was made, and Kelly was glad, because he thought he couldn't stomach seeing it bare. This way, it held the illusion that Nina was coming back to it one day, although he knew full well that wasn't true.

When Kelly came home the night before the election, he noticed the rest of the house was pristine as well. After his initial breakdown, Teo had obviously picked up the pieces. He'd called ahead of time, telling Teo when he'd be home, so when he walked in, he was greeted by the smell of soup and pasta with a tomato sauce. Teo was behind the stove in the kitchen.

"Smells great."

Teo looked over his shoulder, a slight smile around his mouth. "*Arrabiata*, just like you like it."

"Spicy?"

Teo nodded. His face grew solemn.

Kelly could practically read what he was thinking and why it made him feel guilty. Teo had always had to keep their food bland, because Nina couldn't take the spicy stuff anymore, although they all knew she loved it. Now they could make their food the old way. Kelly put his hand on Teo's shoulder, and before he could react, Teo had turned around and pressed himself against Kelly's chest. A little hesitantly, Kelly enfolded the young man in his arms.

"It's okay. You're allowed to grieve, just like anyone else."

Teo squeezed him tight, his lithe frame shaking in Kelly's arms. "It's my fault."

"No, it isn't. We knew this could happen. The doctors told us last year it wouldn't be the last time."

"I made her chervil soup. It makes her throat itch."

Kelly chuckled, just to get the tension out of his shoulders. "It makes me cough too. Doesn't mean I don't love your chervil soup. And so did Nina. I bet she asked you to make it, right?"

Teo nodded, his face buried against Kelly's neck.

"No matter what you did, no matter what happened, it wasn't your fault, Teo. She was ready to go. She told us at the hospital." He ran his fingers lovingly through Teo's black curls, and this made Teo look up at him. The look in his teary eyes was one of total devotion, and Kelly had to resist pushing him away. Instead he opted for, "Let's eat. I'm starving."

The food was good, but something had raised the tension in the room. It took Kelly a little while to realize Teo touched him every chance he got. They were little gestures, a hand on his shoulder as Teo passed behind him, a soft touch on his forearm to prevent Kelly from reaching for the pasta bowl so Teo could serve him. It took Kelly even longer to realize why it made him uncomfortable. He hadn't felt such attention since before Nina had gotten sick. It felt too domestic coming from Teo. He didn't want to call Teo on it, though. Maybe Teo simply needed the comfort.

Later that night, after he'd gone to bed, Kelly woke up when he felt something behind him. Correction: someone.

"Teo?" He flicked on the light and saw Teo lying next to him in his bed, dark eyes squinting against the sudden influx of light and bedding pulled up tight. He didn't look directly at Kelly. "I think you better get back to your own bed."

Teo sat up but didn't move to leave.

"Teo, please, this isn't right."

"Nina told me about you," Teo said, a little hesitantly. "I know you can't come out and say it, because of the election and all, but I can stay quiet. You don't need to tell anyone about us."

"I don't need to tell anyone because there isn't an 'us.' I don't know where you got the idea."

Teo sat on the edge of the bed, with his back to Kelly. "When she hired me four years ago, she said she liked the fact I was gay. When she asked me whether I'd move with you when you came here, she told me you were gay too and that you had a marriage of understanding with her. Then just last week, she asked me whether I'd continue to take care of you after she was gone. I figured she wanted me to do this. She knew I had a soft spot for you."

Kelly sighed audibly. He wanted to reach out and console Teo, let him down gently, but he knew it would be misconstrued. So he didn't. "Teo, we moved here because the man I love lives here."

This time Teo did turn around to face him. "Who is he?"

"It's someone I knew from… before. Nina found out that this was where he lived, and when the opportunity arose—when the sheriff's position opened up—we moved here." He wasn't about to reveal to Teo that he'd met the man, had served him beer on the back porch and dinner in the house, not when nothing could possibly come of the re-acquaintance.

"Is he your lover?"

Kelly didn't immediately know how to answer that. Despite the night they'd spent together, he didn't know what Cooper was to him right now.

"Was that where you were when Nina got sick? With him?"

Teo's tone wasn't accusatory, but Kelly's first instinct was to lie anyway. How had Teo managed to pinpoint the exact source of his guilt? It didn't mean he was going to admit to it, so he decided to ignore the question. "Give it a rest, Teo. He doesn't want to be my dirty little secret, and I can't blame him." Even though it was mostly the truth, now it was Kelly's turn to avoid eye contact with Teo. Which is why it startled him when Teo started speaking.

"I told you *I* wouldn't mind. You wouldn't have to take me anywhere. We'd have the perfect alibi. I'm your housekeeper."

Kelly looked at Teo as Teo got off the bed. Fortunately he was wearing pajama bottoms. He'd never thought of Teo as boyfriend material, but even after his generous offer, Kelly still didn't see himself starting anything with Teo. Even if he could never make it work with Cooper, he couldn't take second best. He hadn't had a lover in almost ten years. He wasn't about to grab the first thing that presented itself to him now. "You're a great guy, but I can't, Teo."

Teo bit the inside of his lip, resulting in a kind of pout, but it didn't last long. He simply nodded, and without saying anything further, he walked out of Kelly's bedroom, closing the door behind him.

Kelly felt relieved but found he couldn't sleep. It kept playing through his mind that Teo had seen through him so easily. And it brought back what he'd been trying to forget. That he was with Cooper when he should have been home hours before that. That Teo had been home with her when she'd almost choked, and he'd been… getting his rocks off.

What kept him awake most, though, was what to do with Cooper. Cooper definitely wasn't the man he'd fallen for in law school anymore. This didn't mean the attraction wasn't there. And it was definitely mutual. Despite Cooper repeating often enough to become annoying that he didn't want to be Kelly's secret, every time they ended up with a little privacy, their lips seemed to lock and they couldn't keep their hands off each other. Just thinking about the night that started on the deserted mountain road was enough for Kelly to grow hard. He rolled to his side in the hope he could wipe the images from his eyes, but with the bedding tucked firmly around him, they only became stronger.

Tomorrow was the sheriff's election, and if he won, one of the dreams he'd shared with Nina would come true. Could his own dream come to fruition as well? Would he be able to tell this town they'd elected a gay sheriff? Or would it be better to quietly cultivate his relationship with Cooper and then let the town slowly realize their sheriff lived with a man, one open-minded citizen at a time?

Kelly longed to hear Cooper's slightly raspy voice tell him everything would work out in the end, just like he'd done in school and just like he'd done in the truck on the deserted mountain road.

Damn, he was going to have to buy Cooper a cell phone.

KELLY woke up at the crack of dawn, knowing he'd slept maybe three hours at best. When he got up and looked into his bathroom mirror while he emptied his bladder, he figured he looked even worse than he felt. A shower and shave later, he looked presentable, figuring the electorate would feel sorry for the poor grieving widower, and looking worse for wear might even procure him a few votes. In any case, he had to go into work to make sure all of the three voting stations were manned and operational and everything was going according to plan. Then he had some paperwork to finish that he'd left on his desk all week. Anything to keep busy.

Once downstairs, he realized the kitchen was empty. No coffee brewing or oatmeal bubbling on the stove. He tried to recall whether Teo's door had been open or closed when he'd passed it and was pretty sure it'd been closed, so he figured Teo had slept in for once. He made himself a sandwich and ate it on the way into town.

—28—

THE day passed blissfully quickly, with an early call to help with throwing a drunk out of the only bar that stayed open until dawn and a traffic accident with luckily only a few fender benders and two very bruised egos. The girl who was in the passenger seat and who looked like jailbait flirted with him and told him she'd voted for him earlier. He smiled back at her until the driver told her to lay off him because he'd just lost his wife. She still smiled at him behind the older guy's back, and Kelly wondered if he was her father or her sugar daddy.

Other people in town also told him they'd voted for him, despite the fact that Bareillas had pulled out the big guns and had plastered the whole town with his posters, occasionally pasting them across election posters for the other available positions. The longer the day lasted, the more Kelly realized that, although he'd miss the work and the town, he'd survive if he didn't win. He'd find something else to do, and maybe not winning would give him a better chance with Cooper. He could see himself renting out his helicopter services for scenic trips to the Tetons, and maybe it would generate enough income to live a quiet life in his house in the woods. Having Cooper there would be icing on the cake.

But he was getting ahead of himself.

After the polls closed, Kelly was about to get into his car and take one last drive around town, when Jennifer walked in carrying food. She stopped him on the way out.

"Uh, uh," she said, shaking her head. "Inside Hanson's office. Now."

"It's a little premature to start celebrating," Kelly replied, protesting weakly.

"It's Hanson's retirement party, you doofus," she said, tongue firmly planted in cheek. "You didn't think we were going to celebrate you, did you?"

Kelly smiled and shook his head. "No, but let's give the old guy a nice send-off."

"That's the spirit."

Kelly took a plate from her. "Who's manning the phones?"

"Well, a woman, of course," she replied, handing him the other plate she was carrying so she could dig the phone out of her pocket.

"Good. I wouldn't want anybody getting ideas that they'll get away with something just because we're all toasting the sheriff."

"Don't worry, sport. Have I ever let you down?"

Her usually defiant look was replaced by compassion, and he didn't like that one bit so he wanted to change the subject. "Where do I put these?"

"Anywhere you like, and there's more in my car."

Always feeling better when he could make himself useful, Kelly carried all the food from Jennifer's car so she could set it up. As people started flooding in, bringing presents for the sheriff as well as more food, Kelly tried to blend in with the furniture and managed quite well. Only a few people came up to him to offer condolences and wish him good luck with the elections at the same time, but more of them didn't seem to know how to behave around him. He couldn't blame them. *He* didn't know how to behave around himself either, sometimes.

At about eight, he saw Jennifer pick up the phone and listen intently. Kelly's heart rate started racing when she climbed on a table, all five foot two of her, and stomped her foot, silencing the party.

"It's time to go to the county election office. The results are in!"

The whole party started walking out of the sheriff's office and down the street, since the election office wasn't that far from the party. Jennifer hooked her arm around Kelly's and smiled up at him. "I'm going to like working for you. Hanson was a great boss, but I have a feeling you're going to be even better."

Kelly wondered if the phone call she'd received had said more than simply "the results are in," but he didn't want to jinx it, even at this late date. He put his free hand over hers, and they walked down the street as if they were an old-fashioned romantic couple. At the same time, Kelly was warring with his own feelings. He might never be able to walk down the street with Cooper this way, but if he wasn't elected, he'd at least be able to be honest about who he loved. As long as he was sheriff, and he was up for reelection every four years, he couldn't risk it.

When they arrived at the election office, he spotted many people he knew, including Grant and Hunter. He tried to look for Cooper, but was distracted by quite a few people who absolutely needed to tell him they'd voted for him. He smiled at them and shook their hands, thanking them for their support. He also shook hands with Hunter and Grant, but just as he decided to ask them whether Cooper was there, the microphone crackled and the portly president of the election committee took to the podium.

"Ladies and gentlemen, fine citizens of Fremont County, I apologize for taking this long after the closing of the polls to bring you the announcement, but the vote was so close on some of the polls we needed to recount quite a few times."

As the guy rattled off the election results for the state representatives and the district attorney, Kelly took a few deep breaths to attempt to calm himself down. As was expected, voter turnout was meager, and he did indeed hear some very tight results. Left and right, people were congratulated, and some trooped off with their entourage. At the other side of the crowd, Kelly had spotted Bareillas with his people and their ostentatious red-and-blue banners, which better suited a presidential election than a sheriff's race, he felt. He was secretly proud he'd kept it low-key and let his actions speak rather than his words. Even if that meant losing the election.

Then out of the blue he was accosted by Jennifer, who flung all of her five foot two frame around him. "Oh, my God! You did it!" She kissed him hard on the cheek, and he must have looked bewildered, because she gave him one of her maternal looks. "Bareillas 1106, Freed 1111," she repeated. "Five votes. Just five votes, Kelly! Ehm, Sheriff Freed, I mean." She even pinched his cheek, although she was about ten years younger than him. "I knew you'd win. Anyone with at least one functioning brain cell would vote for you." She pulled him into a tight hug again while people around them patted him on the back and shoulder. It was slowly sinking in that he'd won. Everything he'd worked for in the last twenty years was coming together.

"Congratulations, Sheriff Freed."

Kelly turned around with a start, only to see the low, sultry woman's voice he'd heard wasn't Nina's. "Calley. What are you doing out here at this hour?"

She smiled, and it made the dark circles beneath her eyes look less unnerving. "Cooper told me how important this was for you."

Kelly swallowed at hearing Cooper's name. "I expected him to be here tonight."

"He dropped me off but didn't want to distract you," she said with a smile. "How's Teo?"

"Teo?" Kelly asked, not sure where the question came from. And then he realized Cooper must have spilled the beans to her. "He's a little lost with nobody to take care of anymore. I think he's looking for another job."

She leaned a little closer to him. "But he's got you to take care of, right? Especially now you're sheriff, you won't have much time to do any housework." She looked at him as if she was trying to push him to admit to something.

"He was Nina's nurse. I don't need a nurse," Kelly replied blandly.

"Fair enough." She looked around for a moment and then asked him in a softer voice than before, "Is there anything you want me to tell Cooper?"

Kelly bit his lip and was glad for the distraction of townsfolk congratulating him, but he knew he couldn't keep Calley waiting. She didn't look like she'd be able to stay on her feet for long, so he guided her to a quieter area, away from the crowd.

"I wish he had a cell phone so I could talk to him," he told her once they were out of earshot of most of the people.

"Well, join the line. I'm tired of calling the main house too, and I'm surprised they're not tired of passing on messages for him, but they do it anyway. He's resisted for so long." She unearthed her phone from her purse.

He eyed it suspiciously but took it anyway.

"I gave him my spare one so I could call him to pick me up again. It's the last number dialed," she said before walking a few feet away and turning her back to him.

With a bit of apprehension and a lot of cold feet, he redialed.

"Where do you want me, Cal?" the voice on the other side answered more quickly than Kelly anticipated.

"Cooper?" Kelly croaked.

The line went silent for a moment, and then Cooper answered. "Hey, Kelly. Did you win?"

"Yeah, by five votes."

Cooper chuckled. "Guess Hunter was right driving the ranch hands into town this morning to vote for you. Congrats."

"Thanks. I'll have to thank him too when I see him." Silence fell between them, not for lack of things to say, at least not on Kelly's part, but because there was too much to talk about. Kelly had no idea where to start, though.

"Listen," Cooper eventually said, "will you drive Calley home, or will she call me herself to pick her up?"

"I'll drive her. Gives me an excuse to get out of here."

Cooper chuckled again. "Thought so. Tell her to take care, okay?"

"Will do." Kelly disconnected and walked to where Calley was standing, watching the celebrating crowd. "I told Cooper I'd drive you home."

She laced her arm through his. "Why, that's nice of you, my dear sheriff. Did you get a chance to talk to him?"

"Yeah." He didn't want to tell her they'd barely exchanged any more than niceties.

"Did he ask you to come by Gable's ranch this weekend to help out with building the addition to their house?"

"No."

"No, he didn't ask, or no, you're not coming?"

"He didn't ask," Kelly clarified.

"Which leaves me to beg you for assistance. Never mind, it's meant for me anyway." She turned to him. "We need guys with some muscle to help with a bit of barn raising. Gable and Flynn are adding a few rooms to their house so the kids and I can stay over there. The guys from the Blue River are all going to chip in, and we wondered if you could spare some of your time as well. Doesn't have to be all weekend, and we'll understand if you get called away."

All Kelly wanted was to be left alone, but he couldn't resist Calley. He figured Cooper had probably organized it just so she'd end up being the one to ask, and he couldn't possibly turn her down. "When do you want me there?"

"Anytime. Someone will be working at the extension all through the weekend, so any time you can spare is great."

"I'll be there."

—29—

THAT Saturday morning, Cooper got up early to do his chores at the ranch before making his way to Gable and Flynn's. When he arrived, he was surprised to see that the guys had started on the foundation already. Hunter and Grant were moving long planks to where they were needed using the forklift they used at the Blue River to move wood from trees they felled. Rory was checking whether the cornerstones were level so the floor wouldn't slant. Cooper knew they'd have their work cut out for them, and he figured they'd need Sunday as well, but depending on how many able hands showed up, they'd be able to make a go of at least the first two rooms.

He parked his truck next to Gable's by the apple tree and walked over to where the other guys were.

"Decided to sleep in, Cooper?" Grant joked.

Cooper snarled at Grant for a moment, but smiled back at him when Grant did as well. He could take the mild taunts. "Someone had to take care of the ranch this morning while you were out here sunning yourselves." He didn't wait for an answer. "So where can I help?"

THEY easily fell into the routine of building again. Just like when they were fixing Tim and Rory's cabin, Grant was the man with the plan, and Rory had the very practical all-round knowledge to get the job done. Hugh, Hunter, and Tim provided the muscle, Flynn and Cooper were the only two comfortable working high up, and Gable did everything that didn't need climbing up a ladder. By the time they were one hour into working, they were a well-oiled team again.

Cooper was on the roof of the existing house when he saw Kelly's car come up the driveway. He yelled down to the others. "Timmy! More muscle coming in."

Tim looked up, shielding his eyes from the rising sun. "Who is it?"

"Our new sheriff."

Tim wolf whistled, and Rory laughed. "Down, boy. He's off limits, remember?" Rory gestured at his ring finger.

Tim grabbed Rory from behind and pretended to bite his neck. "With all due respect, I'm not going to stop having fun because he just lost his wife," Cooper could just hear him say, although he clearly didn't mean to broadcast it. "If he's here, that means he needs to get his mind off stuff, and that's what we're going to give him, right?"

Rory pulled out of Tim's embrace and walked toward Kelly as soon as Kelly got out of his car. Cooper saw Rory's warm greeting but couldn't hear what they were saying. He was glad to see Kelly wasn't in uniform, which meant he was technically off duty, and stopped to admire the torn jeans and paint-stained shirt that appeared when he took off his sheepskin coat. Rory brought him to where Tim was so he could round out the muscle team.

"You okay, Coop?"

Cooper peeled his eyes away from Kelly to face Flynn. "Yeah, fine. I didn't think he'd show."

"If you want to go downstairs and say hello, I got it covered here."

Cooper pinched his lips and shook his head. "Let's finish this. Two can do more than one."

Flynn raised his eyebrows at him. "We have all day."

Cooper shrugged in the hope Flynn would think he was indifferent. Judging by his slight smile, he didn't believe him, but at least he didn't insist.

After finishing the preparations on that side of the roof, they came back down to the ground. Despite the cool weather, all the men were working up a sweat, and Izzie was handing out cups of water instead of the coffee she'd started out with.

"You're a godsend, Izz," Cooper said after he took a cup from her.

"Here, take both, and give one to Kelly."

Cooper narrowed his eyes at her. "Stop matchmaking, Izzie. He still has to bury his wife."

She shrugged innocently. "Just because you bring a man a drink doesn't mean you have to seduce him, Cooper. If it did, Hugh would never allow me to do this."

Cooper grinned wryly at her. First Flynn and now Izzie. Cooper wasn't entirely comfortable with everyone's agenda here today. He admitted to himself that he'd been wrong dismissing Kelly's advances because Kelly couldn't be out, but this wasn't the time or the place to make amends. They'd all agreed to invite Kelly to get him out of his empty house, and that was all. Cooper wondered how much everyone here knew about the two of them. He was pretty sure most people were aware of their history by now. Maybe that was all they were aiming at? Maybe they figured, since he was an old friend, consoling Kelly would be his task. If only Kelly would let him come near.

After one more dismissive look, Cooper started to walk toward Kelly, who was helping Hunter line up some of the beams they were going to be using to make up the frame of the house extension. He waited until Kelly's hands were free and was glad of the fact that Izzie was near Hunter, handing him water, so it didn't look strange that Cooper was doing the same for Kelly. Kelly accepted the cup with a murmured thank-you, drank his fill, and then handed the empty cup back without looking at Cooper.

Cooper dared one look at Izzie and saw compassion, so he decided to avoid her the rest of the day. He hadn't counted on Calley being in on the whole matchmaking idea as well. Since there wasn't enough space for everyone to eat at the same time, Calley had arranged for shifts, and Cooper and Kelly just happened to end up in the same shift with Tim and Rory, who, despite having been together for more than three years, only had eyes—and attention—for each other, leaving uncomfortable silences between Cooper and Kelly.

"Thanks for coming to help us today," Cooper said in between bites of a delicious turkey sandwich.

"Well, you know me, always willing to chip in."

Cooper felt Kelly was way too focused on what he was eating, but didn't push. "Well, the guys all appreciate it, and Calley will find a way to pay you back."

"She doesn't need to."

Cooper couldn't stop looking at Kelly, even though Kelly didn't return the gaze, or maybe because Kelly kept looking at his turkey sub and thereby gave Cooper the chance to feast his eyes.

"We should get back to work," Kelly said as soon as the last bite was in his mouth. He didn't linger and left the table, taking his mug of coffee and his empty plate with him. Tim and Rory stared at him, silently admitting they had been following their entire conversation. By then, Cooper didn't care anymore.

THEY worked in teams all afternoon, until the basic frame of the extension was secure and they all had a good idea what the four extra rooms were going to look like. Just like the rest of the house, the rooms weren't huge, but they'd fit beds and some additional storage. The sitting room faced southwest, so Calley could see the setting sun, and could easily fit a sofa and a dresser.

They'd just started building up one of the walls when Kelly's phone rang, and he walked away from the construction site to answer it. He took a long time to return, and after a while, Cooper walked out to see whether he was still there.

Kelly was standing in the middle of the field, looking at the horizon, his cell phone still in his hand.

"Everything okay in town?" Cooper asked after walking a little closer.

"Jennifer just needed some advice," Kelly answered flatly.

"So you don't need to leave?"

"No."

"Good," Cooper said a little too enthusiastically.

"Just leave me be, Cooper."

Cooper watched Kelly walk away from him. He stood with his hands on his hips, hoping against hope Kelly would turn around again and walk back. When he didn't, Cooper knew he couldn't leave it like that. "You're not the man to walk away from things, Kelly. I'm the coward. I'm the one who runs when it gets hot under my feet. Not you."

Kelly stopped in his tracks. His head sagged, and Cooper could see him deliberately taking breaths. When he turned around, his shoulders were squared and his eyes shot fire. "You have no idea, Cooper."

"So explain it to me, then."

Kelly paced over to him and shoved him back. "Every time...."

Cooper waited for Kelly to string his sentence together, but as Kelly lowered his head, Cooper realized it wasn't going to happen. "What?" he asked tentatively.

When Kelly raised his head again, his eyes were softer and so full of hurt. "Every time I as much as think of you.... Every time I jack off to the memories of you and me together that night.... Every time I think about how that one night was so much better than all the memories I have of our year together in school.... And you know how memories are, Coop, you only remember the good things, not the bad...."

Kelly mimicked Cooper's stance and put his hands on his hips while kicking the dirt with his boot. All Cooper could think was that it looked a lot better on Kelly than it did on him. He wished Kelly would get his point across, though.

"She was choking while you and I were fucking, Coop."

Kelly's eyes shot full of tears, and Cooper pulled him closer and into his embrace. He was standing with his back to the house, but he figured the guys were within earshot and probably covertly watching them, so to save Kelly embarrassment, he turned them around. He could see Rory watching them with concern in his eyes and Tim urging him not to. Grant was calling the others away from the open part of the building site, and Cooper was grateful for the relative privacy while Kelly sobbed in his arms.

Much sooner than he expected, Kelly pulled away from him, wiping his hand over his face. His entire face was bloated, and Cooper wondered how many times he'd cried like that when nobody was watching.

"Let's get back to work."

Cooper raised his eyebrows. "Maybe it's better if you calm yourself down some more first."

When Kelly looked him square in the face, Cooper tried not to think how kissable his puffy lips were. Instead, he gestured at Kelly. "Sit down on the back porch. I'll go get us some water."

When he returned, he stopped a few feet away and watched Kelly, sitting with his eyes closed and facing the setting sun. His face seemed more relaxed and less bloated than a few minutes earlier. "Here you go." He could swear Kelly was trying on a smile when he took the cup of water from him, but not everyone would agree. He knew that.

"Didn't have anything stronger?"

Cooper sniggered. "You said yourself that you were on call in case something happened. Can't have our newly minted sheriff show up drunk at a crime scene."

"True," Kelly replied. "Although right now I'd give my right arm to get plastered and drink my misery away for once."

"You don't even drink coffee, Kells. Don't think your stomach could take the alcohol any more than it did in school."

"I was always a cheap date."

"So am I, these days." Cooper looked at Kelly sideways. "I sank pretty deep after Marty's death. If it wasn't for Hunter, I'd have probably killed myself drinking."

"Was the guilt eating at you?"

Cooper nodded. "And the injustice of it all. If I'd been a woman, Martin would have made a public apology, stayed with his wife, and that would have been the end of it. Now he was a deviant, a monster, in their eyes. He didn't see any other way out. If his wife had been a stronger woman, she would have been okay, but she wasn't, so I ruined a lot of lives, Kells."

"What happened to his kids?"

Cooper shrugged. "I'm sure she had family. At least after Marty… they whisked her away from here. I never saw the two kids again, or the baby that arrived later."

Kelly sat, his elbows resting on his knees, slowly sipping his water. He looked a lot more relaxed than before his outburst, and Cooper was glad he'd been able to let those feelings air. The fact he had to actively will himself not to touch Kelly made it hard for him, but he could live with that.

"Do the guys know about us?"

Cooper frowned at the sudden change of subject. "If they didn't before, well, you shouted loud enough for all of them to hear." Cooper chuckled. "I'm sure it didn't surprise them to hear I was fucking a guy, but you, well, that was news for most, I think."

"Not Gable."

"He may be the quiet, brooding sort, but he sees and knows everything. We practically had to spell it out for him when Flynn was mooning over him, but other than that, yeah, he'd probably have figured out which side your bread was buttered on before you had, if he'd known you back then. It doesn't matter all that much, Kells. Even the straight guys know not to talk about it to anyone outside these two ranches. All of them have seen how hard it is to be out and proud in this neck of the woods. Hell, most of them have family that would disown them if they found out they were working for gays. They won't tell. Which doesn't mean news won't travel. Eventually." Cooper looked at Kelly to gauge his reaction, but Kelly remained neutral.

"I need time, Coop."

"I know," Cooper answered.

"No, that's not what I meant."

Cooper leaned forward when Kelly didn't immediately elaborate.

"I can't come out and tell people who need to reelect me in four years' time that I'm gay all of a sudden. You said yourself that they won't take kindly to something like that, and I like my job."

"Like I said, I understand."

"Don't…." Kelly sighed. "Just let me finish, please?"

Cooper nodded.

"I need time to get used to this. I have a funeral to get through first."

Cooper nodded again, holding his tongue because he'd promised to let Kelly speak without interruption.

"I need to feel comfortable with you again. I can't be open or even proud unless I feel it here first." He struck his chest with his fist.

Cooper tried to suppress the butterflies he suddenly felt fluttering around his stomach. Kelly wasn't pushing him away. He was saying he wanted to take it slow, but he was definitely taking baby steps toward them being together, and it actually made Cooper feel happy. To hide the smile that was impossible to stop, Cooper scratched his scruffy chin. "So you're saying you want to play it by ear and ignore any questions this might raise with your constituents?"

"Pretty much."

"You're willing to be seen with me in public, without explaining anything to anyone?"

"Well…."

"Look, Kelly, it's not like we'll be holding hands."

Kelly chuckled nervously. "I didn't think you were the type."

"And it's not like we'll be doing any necking in public either." Cooper playfully eyed Kelly sideways.

"Unless you consider a truck at the mountain pass vista point a public place, no."

"I figured," Cooper said, pursing his lips.

"Unless you want to move in with me. I've got this huge, empty house and—"

"Wow!" Cooper interrupted. "Step on the brakes there for a minute, Sheriff. Let's take it one step at a time, okay?"

"No problem. As long as you come visit occasionally."

"So we're just going to do things in private, and if people draw the conclusion that you and the town queer are an item, then that's their imagination?"

Kelly looked past Cooper at the unfinished house extension, where quite a few of the guys were still hanging around, and then looked at Cooper. "I'm sorry to have to tell you this, but you don't qualify as the town queer anymore, Coop. There are six other guys who all live in this town and are actually in an established relationship with someone of their own gender."

"And let's not forget you."

"Yeah," Kelly replied, looking more relaxed than he'd been all day. "Let's not forget the queer sheriff."

"But the whole point was not to let the town catch a whiff of that, right?"

Kelly smiled. "That the town sheriff is one of the queers? No, I guess not. At least not for a while. Not that I'd deny it if I was asked directly."

"As if someone around here would have the nerve to ask."

Kelly shrugged. "I figured they wouldn't. Talk behind my back, yeah, sure, but not to my face."

Cooper put his hand on Kelly's thigh and squeezed it. Kelly looked at Cooper's hand and then proceeded to lean forward and gently kiss Cooper full on the mouth. Cooper kissed him back, and then he heard someone wolf whistle behind him, and he chuckled.

"They're jealous," Kelly said, looking over Cooper's shoulder with obvious delight.

"Who is it?" Cooper asked without turning around.

"That's for me to know and for you to find out."

"Bastard," Cooper hissed.

"So look behind. He's still standing there."

"I don't think I want to know." Cooper pulled Kelly closer and kissed him again, this time deepening the kiss like he'd wanted to the first time.

When Cooper finally let go of Kelly and turned around, the guys had given them their privacy. On the way back, Cooper took Kelly's hand but let go again once they reached the building site.

—30—

KELLY was tidying his kitchen when he heard a truck. Drying his hands, he walked outside and around his porch. It still stung every time he saw the ramp and was reminded of why it was there, and of the fact it was no longer needed. Seeing Cooper walk up it made the smile return to his face, though.

"It's late. Don't you have chores early in the morning?"

Cooper looked serious. "Do you have a minute?"

"Sure."

Cooper followed Kelly inside.

"Teo gone to bed already?"

Kelly wasn't quite sure how much he was going to tell Cooper, but then he wasn't one to keep secrets. Especially not from the important people. "Teo left. He, ehm…. After Nina…." Damn, this was hard. "He made a pass at me, and I made it clear to him I didn't see him in that way. I managed to mention that we moved out here so I could be closer to the man I loved, and I guess that sealed it for him. He left the next morning."

"I'm sorry to hear that," Cooper said. "I know you depended on him."

"I'll live."

"I'm sure you will. You're always welcome at the Blue River for dinner. I'll cook for you."

"Or you can come cook over here occasionally." Kelly knew he was teasing, especially after not following up on the agreement they'd made on Saturday, but he wanted to keep all possibilities open between them, while at the same time taking things slow enough for him to catch up. "So what brings you here?"

"I can't believe how blind I've been. It's been in front of me all this time, and I never saw it. Or maybe I didn't want to see it."

Kelly had no idea what Cooper was rambling about, and it must have shown in his face.

"What is Ryan and Noah's last name?"

"Hang on." Kelly walked to the hallway, where he retrieved his notebook from his coat. He came back leafing through it. "Here it is. Ebersole."

Cooper smiled widely. "I knew it."

He stood in Kelly's kitchen smiling, hands on his hips, shaking his head. Kelly wanted to shake him to get him to talk. "What?"

"I drove Calley home after we finished at the building site, and she asked me to go over the contract she was going to offer Sadie to run the store. It had the name Ebersole on it."

"So Sadie is related to Ryan and Noah?"

"Mmh."

"Cooper Nelson, cut to the chase, will you?"

"I caught Sadie and Ryan hugging in Calley's storage room, and I thought they were… you know, boyfriend and girlfriend. They're not. Sadie is Ryan's sister."

"So he has a grown-up sister. That's good, I suppose." Kelly's mind started whirring with the possibilities. He'd have to have a talk with her about where the boys would be staying, since the social worker would prefer them to stay with family instead of strangers. The only way Noah could stay with Calley's twins was if Sadie was unable to take Ryan and Noah in. His train of thought was stopped by Cooper's serious face. "What's wrong?"

"Ebersole was Emilia's maiden name."

Kelly shook his head to signal he didn't know what that meant.

"Emilia was Martin's wife. Sadie, Ryan, and Noah are Martin's kids."

—31—

"HOW could you not know?"

Cooper shook his head. "Martin kept me far away from them. He always called his son Ry, not Ryan, and I thought his daughter's name was Sandy or Sandra. I never knew Noah. Emilia was pregnant when Marty… died."

"Do the kids know?"

"I wish I could say they didn't, but the first time Sadie looked at me she froze, and you know Ryan doesn't like me."

Kelly took two beers out of the fridge, opened them, and handed one to Cooper. He leaned against the counter. "Did I ever tell you what Ryan said to me when we picked the kids up after Calley got sick?"

Cooper shook his head.

"He called you a pervert. Told me you couldn't be trusted around the little ones."

"Wow." Cooper stalled for time by drinking his beer. "I suppose I could bury my head in the sand and pretend he's just reacting to the fact I'm gay, but I'm afraid this sounds like he knows from someone who's been there."

"His mother," Kelly agreed.

"Well, he was eight when his dad killed himself. I'm sure he wasn't totally oblivious to the circumstances."

"I wish I'd asked him why he thought you were so dangerous, but I purposely ignored it because we had to get the kids safe, and they know you better than they knew me."

"And you trusted me with them?"

"Of course I did."

Cooper walked closer to Kelly without directly looking at him. He joined him in leaning against the counter so their shoulders touched. Although Kelly had made it clear to him he wanted their relationship to start again, he was sure it wasn't in his best interest to make the first move. At least Kelly wasn't pulling away.

"It does put a few things in perspective," Kelly said after a long silence. "The whole business with Kaye Simmons."

"As in, it explains Ryan's overly dramatic response to a possible overture by the guy?"

Kelly shrugged. "Well, either he's gay like his dad, but he's seen how that turned out, or he's straight and was so freaked out about the pass Kaye made at him, it made him react the way he did. Suppose we can be grateful it didn't result in violence."

"I suggest you stay in the closet for now," Cooper quipped. "You're one of the few people he still respects and occasionally talks to."

"He lives with Gable and Flynn. Would he stay there if he had a problem with them being gay?" Kelly wondered out loud.

"So it's me, then? He just doesn't like me? I'm the only pervert?"

Kelly turned toward Cooper, his eyes closed and his forehead creased. He put his hand at the back of Cooper's neck before pressing his lips against Cooper's. When he broke away, he didn't move back, but let his forehead rest against Cooper's. "Maybe we should persuade him that we're not perverts?"

Cooper wanted to call him on the "we," but didn't. Baby steps. "How do you want to do that?"

This time Kelly did pull away. He sighed, defeated. "You're probably right." He took a big swig from his beer bottle. "It'll be easier to get to the bottom of this if he thinks I'm straight."

Cooper nodded, but without conviction. He had to admit Kelly was probably right, but that didn't mean he had to like it. "So are you dropping by the building site after work this week? Ryan was working at the store this weekend, but he's helping out with the building after school."

"I'll see what I can do."

Now the heat between them had died again, Cooper changed the subject. "I got the lowdown on how Bill Haines's termination of parental rights should go from Sean and Norm Goddard, and they gave me the information documents to show him. Calley and Gable got the blood work done, so all we need to do now is confront Bill with it and ask him to sign the papers."

"You think he'll do it?"

"Would you?"

Kelly shrugged. "I don't know. I would never have walked away from those kids in the first place. Given half a chance, I want kids. It wouldn't matter that much if they were mine biologically. So in my mind, he doesn't care for them. Why wouldn't he sign?"

"To make life hard on Calley?"

"Guess we'll just have to give him all the facts, then. From what I've found out, he's barely looked at these kids since they were born, but if he doesn't sign away his rights, his'll be the first door they come knocking on if Calley can't take care of them anymore."

"God, I hope that cranks the deal." Cooper wasn't at all sure.

"You know the man. I only know him by reputation. All I've heard is that he's a great vet."

"And quite a character. I don't know how Calley lasted so long, the way he treated her."

"Abuser?"

"Not physically. At least I don't think so. He had a way of ordering her around, though. And he didn't exactly treat her with the respect she deserved."

"Love is blind."

"Yeah, tell me about it."

Cooper was looking at his feet, and Kelly playfully kicked him so he'd look up. "Part of me wants to ask you to stay the night."

"But?"

"Why does there need to be a but?"

"It sounded like you were going to give me a but."

Kelly took a step closer, and Cooper automatically spread his legs a little. "Oh, you want a butt, hey?"

"Always."

Kelly took another step closer, and Cooper grabbed his ass cheeks, pulling him closer still. Kelly took Cooper's head in both hands and kissed him again. It was a sweet kiss, but neither tried to make it any more than it was. Cooper didn't want it to end. He didn't want to stop feeling Kelly's bulk leaning against him and moved his hands to the small of his back in the hope he wouldn't pull away. He wanted to continue tasting Kelly's sweet taste and feeling the rasp of his stubble against his skin. When he inhaled, he committed Kelly's my-last-shower-was-this-morning-and-I-worked-hard-all-day scent to memory. Despite Kelly's confession of the day before, Cooper still played it safe in case Kelly changed his mind, because he knew he was going to. At least temporarily.

"You were right," Kelly said after breaking the kiss. "There is a but."

"I knew it," Cooper replied, and it surprised him that he could keep the hurt out of his voice.

Kelly ran his fingers through Cooper's hair, making a curl flop onto his forehead. "I still feel guilty about not being here when…." He shook his head. "I need to sort things out in my mind before we rush headlong into something that will be sexual and very little else."

"Oh, I think we passed that stage years ago, don't you?"

"Maybe you have, but God, Cooper, I can't even close my eyes at night without dreaming about you!"

Cooper couldn't hide the fact he was flattered, but he understood how hard this was for Kelly. He kissed him quickly and then reluctantly wiggled from between the counter and Kelly's muscled frame. "I better go, then. Chores in the morning and all."

Kelly nodded. "I'll drop by Gable's after work. See if I can talk to Ryan."

"Yeah, and we can figure out what to do about Bill as well."

Cooper took one more look at Kelly and then walked through the back door, to his truck. Just before he backed out of the drive, he saw Kelly standing on the porch, but he didn't acknowledge him. He had to leave and deal with his feelings on his own.

—32—

ALTHOUGH it had always been his dream, being the town sheriff was a little strange at first. He was already used to making most of the decisions at the office. Hanson had barely come into work during the last six months of his tenure, and Kelly had all but taken over long before he'd actually been mandated to, but now Kelly got the cushy corner office, and they were putting his name on the door. Although he tried not to change his attitude, he was clearly no longer one of the guys. Although he'd never asked them to, the deputies called him "Sir" and they didn't include him in the office gossip anymore. Luckily, Jennifer was still Jennifer.

"The ladies—and one gent—from the book club are reading a cop story, and they invited you to tea." She looked up from her notepad. "I know you like this sort of stuff, but I asked for a rain check because it's Wednesday."

Although he didn't want to think of Wednesday and Nina's funeral yet, he couldn't help but smile at his office assistant. They'd had a rapport since the first day he'd arrived, and she hadn't changed one bit since he got elected. She was still this curious mix of irreverence and mother-hennishness, and he knew she'd always have his back.

"Of course, now they know why you can't come, they'll probably make a day trip out of coming to the funeral, but I figured they all had your best interest at heart, so no harm done."

"Did you get the funeral details out to the local news channels?"

She sat down on the side of his desk. "Mike and Len are going to be there to keep the onlookers at bay. I don't want them turning this into a media circus, Kelly."

"It's the deal I made with them the day Nina died. My privacy in the first few days for their access to the funeral."

She sighed. "That doesn't mean they get the run of the place."

"It's their job to report the news. And it's my job, not yours, to run this office."

"But it is my job to make it easier for you to do yours, and if that means coaxing two of your most trusted deputies to volunteer to go to the funeral, then this is what I do." Her mouth was a thin line, and her eyes were dark with determination. "Everyone else will be working as usual, so I don't want you anywhere near this station, or anywhere else in the county in an official capacity, for that matter."

His initial anger at her taking charge had abated as he saw her determination rise. He knew she meant well. "Will you be coming to the funeral?"

"If you want me there," she said, much more subdued than before.

"Yes," he said softly, but not without conviction. "I'd like it if you could have my back there as well."

She smiled at him as if she'd just won a bet. He decided not to call her on it.

WEDNESDAY came too soon.

Kelly knew exactly when Nina had been cremated and had said good-bye to her one last time just before. The funeral itself was just a formality. Nobody of Nina's small, estranged family had expressed any interest in attending, although Kelly had postponed the proceedings so they would have the time to make the trip. His family had come up with excuses not to show up either. Kelly didn't really care. An old professor who was now living on the West Coast had accepted the invitation, and Kelly had received a few nice, polite but impersonal letters from some of Nina's ex-employers, so none of them would be coming. He was expecting a few people he'd become close to over the last months, but only one would be able to console him, and he couldn't do it in public.

Kelly greeted the people who came to the funeral home by shaking their hands and accepting their condolences. Most people he recognized as having met them on the job at one time, and he was surprised how many he remembered by name. The Blue River troupe came together. Hugh with Izzie and their girls, Grant and Hunter with their son, Matthew. Christie joined them without her kids, since they were in school. Gable and Flynn came with Calley and her twins. Kelly waited for Cooper, but tried not to be too disappointed when he didn't see him emerge from the line.

The reporters were there as well, but Mike and Len kept them in the entrance hall and away from Kelly and the others attending. Kelly noticed Jennifer talking to them, and he hoped she'd do a good job. He had briefed her in the anteroom before the proceedings and knew he had to trust her, since he didn't feel like talking to them himself.

The service was short, and Kelly barely listened to what the nondenominational minister was saying. The woman spoke in a soft, soothing voice about all the things Kelly had told her, but this service had been Nina's wish, not his. Emotions bubbled up nevertheless, although he kept them from showing for the longest time. Just when sitting alone on the front bench was getting to him, movement made him look to the side. Cooper was sliding in next to him. He was wearing the same dark gray suit he'd worn to Jack Conroy's wedding, and just like then, he'd cleaned up nicely. They exchanged looks of gratitude and understanding, but Kelly resisted taking Cooper's hand, although God knows, he wanted to. He contented himself with feeling Cooper's warmth instead.

After the service ended, two of Nina's doctors came to greet him, but soon enough the hall emptied. Cooper was standing discreetly to the side, and this time Kelly didn't resist his urge to talk to him. He knew they needed privacy, though, so he dragged him into the anteroom he'd used before the service.

"I was waiting for you before we started," Kelly said just after he closed the door.

"I didn't want to intrude."

"I did this for you, Coop. I didn't want a service, but Nina insisted I have one because of you. She said she wanted you to have a chance to say good-bye together with me. She said we were the only ones who'd care. Well, she included Teo as well, but he's flown the coop early."

"I said my good-byes at the hospital, Kells."

Cooper was calm and collected, and a lot better at hiding his emotions than Kelly was. Then again, Kelly had always been the crybaby. When Kelly took a step closer, Cooper was the one grabbing Kelly and enveloping him in an embrace. It broke the dam, and Kelly felt tears in his eyes.

"I miss her too, baby. I wish I'd had more time with her, but she went on her own terms."

"I know," Kelly managed to squeeze out. "That's why I needed you. Because we're the only people here who actually knew her." Cooper ran his hand over Kelly's hair, and Kelly pulled back to look at him. He felt the uncontrollable urge to kiss him. He didn't hesitate. It was a desperate kiss, and Kelly hoped he was conveying the need he felt for contact with Cooper. It was also comforting to feel Cooper holding him tight and kissing him back. Cooper was there for him.

"Kelly, would you consider consenting to...."

Kelly pulled away from Cooper as soon as he registered that the door had opened and the words spoken belonged to Jennifer. The fact she'd stopped talking, together with the utter consternation in her face, made it clear to Kelly they hadn't pulled apart fast enough. She'd caught them kissing, and she wasn't taking it well.

Looking to the side, he saw Cooper standing about ten feet away from him, his eyes trained on the floor. Jennifer was still holding the door open.

"It's not what it seems, Jen." *Boy, was that the best he could come up with?* "Cooper knew Nina from law school. We were both upset." From the corner of his eye, he could see Cooper cringing. Jennifer wasn't buying it, and he was hurting Cooper with his denial. Jennifer was on his side, right? The damage was done; she'd seen them kiss. He had to play straight with her now.

"Jenni, I'm gay."

Jennifer swallowed but didn't move, her eyes the size of saucers.

"Could you close the door before one of those reporters catches some of this, please?"

She closed the door as if she was an automaton.

"Jenni, please talk to me. I'm still the same guy. I'm still just Kelly."

"You're not!" she shouted. "You lied to me. It's your wife's funeral, for heaven's sake. And I voted for you!"

"Nina knew, Jen. She's always known. Cooper was my boyfriend in law school. The three of us were the three musketeers. She was there for me when Cooper left me. I loved her, Jenni. I never stopped loving her, but she knew."

All through his speech, Jennifer was shaking her head as if she still couldn't believe what she'd seen.

"I'm still the same person, Jenni."

"No," she said just before turning around and walking out the door.

Kelly stood defeated. He didn't move until Cooper closed the door. Then he realized he was crying again.

"Hey."

Kelly looked into Cooper's soft blue eyes and shook his head. "If she can't accept it, how can I expect strangers to accept me, Coop?"

Cooper was biting his lip. "I know this doesn't feel good right now, but thank you for being honest with her."

"What if she goes to the press?"

Cooper rubbed Kelly's arm. "I'm not going to say I didn't think about that too, and I wish I knew her well enough to say she won't, but if she does, we'll survive that too. *You*'ll survive that too. And I'll be here for you."

"Even if they run me out of town?"

"They won't."

Kelly raised an eyebrow.

"They didn't run *me* out of town. And I caused someone's death."

"They won't want me to be their sheriff anymore."

"Sure they will. It'll cause a storm, and when it dies down, you'll have four years before there's another election. Four years of saving kittens and catching teenagers making out in cars at the vista point. And if you're lucky, you'll get another chance to stop two guys from shooting each other."

Kelly smiled. "Rory won't do it again. I'm sure of that."

Cooper chuckled. "There are plenty of Rorys where he came from. And they don't all have a Tim to turn them around."

"True."

"So will you be okay to go home?"

"You have to work?"

"'Fraid so. And since I drove up with Hugh and Izzie, could you drop me off at the Blue River?"

"Only if you come to my house after work."

"I have groceries to distribute as well."

"I can wait."

Cooper squeezed Kelly's shoulder. "Deal."

—33—

THE sun was setting when Cooper arrived at Kelly's house. Every time he parked his truck there, he still expected to be greeted by Teo and guided to the back porch to visit with Nina.

Neither was there anymore. Now it was just Kelly, and this was both sad and immensely liberating. He was going to have Kelly all to himself, whatever that meant. He was packing lube and condoms. Just in case.

Kelly walked out just as Cooper was getting out of the truck. "Go inside. It's cold."

Kelly was in his shirtsleeves and had his arms wrapped around himself. "I'm okay. Hurry."

Cooper looked around when he thought he heard something, but couldn't make anything out, so he followed Kelly inside.

"Have you eaten?"

Cooper nodded. "I grabbed a sandwich in between deliveries. You?"

"Not much," Kelly admitted.

"Let me fix you something, then."

Kelly shook his head. His eyes were puffy, and he was sniveling like he had a cold, but Cooper knew he'd probably been crying. When he made a half-assed attempt to touch Cooper without actually coming closer, Cooper enveloped him in his embrace. It never ceased to amaze him how this big bulk of a man could turn into such a puddle. They stood in the kitchen for a long time until Cooper felt Kelly relax somewhat. "Better?"

"Come to bed with me."

Cooper agreed silently and followed Kelly to the back of the house, where his bedroom was located. They silently undressed to their boxers and wifebeaters and dove under the cool sheets and blankets. Almost immediately, Kelly crawled into Cooper's arms, and Cooper was transported back to law school, when this was how they'd almost always fall asleep. Only then it was always after making love, and they'd both be in their birthday suits. This time Cooper knew there'd be no need for him to unearth his supplies from his jeans pocket.

If he was honest with himself, he had to admit he liked it this way too. This was comfortable and familiar and soothing in a way sex would not have been. This was also guilt-free, and Cooper knew how important this was for Kelly right now. Feeling Kelly snuggle even closer, Cooper smiled to himself. Kelly was still his big teddy bear, and he only now felt how much he'd missed this contact. In lots of ways, Kelly still felt the same. He was a little bulkier, but the skin covering the muscles was still soft and fairly hairless. And he still smelled the same.

"Think you can sleep this way?" he asked Kelly.

Kelly nodded without looking up.

WHEN Cooper woke up in the morning, Kelly was sitting on the side of the bed, bent over. He reached for him, which made Kelly startle.

"Did you sleep well?"

"Yeah, I did," Kelly drawled. He forced a smile. "But now it's morning, and I never thought this could ever happen, but I don't want to go to work."

"Jennifer will rise to the occasion," Cooper said, turning to his stomach so he could keep the physical connection between his hand and Kelly's side.

"And what if she doesn't?"

"Then you fire her."

"I can't fire her because she's a bigot!"

"Sure you can. If she's impossible to work with, you can fire her. If she goes to the press to spill personal secrets of yours, you can can her too."

With a start, Kelly got up and walked out of the bedroom. Unsure what had happened, Cooper followed him. Kelly was standing in front of his flat screen TV with his remote control in hand, flipping through the news channels until he stopped on the local news.

"Yesterday afternoon, newly sworn in sheriff of Fremont County Kelly Freed held funeral services for his wife, Nina Alexander, a former assistant district attorney for the city of Boston, Massachusetts. Mrs. Freed was thirty-eight, and succumbed after a long battle with motor neuron disease. Jennifer McCarthy, spokeswoman for Sheriff Freed, had this to say."

The image cut to Jennifer being interviewed.

"Sheriff Freed has always served his county, even when Nina was seriously ill, and he will continue to do so. He's taking today off, but he'll be back in the office tomorrow. He appreciates that he's given the space to mourn his wife in private." It cut back to the studio.

"Guess that seals it, then. You need to go back to work."

"Ssh!" Kelly cut him off.

The anchorwoman continued: "Sheriff Freed was joined by many people from his county, and the funeral home was packed. It's good to see that, although the election results were not that outspoken, the people of Fremont County clearly stand behind their new sheriff. Now over to Stacey and the weather."

Kelly let out a breath.

"Jennifer didn't go to the press, Kells."

"I know."

Cooper put his hand between Kelly's shoulder blades and felt the tension in Kelly's back. It didn't ease in the time it took Kelly to pull away from it and turn around to go back to the bedroom. When he reappeared, he was dressed in his everyday sheriff's uniform, and the defeated look was gone.

"I'll lock all the doors. Just go out through the front door and close it behind you. It locks automatically."

Cooper nodded. Kelly was back in his don't-mess-with-me headspace, just like he was supposed to be, wearing that uniform.

COOPER finished his morning chores at the Blue River and then joined the rest of the gang at Blackwater to work on Gable and Flynn's house extension. Enough of the downstairs work was finished for them to start on the roof, and that meant he and Flynn would be up there for a good part of the day. The sun was shining, so, despite the cold weather, both men were in T-shirts, working up a sweat.

"So how is Kelly doing?" Flynn asked as they were securing a crossbeam.

"He's okay, I suppose. It's understandable that he has trouble with the house being so empty."

Flynn nodded, a mischievous smile playing around his lips. "I'm sure he appreciates you helping to make the house less empty."

"What do you mean?" Cooper had answered before he realized how futile it was to lie to Flynn. Usually it was Gable who uttered the simple truths, but Cooper figured something must have rubbed off. He threw Flynn an annoyed look.

"Come on, Coop. We're all friends here. I get that Kelly can't just burst out of the closet, but among us guys, there's no need to hide."

"There's also this thing called privacy."

"Fair enough," Flynn responded. "I'm just saying that Gabe and I are okay with the two of you being together, and if you ever need a place to let your hair down and not worry about what other people think, you can always come knocking on our door."

Cooper grumbled "Yeah right" under his breath and continued hammering away.

Flynn stopped him. "I'm serious, Cooper."

Cooper looked down between the rafters and saw very few people within earshot. He sighed. "Ryan doesn't want me around. With good reason."

"I can't imagine why...."

"Ryan is Marty's son."

"Who's Marty?"

Cooper sighed, figuring Flynn was new enough not to know the whole story. "Eight years ago, I was disbarred as a lawyer because I had an affair with the DA. He killed himself over it and left a pregnant wife and two kids behind."

"Marty. And Ryan, Noah, and Sadie are the three kids."

"You know about Sadie?"

Flynn nodded. "From Calley."

"So you see, I can't bring Kelly to your house. He's one of the few people who can still get through to Ryan, and if Ryan finds out Kelly's gay...."

"Ryan isn't a homophobe, Coop. He's uncomfortable when Gabe and I get too close—he caught us kissing the other night, and he looked like he wanted to wash his eyes out with soap—but other than that, he doesn't give us a hard time over it. In fact, he and Gabe talk about all sorts of stuff. Just give him some time."

Cooper leaned back on the beam he was straddling. "His father killed himself over me, Flynn. His mother couldn't hack it, and they ended up in the system. People are hated for a lot less than that."

"So work on Ryan through his sister."

"Sadie practically shot me with her eyes when she first saw me."

"She's a lot more open-minded than her brother."

"Lesbian?"

Flynn laughed. "You're asking me to read a woman? So not going to happen. Seriously. I overheard her telling Maxie that she thought we were all cute. 'The guys from those two ranches who all love each other.' I wasn't too thrilled when I heard her talking about us like that, but I guess it's to your advantage."

Cooper thought about it. He didn't know what to do with it yet, but he figured it wouldn't hurt to strike up a conversation with Sadie. "Good to know in any case."

"Hey, you guys sunning yourselves up there?"

Cooper looked down and saw Gable standing near the porch, his eyes shielded from the sun.

"We're working, Gabe!" Flynn yelled down. "But we're also thirsty."

"I'll send Ryan up."

"Shit," Cooper muttered.

—34—

THURSDAY night, Cooper didn't have a grocery run, but he went by the store anyway. Like he hoped, there was nobody in that late.

"I'm about to close," Sadie warned.

"I know," Cooper said as he approached the counter. "I'm hoping to talk to you."

Over the weeks, Sadie had grown more comfortable around Cooper, but now she tensed up again. Cooper raised his hands. "I just want to talk. If you want me to leave, I will."

She shook her head vigorously, but Cooper could tell she was extremely cautious, so he decided to cut to the chase. "You're Martin's daughter, aren't you?"

Her look softened. "How did you know?"

"You took your mother's maiden name. It's not a very common name."

"And you're the reason my father killed himself."

"Yes, I am," Cooper croaked. He cleared his throat.

"I used to hate you."

"Used to?"

Sadie nodded. "Mom blamed you for everything that went wrong. Some of the things were ridiculous, but I was fourteen. I believed her. She changed our names and took us away from here. I didn't want to leave my friends, but I had no choice. And then she had Noah, and she lost it. She was angry because Noah was a boy and would grow up 'just like his father.' They took us away from her because she threatened to hurt us."

"And then you got separated?"

"There was a couple who wanted the boys. I was sixteen by then and in a good foster home. I figured I could stay in touch with them."

Cooper could feel the sadness in her as she moved to the side of the counter.

"Ryan made it hard for them. And Noah wasn't an easy baby either. Ryan wanted to see me all the time, so they moved away, hoping if they severed contact he'd turn around."

"They didn't know him very well, did they?"

She chuckled. "No, they didn't."

"The next time I saw them was here, three months ago." She took another step closer to Cooper, and Cooper held his ground, unsure how to react.

"Did Calley fill you in on what happened in the meantime?"

Sadie nodded. "As much as she knows. Ryan isn't much help either."

"Yeah, getting Ryan to talk is like drawing blood from a stone."

She smiled. "I guess he'll tell me when he's ready."

Cooper cocked his head. "I'm glad we cleared the air between us, at least."

"My dad loved you."

Cooper swallowed away a big cotton ball.

"Mom turned it into something sordid, and I can't blame her for that since she was on the receiving end of the whole mess, but I can't forget it lasted five years. You and my dad, against all odds, always afraid of being caught. He. Loved. You."

"It wasn't perfect, Sadie."

"Love never is, but that doesn't mean he didn't love you. He couldn't see himself leaving mom for you, but if the outside world would have understood, he would have. As it was, he would have lost everything. The job he lived for. Us. He needed both. But he needed you too."

Cooper put his hands on his hips and shook his head. He didn't want to deny what she was saying. He was just trying to keep his emotions at bay.

Sadie stepped closer, hooked her arms under Cooper's, and hugged him around his waist. For a long moment, Cooper didn't know how to react, but then he hugged her back. She fit right under his chin. Cooper felt paternal toward her, as if he was compelled to take Martin's place and protect her against the big, bad world. "You've done well for yourself," he whispered. "Your dad would be proud."

"I can't take care of the boys yet, Cooper," she said, looking up at him without pulling out of the embrace. "I'm just getting back on my feet. Calley is great with them, even with Ryan, but I know how sick she is, and I want to make sure they don't go back into the system."

"We can try to persuade the social worker that the boys have a great support system, and I think you should be a part of that."

Sadie pulled away from Cooper, as if she'd only just realized she'd invaded his personal space. Cooper felt the same, so he didn't mind. He was just glad they were connecting.

"What does this entail?"

"Why don't you close the shop, and we can talk about this over a cup of coffee?"

TALKING to Sadie was surprisingly easy. Cooper recognized a lot of her father in her, and that was surprisingly painless. She had tons of questions for him, and in return he learned she'd dropped out of law school and had an acrimonious divorce under her belt. Hence the reason she needed to get back on her feet.

"It's not that I don't want to take care of Ryan and Noah, but they're doing great with Calley, and I'm only just getting to know them again. Ryan is still working on forgiving me for leaving them, and he needs someone he trusts."

"Tell the social worker this, Sadie. Make her see you have their best interest at heart, but that when push comes to shove, you're there for them."

"I don't want anything to happen to Calley, Cooper. She said you were helping her get her affairs in order?"

Cooper nodded. "Have you gotten to know Gable and Flynn?"

"A little."

Cooper wasn't sure how much he could divulge to her, or what Calley had already told her. "Then you know, if she can't take care of her kids anymore, if she needs to go to the hospital or worse, that she wants Gable and Flynn to take care of her kids, right? And this includes Ryan and Noah?"

"She told me Gable was her kids' father."

"We're trying to sort that out legally, right along with the fostering situation. They're two different things, though, and I could use your help for your brothers."

"You've got it," Sadie said with a smile.

"Now on a more personal level…." He'd said A, so now he had to say B, but boy, was it hard. "I get that Ryan doesn't like me, and I already give him a wide berth, but I have his best interest at heart, Sadie."

"He knows that, but he's struggling with so many things at the same time."

"He's a teenager," Cooper tried.

"And he's in love, although I told him it was inappropriate."

"In love?" Cooper feigned innocence, but she didn't believe him.

"Your friend intervened. Sheriff Freed?"

Cooper nodded but didn't say anything.

"I told Ryan that a sixteen-year-old boy in love with a twenty-eight-year-old schoolteacher was going to cost that schoolteacher his job."

"Kaye Simmons."

"Yes. I also told him it didn't matter if it was consensual, because, according to the law, he wasn't old enough to consent."

"They had sex?" Cooper asked, his voice barely a whisper.

"Oh, like I'm going to tell you what Ryan told me in confidence. I only have his side of the story, and I wouldn't tell you either way."

Cooper raised his hands. "Fair enough. I'm the last person to intervene, but since he's talking to you about it, could you keep him safe?"

"Yes, Dad," she said with a twinkle in her eye. "But you can see how this is screwing with him, right? He's gay, just like our dad, and all he's seen happen to gay men is misery. It cost you your job and Dad his life. He sees good things at Gable and Flynn's, but he hears the kids at school sneer and make fun of the 'gay ranches' and he doesn't see the light at the end of the tunnel."

"Is there any way you could get him to talk to me? I could tell him about his dad, show him it isn't all misery."

"You're not exactly a shining example, Cooper. If I didn't know any better, I'd think he was your son instead of Dad's. Just like him, you're always grumpy."

"He's so angry at the world."

"Wouldn't you be if you were in his shoes?"

"Probably," Cooper conceded. "But he still needs to wait until he's eighteen to get that boyfriend."

"He knows." She was fiddling with a napkin. "Would you take Noah in if Calley couldn't anymore?"

"I'm not daddy material, Sadie."

"You don't give yourself enough credit."

"A crew house on a stud ranch is no place for a little boy. Besides, he loves Calley's twins. Gable has already said that Flynn will castrate him if he doesn't keep Noah and the twins together."

"So Noah is taken care of?"

"Yes, I'd say so."

"Good."

They said their good-byes, and Cooper couldn't wait to get over to Kelly's.

—35—

A TRUCK stopped in front of his house, and Kelly hoped it was Cooper. It was late, but they'd agreed that he would return, no matter what time. He purposely didn't look up from his book when the screen door to the kitchen opened and closed, despite the fact he realized it could be anyone, from a reporter to a burglar.

"So how was your day, Sheriff?"

Kelly looked up to see Cooper standing in his living room. "Jennifer called in sick."

"So you had a stay of execution."

Kelly sighed, feeling some of the tension leave him. "Yes. Which means the torture starts again tomorrow morning. So how was your day?"

"Oh, you know. Muck out stalls, put a roof on Gable's extension, talk to Sadie about Ryan and his love for a certain schoolteacher."

"You talked to Sadie?"

Cooper shook his head and smiled. "No, Kelly, the correct response is: so I was right that Ryan was sleeping with Kaye Simmons?" He plopped down on the couch next to Kelly.

"I don't want to know that, Coop. I'm sworn to uphold the law. If I find out a twentysomething schoolteacher is sleeping with a sixteen-year-old boy, that is statutory rape. Nobody is going to be interested in whether it's consensual or not, and even fewer people will think it's love."

"All I know is it *is* love. Sadie won't tell me what she knows, and I didn't press her for more. I don't know if it's just infatuation or a kiss happened or… something more. When I talked to Simmons right after it happened, I had the distinct impression it was mutual, so that's good enough for me."

"It's still—"

"Yes, statutory rape according to the law," Cooper interrupted. "I know, so I asked Sadie to keep Ryan safe. I know better than to try and talk to him. I think that would have an adverse effect."

Kelly moved a little closer to Cooper on the couch, eager to connect with him, receive some of the comfort he'd felt all night sleeping close to him. "So tell me about Sadie."

"She's on our side."

Kelly felt his throat constrict. He sat up. "*Our* side? Did you tell her about me?"

"Relax, sport. I didn't divulge your dirty little secret."

Kelly couldn't help feeling relieved.

"Whenever I went into the store to pick up the groceries to deliver, there was always this tension between us. I wanted her to know I knew who she was, since she obviously knew who I was."

Kelly allowed himself to relax again. "I gather it went well?"

"We went out for coffee. She's a smart kid. She wanted to talk about her dad. She told me she knew he loved me, but that for the longest time, her mother made it impossible for her to acknowledge it. She's going to help us establish a good support system for Ryan and Noah so they won't need to go back into the system if anything happens to Calley."

"That's good, right?"

"It's a start."

Kelly snuggled closer to Cooper. "You staying over tonight?"

"If you want me to."

"Duh!"

Cooper tickled him, and Kelly bent over. When the assault stopped, Cooper kissed him, and he was all tenderness again.

"I loved sleeping next to you last night."

Cooper went shy on him, his mouth twitching.

"I wouldn't mind a repeat of that." Kelly wished there was more light in the room, because he thought Cooper was blushing.

"I'm going to have to start bringing clean underwear and a toothbrush here," Cooper murmured.

"You can borrow mine."

Cooper chuckled as Kelly tried to kiss him. "You think me walking around in your underwear is going to help my hard-on?"

Kelly pulled back. "I'm sorry."

"For giving me a hard-on?"

"For asking you to sleep here and then not putting out."

Cooper ran his hands over Kelly's cropped hair. "We're not kids anymore, Kells. You don't need to put out for me to want to be here."

Kelly snuggled back into Cooper's embrace, where he felt safe and still a little insecure at the same time. "It just feels surreal, like it's all going to be snatched away again at a moment's notice."

"It won't," Cooper whispered against Kelly's forehead. "Let's go to bed. Early rising tomorrow."

WHEN Kelly woke, it wasn't even light yet. Despite it being a mild winter, days were still short in Idaho. He could feel the warmth radiating off Cooper's body and turned to get closer. Cooper was lying with his back to him, head slightly forward and his neck exposed. Kelly pushed his nose against it and inhaled Cooper's scent.

"Time to get up?" Cooper grumbled.

"Not yet. Just go back to sleep."

"Kinda hard with your hands where they are."

Kelly withdrew his hand from underneath the band on Cooper's boxers and opened his eyes. "I should let you sleep." He got up and put the blankets back around Cooper so he'd stay warm.

Kelly had barely turned on the shower when he saw Cooper standing behind him.

"What's up?"

"I didn't mean to wake you. I just wanted to feel you," Kelly admitted.

Cooper pulled his T-shirt over his head and stepped out of his boxers before joining Kelly in the shower. "So feel."

Kelly didn't need another invitation. He pulled Cooper under the spray with him and kissed him ferociously, all the while letting his hands travel over Cooper's body. Kelly's skin started to tingle as Cooper returned the gesture, and before long he felt Cooper's erection push against his hip. Instinctively, he rubbed his groin against it, eager for more contact.

"Stop teasing," Cooper grunted before pushing Kelly against the wall and sinking to his knees.

There was nothing hesitant about Cooper's actions as Cooper swallowed Kelly's erection, and Kelly grabbed for purchase against the slippery tiles of the shower. Kelly looked down and past what Cooper was doing to him to what Cooper was doing to himself. Kelly thought he'd never seen anything quite as sexy as Cooper fisting his own erection while he was expertly blowing him. And then Cooper looked him straight in the eye, and he had a new favorite view. It was all becoming a bit much, so Kelly gestured at Cooper to stand up. Cooper wanted none of it and upped the ante, making the image in front of Kelly's eyes swim as he felt his spine tingle and his hips jut forward of their own accord. Kelly closed his eyes as Cooper swallowed all Kelly gave him and then some.

Kelly didn't get the time to catch his breath as Cooper pushed his lean body against his and smothered him with a kiss. It had been ages since Kelly had tasted himself in another man's kiss, in Cooper's kiss, because Cooper was the only man he'd ever met who liked to share like that.

"Now dry off, put on that uniform, and go tell the Jennifers of this world who's boss."

As conscious thought slowly returned to his brain, Kelly knew he needed to do one more thing first. He grabbed Cooper and turned him around before grabbing a hold of Cooper's distended erection. "I need to turn you to mush like you did with me." As he started off slowly but firmly stroking him, Cooper's smug look was replaced by a softer one, and as Kelly sped up his movements, Cooper's eyes started to glaze over. Cooper's reactions made the fatigue that usually overtook him after coming evaporate, and Kelly found his strength again. He switched his grip so he could go even faster and saw Cooper cave in as he came in big gusts.

Kelly slowly moved them so they were standing under the spray and could let the water wash the evidence of their lovemaking away.

"You can still make me feel so good," Cooper drawled. "Now go to work so I can leave too. We can't be making out all day."

"We can't today, but we can on Sunday." Kelly wiggled his eyebrows at Cooper.

"Sunday is for finishing Gable's house."

"Damn!" Kelly shouted playfully before stepping out of the shower.

IT TOOK Kelly longer to get ready since he had to shave, but he was considering letting the stubble stay because he was feeling the whisker burn from Cooper's kisses. He figured it was a small sacrifice. When he arrived in the kitchen, Cooper was making tea and sandwiches.

"I helped myself. Hope you don't mind."

Kelly handed Cooper the cell phone he'd been holding. "I don't mind."

"What's this?"

"It's a cell. You can call people with it and get calls, you know." Kelly bit his lip. "It used to be Teo's. He left it here, and I put a prepaid card it in."

"Okay," Cooper said a little hesitantly.

"I figured we'd come to a point where I couldn't tell Tim or Grant everything I wanted to tell you, so now we can talk directly. It's kind of hard to ask Hunter to ask you whether you want to stay the night."

Cooper smiled. "Fair enough."

Kelly drank from his tea and grabbed a sandwich. "Thanks for this. Now I need to go."

"Stand your ground, Sheriff."

THE little detour in the shower had distracted Kelly for a while, but as he drove into town while the sun was rising, the anxiety about dealing with Jennifer returned. He knew he had to bring things out in the open, just like Cooper had cleared the air with Sadie.

He walked in past the duty deputy and checked the night registry. Nothing major had happened, so he walked through to his office. He was early, so he hadn't expected Jennifer to be there already, but she was.

"Glad you're feeling better today, Jennifer."

She looked up, her lips tight lines. "I came in early to catch up on yesterday," she said flatly.

He figured that until he could talk with her alone, he'd have to act as if it was all business as usual. "Could you call Bill Haines for me, please? Make an appointment for me to talk to him."

"What shall I tell him it's about?"

"Just tell him you don't know the details, but that I'd like to talk to him." Kelly walked into his office and then reconsidered. "Tell him he didn't do anything wrong, but I just want to talk. Over coffee somewhere, maybe. He can choose the place."

She nodded, so he left her alone.

Just after ten, she came into his office with a note that said, "Barnaby's, twelve thirty." She handed it to him without a word, so Kelly gathered all his courage. "Jennifer, do you have a minute?" He didn't wait for her to answer in case she said no. "Close the door, please."

Jennifer looked like she was about to be executed, so Kelly got up from behind his desk and offered her a chair. She sat. Then he went to his cabinet and poured two cups of tea. "I know you prefer coffee, but I don't have any, and I noticed you hadn't made a pot this morning. Do you want me to go get you a cup from the front desk?"

She shook her head. "This is fine."

"No sugar, right?"

She forced a smile before she took a sip. "It's hot."

Kelly sat down on the chair next to her and took a sip as well. He didn't want to prolong the agony. "I want to talk to you about Wednesday."

"I know."

"You were angry with me."

"I still am."

"Why?"

"You need to ask?" Her eyes were wide.

"I did nothing wrong, Jenni."

"Well, that depends on your point of view."

"Will you let me explain mine?"

Her chin and lips tense, she nodded.

Kelly cleared his throat. He looked into his tea mug as he started talking. "Nina found me this job. She was the one who found out Cooper was living here, and she knew Hanson was close to retirement. The three of us were in law school together. Cooper and I were together, and she was our friend. When Cooper left for a job on the West Coast, she stayed. I loved her, Jennifer. When she got sick, I didn't think twice about taking care of her. I still love her. She accepted me for what I was. She never knew me any other way than gay, but she also knew they'd never hire me if they knew. Hanson's a great guy, but not exactly Mr. Open-minded."

"Neither are the rest of the people who voted for you."

"Including you?"

She didn't answer right away, so Kelly was forced to look up.

"I don't know you anymore."

"I'm still the same guy."

"But you do… things… with him."

"If you mean I love him, then, yes."

"You *love* him?"

"Yes, Jennifer, I love him." Kelly knew he had to stay calm. If he could keep his cool while two guys were squaring off with guns to each other's head, he could stay calm while his assistant was playing the bigot card. "I feel exactly the same things for him as you do for your high school boyfriend, who was good enough for you to marry him. I wish I could marry Cooper. I wish I could hold his hand walking down Main Street. I wish I could show everyone that he's my man. You're trying for kids with Billy, right?"

She nodded.

"I want to raise kids with Cooper too. None of this is going to happen. Even if I wasn't the town sheriff, Cooper and I would never be accepted as a couple. Can you imagine how they'd treat a child we adopted? Can you imagine what would happen if we walked down Main Street the way you do with Billy on date night?"

"I suppose they'd be uncomfortable."

"And you?"

She shook her head, indicating she didn't understand him.

"Would it make you uncomfortable if we walked down the street holding hands?"

"I saw him kiss you!"

"Who says I wasn't kissing him? Do you ever kiss Billy without him kissing you? No, you don't. You kiss each other. Cooper and I were kissing each other too." Kelly took a few deep breaths because he felt he was leaning a little too hard on her. He was about to give up on her, categorizing her as a lost cause.

"I don't know any other gay guys."

Kelly looked up at her with wide eyes. "Hunter and Grant? Gable and Flynn? Tim and Rory were in this station after Rory broke his parole. You've seen how much those two love each other!"

"I didn't want to see it, okay!" Jennifer jumped up from her chair and put some distance between them. "I was raised to think it's wrong. In church on Sunday the minister has sermons about it. He calls them by name. The ranches with the deviants."

"And what do you think?"

"I don't know."

"You told me you like Rory. You told me it was sweet how Tim doted on him."

She nodded. "I never thought you'd be like them."

"I am, but I'm just the same guy I always was."

She looked at him. "I know."

"Jennifer, do you still want to work for me?"

"I can't afford to lose my job."

"That's not what I asked. If you no longer feel like you can work for me, we'll find you another job, but I'd hate to lose you because you're the only one who talks back to me."

For the first time since the conversation started, Kelly saw her genuinely smile. "And you like that?" She sat back down.

Kelly nodded, unable to hide a smile.

"I'd like you to continue doing it—within reason—but you need to know that, although I won't tell the world about this, I am who I am. You'll be one of the people keeping the secret. For now."

She nodded.

"Hopefully you won't need to keep quiet forever." He got up from his seat.

"Kelly?"

He turned to face her.

"I need some time to get used to the idea."

"Fair enough."

"Can I go now? I still have a lot of work to do."

He opened the door and let her out. He winked at her as she passed.

After the door closed, he understood the relief Cooper had felt after clearing the air with Sadie. He picked up his phone and dialed Cooper's number.

"I'm taking you out to lunch. This is for Calley too. We have a date with Bill Haines. Bring the termination papers."

—36—

IT DIDN'T take Cooper long to spot Kelly sitting in a booth at Barnaby's. He was wearing his tan uniform, and his hat was on the table beside him. He wasn't the only man sitting alone, but he was the only one tapping on his smart phone.

"Hey, city boy," Cooper greeted him.

"City boy? Where did that come from?"

Cooper gestured at the other patrons, reading the newspaper or drinking beers at the bar. "You stand out with your fancy phone."

"Well, aren't you happy I didn't get you one of those fancy ones?" He tucked his phone into his back pocket.

"Ecstatic."

"At least I can call you now," Kelly said in a softer voice as Cooper scooted into the booth next to him.

Despite having only missed him for a few hours, Cooper needed to touch Kelly, and he squeezed Kelly's thigh under the table. Kelly only veered up a little. "So when are we meeting Haines?"

"He's coming here in about half an hour. I figured we could have lunch first."

Cooper leaned a little closer. "Is this a date, Sheriff?"

Kelly playfully sneered at him, but moved his leg so their thighs were touching. His face turned to neutral pretty quickly, though, as the server joined them at the table.

"Hi, I'm Linsey, and I'll be your server today." She handed them the menus. "The specials are up on the board. Can I get you something to drink to start you off?"

"I'll have a beer," Cooper said.

"Just water for me, thanks," Kelly added. They waited for her to leave. "So let's talk strategy," he said, turning to Cooper.

"He's never cared for the children because they're not his. He's never looked after them or even looked at them twice. Calley has never asked him for anything," Cooper summarized.

"Are we sure about that?"

"We'll have to play it by ear, but I'm pretty sure." Cooper stopped talking when the waitress brought their drinks.

"Are you guys ready to order?"

Neither had looked at their menu yet, but Cooper spotted a country omelet on the specials board and ordered that. Kelly followed suit.

Cooper waited until she left to start speaking again. "She's always told me she had to keep her store open no matter what, because she's the sole provider for those kids. I know Gable will chip in if she needs it, but apparently she's okay financially."

"But this might change because she's going to be sick for a long time."

Cooper nodded. "She's a good businesswoman. Sadie gets paid on a sliding scale, depending on whether she can keep the store profitable. I work for free. She has lots of others volunteering because they know she's trying to stay afloat with four and soon five kids depending on her."

"Now we just have to paint a bleaker picture for Bill and make it clear to him that if he doesn't sign the papers, he's going to be asked to help out financially."

"That should work. I hope," Cooper said as the waitress brought their food.

They'd only had a few bites when Kelly's phone rang. "Kelly Freed. We're having lunch. Seriously?" He sighed. "Text me the address. We'll drive up there." He disconnected the call. "Haines isn't coming. He's treating a horse with colic and can't leave, so I said we'd drive up there."

"You really want this over with, don't you?"

Kelly chuckled. "I'm Andy Griffith, remember?"

THEY drove to a cattle ranch forty-five miles away and were directed to the barn, where they found Bill Haines in the back, washing his hands.

"Your secretary said you'd be coming by," he said, smirking. "I'm at a point where I don't believe her anymore. What did I do, Sheriff?"

"Nothing, Mr. Haines, just like she said," Kelly replied, wearing his kindest smile. "We're here to talk about Andrew and Victoria. Your name is on their birth certificate."

"And what of it?"

"Mrs. Haines had a paternity test done on the children, and you are not their biological father."

Bill Haines squared his shoulders and put his hands on his hips. "She didn't need a test for that. It's no secret to anyone that Gable Sutton sired them."

"She'd like you to terminate your parental rights."

"And why would I do that?"

Cooper, who had stayed in the back, not exactly out of sight but not close enough to cause interference, was starting to worry. Bill's indifference to the children was clear, but he didn't seem to want to change anything about the current situation.

"Because the way the situation is now, you could be asked to provide financial support for the children."

Bill turned away from Kelly to pick up his bag of supplies. "Calley has her own business. She's made it very clear that she doesn't need or want my money."

"She's sick, Bill."

Bill looked up and put his bag back down. For the first time, Cooper saw some interest.

"Sick?"

"Yes, to the point where she can't manage the store anymore and she's had to hire someone to do it for her."

"Must be serious, then, if she's willing to leave the shop to someone else. I wasn't even allowed to unpack a crate."

"Yes, it is serious."

Cooper liked the fact Kelly wasn't revealing anything about the nature of her illness. He agreed it wasn't any of her ex-husband's business.

"And Gable doesn't want to help her." It wasn't a question. "Figures."

"Actually, Mr. Sutton would like nothing more than to help with the children, but as it stands, he can't, at least not in an official capacity."

"So you're saying that if I don't sign this piece of paper, I'll get asked to pay for kids that aren't even mine?"

"That's what it boils down to, yes."

"So what do I do?"

Now Cooper really had to prevent himself from interfering. Kelly knew what the procedure was and he was on a roll, so he didn't want to jinx it, but it was hard to stay in the back.

"You have to make an appointment with the district judge. He'll ask you some questions, and if the answers satisfy him, you'll need to sign an official paper."

"Can't I do it here?"

"It needs to be witnessed by a judge."

"And this will make sure I won't be called on to pay for them?"

Kelly nodded.

"I'll need to run this by my lawyer."

"Fair enough," Kelly said. "We have examples of the questions you'll be asked and the papers you'll need to sign. I'm sure your counsel will corroborate this." He gestured at Cooper to give him the papers.

Kelly handed them to Bill. "The number of the district judge's chambers is on there."

Bill looked at the papers. "I'll consider it."

"That's all we can ask for." Kelly held out his hand, and Bill shook it, although he didn't look like he trusted it. "So do you trust us now when we say you didn't do anything wrong?"

Bill chuckled. "I suppose."

"Unless there's something you want to confess?"

"No, no," Bill was quick to answer.

A horse whinnied in the stall next to them.

"We'll leave you to your work, then."

Kelly saluted Bill and turned on his heels, gesturing with his head for Cooper to follow. Once they were outside the barn, Cooper had to practically run to keep up with Kelly. They both got into Kelly's car and drove off. Kelly didn't speak until they were on a deserted country road and he'd stopped on the soft shoulder.

"It can't be this easy, right?"

Cooper shrugged. "A lot of things can still go wrong. His lawyer could tell him this is a bad idea."

"Would you?" Kelly held up his hand. "And don't tell me you're not a lawyer anymore."

"No, I'd tell him to get this arranged ASAP. He still has to make the appointment."

Kelly casually placed his hand on Cooper's thigh. "I'd let my lawyer make the appointment. He probably knows the judge."

"Good point. The judge could ask all the wrong questions and freak him out."

Kelly smiled, his hand moving back and forth. "Haines doesn't look like the kind of guy to freak out."

Cooper clamped his hand over Kelly's. "If you don't stop this right now, we're going to end up making out in the middle of an open field in a car with 'Sheriff' written on it in big letters."

Kelly pulled his hand away and looked at the road. He was still smiling, though. "We better wait for tonight."

"Should we go tell Calley?"

Kelly cussed and fished his cell phone out of his pocket. "Damn, three missed calls." He thumbed through them. "We should go see Gable first." He held the phone up to Cooper.

"I didn't hear it ring."

"It didn't. I set it to vibrate so we wouldn't be disturbed."

Cooper raised his eyebrows, not even pretending to understand what that meant, as Kelly started the car again and drove in the direction of Gable's ranch.

—37—

GABLE jumped up as soon as he heard a car stop in his driveway, but Flynn beat him to the porch.

"The social worker was here," Flynn blurted out while Cooper and Kelly were walking toward the house. "She wanted to see where the boys were going to live."

"You can imagine this was the worst possible time. We live in a war zone," Gable added, pointing at the building site next to their house. He couldn't believe everyone stayed so calm.

"She's a good woman, guys," Cooper said. "She'll take into account a lot of it isn't ready yet."

"She'll give you recommendations on what to think about while finishing it, so in fact she came at the right time," Kelly added.

"But what if she says the boys can't move here?"

Gable put his hand on Flynn's shoulder. "We didn't have time to prepare."

"That's the idea," Kelly explained. "And she won't tell you the boys can't live here. Like I said, she'll give you recommendations. Some of them may not be easy to accomplish, but she won't expect everything to be perfect. So did you explain to her what you're doing here? Did you show her the plans Grant drew up?"

Gable nodded and felt his anxiety die down a bit.

"We have some other news too," Cooper said.

"Let's go inside and get some coffee."

GABLE kept busy making tea for Kelly and coffee for everyone else, and letting Flynn do the talking. He was better at it anyway. Having Cooper and Kelly in the house, calmly explaining what they knew about the whole fostering experience, rubbed off on him too, and he started feeling like himself again. Maybe he'd gotten carried away by Flynn's fear of being told they just weren't good enough to have kids in the house.

"She went into everything," Flynn rambled. "She wanted to know what kind of food we had in the house, whether we were going to give the kids sodas, where they were sleeping right now. She wasn't too thrilled that Ryan only had the sofa to sleep on and Noah slept on a blow-up mattress. At least it was better than telling her that the three kids slept in two beds because we can't keep Vicky from crawling into her brother's bed." Flynn was actually gasping when he stopped talking,

"So what was your big news?" Gable asked as he put down the four mugs.

Kelly looked at Cooper, gesturing for him to tell them.

"We drove up to talk to Bill Haines today."

"To talk about his parental rights?" Gable asked cautiously. He ignored Flynn's worried stare for a moment.

"Yes," Cooper replied.

"He didn't seem averse to the idea. He said he'd run the papers by his lawyer."

"Can't we just ask the courts to rule on this? We have the paternity tests to prove that Gable's the father."

"Calley would have to start the petition to have Bill's parental rights taken away. It takes a lot of time Calley might not have."

Gable felt his throat grow tight. He hated to be reminded of the fact that Calley could die. He took Flynn's hand for comfort.

"If Bill voluntarily gives up his parental rights, it goes into effect from the moment the papers are signed," Cooper continued. "It will be better for everyone."

"So when do we know?" Gable asked.

"The judge is going to call Calley as soon as Bill's been to see him to sign the papers. It could be soon, or it may never happen. We just don't know. The ball is in Bill's court."

"God, I hate waiting," Flynn lamented.

Gable squeezed Flynn's hand to comfort him. "Thank you for all you've done, guys. If it hadn't been for you, we wouldn't have known this was possible."

Kelly got up from the table. "We'll celebrate when everything is settled. And don't worry about the social worker. She's got a lot more difficult cases to manage than yours."

They shook hands, and Gable and Flynn waved Cooper and Kelly off from the porch. When Gable looked at Flynn, he was smiling.

"Your mood picked up," Gable said.

"Just think about it. If Bill forgoes his parental rights, that means Calley could put you on the birth certificate. You'd actually, legally, be their father."

"It won't change that much," Gable said calmly.

"Yes, it will. If anything happens to Calley, they'll come knocking on your door and not Bill's."

"Don't talk about that, okay?" Gable knew how important that security was to Flynn, but he really didn't want to think about what needed to happen for Flynn to get his wish. They basically had the kids full time anyway, especially on the days when Calley was in the hospital. "Let's go pick them up from Hunter's."

AT THE Blue River, the twins were nowhere to be found, so Gable and Flynn walked into the kitchen, where Christy was fixing dinner for the ranch hands.

"Hey, guys, how ya doing?"

"We're good. Thanks for looking after the twins for us on such short notice."

"No problem, Gable. They're no bother, and Matty loves having them over for a play date."

They heard the front door bang shut and excitedly stomping feet approaching. When the door opened, it was Hunter with three kids. "I thought I heard your truck. Here are your munchkins." Vicky and Andy immediately made their way to Flynn, but Matty needed more time to get into the kitchen, using his walker. Once he settled in his corner, surrounded by his fire trucks and toy cars, the twins joined him there.

"So how did it go with the social worker?"

"I think it was the most nerve-wracking two hours of my life," Gable answered. "She dissected our lives with a pitchfork."

Hunter chuckled. "I know the feeling. They were happy to let me take Matty home, but before all the papers could be signed, we had to endure a home visit as well. I had nightmares about having to bring him back to the hospital because we didn't pass muster. Should be easier for you since Calley will be there. You're not adopting. They just have to make sure the temporary situation is safe enough for Ryan and Noah."

"But you know what our house looks like right now. Neither boy has a decent bed to sleep in. How is she ever going to approve that?"

"By adding a shitload of recommendations to the approval. Some of them will be mandatory, some not. We didn't have a house ready for a less-abled child either at the time, so don't worry. She has hotter potatoes to rescue from the fire."

"That's what Kelly and Cooper were saying."

"Ah, you've had the latest addition to our gay happy family over as well?"

"See, I told you I wasn't alone!" Flynn interjected. "Hunter thinks they're sleeping together as well. Besides, Cooper all but admitted it to me."

"Flynn," Gable cautioned, but Flynn kept smirking.

Christy intervened. "Cooper is sleeping somewhere, and it ain't at the crew house!"

"For heaven's sake." Gable sighed. "Kelly just buried a wife."

Hunter leaned across the table. "And you of all people should know the difference between loving a woman and loving a guy. How is Calley, by the way?"

Hunter had a point. "I was going to go over to see her this afternoon, but the visit interrupted that."

Hunter gestured outside. "You can leave if you like. Grant's gone to pick up the kids from school, and he was driving back up to your place to do some more work, anyway. We can take Flynn and the kids home."

"Go on," Flynn said. "Go see your girlfriend."

Gable sneered at Flynn before giving him a quick kiss. "I'll be home for dinner."

—38—

BY MONDAY evening, Cooper felt in dire need of a holiday. They'd worked nonstop all through the weekend in an effort to get the extension to Gable's house livable for when Calley came home from the hospital, and had just moved beds and wardrobes from Calley's town house to the ranch. Like he had every evening for the last week, he didn't return to the crew house, but went home with Kelly, only for the two of them to crash on his bed and do nothing but sleep until they had to get up again at the crack of dawn.

Kelly was in the shower when Cooper's rarely used cell phone rang. "Cooper Nelson."

"Cooper, Jim Davies here. I was trying to reach Calley Haines, but I can't seem to. I'm hoping I can rely on your lawyer-client confidentiality for a moment?"

"Sure," Cooper replied to the district judge, not at all feeling at ease.

"She's all right, I hope?"

"Yeah, she's being closely monitored. In fact she's coming home this evening."

"Good, because I had Bill Haines in here this afternoon. He signed papers to terminate his rights to his children. I suggest she gets over here with her paternity tests and gets those birth certificates amended ASAP."

"Wow, he didn't exactly let it lie, did he?"

"Nope," Davis said. "Sounds like you gave him some compelling arguments to get it dealt with fast. His lawyer came along to expedite everything, but there was no need thanks to all the prep you did. Bill even memorized the answers to all the questions I had to ask him. He was that eager."

"Thanks, Jim. I'll tell Calley in the morning."

After disconnecting, Cooper hurried into the bathroom, to find Kelly drying off. He started taking his clothes off. "My turn, because I'm so going to celebrate this evening."

"Huh?"

"It's all done. Bill signed the papers. Jim just called."

"Already?"

Cooper nodded before receiving an armful of wet man, not that he was complaining. "One point for us. You bet we'll be celebrating. I don't care how sore or tired we are. We'll call in sick tomorrow if we have to."

Kelly pushed him into the shower, despite the fact that Cooper was still wearing his underwear, and kissed him madly while trying to get him out of it.

As Cooper grew more and more aroused, Kelly pulled away and started lathering him up, focusing especially on his nether regions. It was thorough and quick and only turned Cooper on more. "If I didn't know any better, I'd think you'd done this sort of thing before," he grunted. Cooper helped to rinse himself off, but the urgency got the better of them and they ended up on top of the bed covers soaking wet. Neither cared. Kelly stopped only to rummage around his bedside table to look for the condoms and lube they hadn't needed before today.

"This is so going to sound like all I want is to get fucked," Cooper said, panting hard.

"I don't care," Kelly replied. "We've been cuddling for a week. Let's get this over with." He ripped the condom packet open and rolled it on with shaky hands.

Cooper turned around and got on all fours. He looked over his shoulder at a nervous Kelly. "It's like riding a bike, Kells. Just go slow and try to keep it together." The lube was cold, the slippery fingers hesitant and nervous, but as soon as Kelly pushed the head of his cock against Cooper's entrance, he knew it didn't matter. He wanted nothing more than to be filled up and then fucked into the mattress.

Kelly grunted as he pushed forward and then grunted again, this time in frustration. "Want to go slow. Can't."

"I'm not delicate, Kells. You won't hurt me." To stress his words, he pushed back, feeling Kelly slip deeper. As Kelly pushed his chest against Cooper's back and wrapped his arms around him, Cooper knew he was truly home.

COOPER turned to his side so he could look at Kelly in the light of early day. He couldn't have slept more than an hour. He didn't want to sleep, but he'd been exhausted, exhausted by the long work hours they'd been keeping and exhausted by the gorgeous man sleeping next to him, his face partially hidden by the pillow. Kelly was lying on his stomach, sound asleep and breathing slowly through his half-opened mouth. A little bit of spit was dribbling out of the corner of his mouth onto the pillow. His far arm was raised over his head, the other one still lying next to him, palm open where Cooper's hand had been as they fell asleep.

Cooper's body was still buzzing. Kelly had always been the man for him. Even the very first time they'd slept together, they'd been perfect in their imperfection. For years after his split with Kelly, Cooper had compared every fresh body in his bed to the striking lawman, and every one of them had failed. Even what he'd felt for Marty hadn't been quite that perfect. Sure, he'd loved Martin, but only after he'd given up on finding another Kelly.

He'd known the time Kelly had walked into the law library that first evening of the study group. Cooper had been charmed by the mix of politeness and respect for others that had obviously been drummed into him in some private school, and by cowboy hick looks in the way he dressed and walked, as if he was raised with a horse between his legs. Cooper had been in lust with Kelly from the moment he'd laid eyes on him. The love had come later, as they worked on arguments for mock court, as they discussed cases they were studying, as Cooper discovered Kelly was pretending to be less smart than he really was so Cooper would tutor him in criminal law.

Cooper shook his head to get rid of the memory. He owed it to Kelly to love the man he was now, not what he remembered from the spruced-up recollections of all the good times he recalled by pushing away the bad times. He had to admit he liked what Kelly had turned into. He'd grown some muscle and still had that washboard stomach Cooper had been so jealous of in law school, but Cooper missed Kelly's long locks, the floppy, bleach-blond hair that was now short and dark blond. He wiped an imaginary hair from Kelly's forehead, knowing he really wanted to run his hand over the crew cut like he'd done earlier when Kelly was on his knees with Cooper's cock down his throat, but he didn't dare. He withdrew his hand when Kelly grunted and stirred. He continued sleeping, though, making delicious comfort noises in his throat.

Unable to resist, Cooper nudged closer, inhaling Kelly's heady scent of musk, sweat, and sex. They'd barely wiped the spunk off their bodies after their first time and hadn't bothered at all after the second time, unwilling to leave each other's side, even for a moment. The reunion had been too intense. For Cooper it had been like coming home. Now he still didn't want to let go and already dreaded the moment Kelly would wake, find it was almost day, and leave to go to work.

"Want to sleep some more," Kelly murmured. Nevertheless, he wrapped his arm around Cooper and pulled him closer before kissing him sloppily on the mouth.

Cooper more than let him. He was turned on and felt incredibly needy. As if their two earlier exchanges had never happened, Cooper felt the hunger for Kelly, the need for him to get so close to Kelly he'd forget they were two separate people. He could still feel Kelly inside him and would gladly repeat the experience, although he knew he wouldn't be able to even think about mounting a horse for the next few days after that. Luckily, he was just a ranch hand, and his horse-riding skills were only occasionally called for.

Kelly's kiss was becoming more insistent, more aggressive. He was practically fucking Cooper's mouth with his tongue, and Cooper gladly aided him in it by sucking. Kelly was the only man Cooper willingly submitted to. And then Kelly pulled away.

"You're turning me on."

Cooper snorted. "Duh."

Kelly was grinding against him. "God! Want you so badly."

Cooper smiled just a little. "Seriously?"

"Why not?"

"Round three?"

Kelly chuckled. "It's like being twenty-two again. Is there another condom?"

"Sure." Cooper slowly felt his insecurities dissipate. Kelly did really want him. He'd learned in the last week that Kelly definitely wanted more from him than just a fuck. He moved away just enough to lean over to the nightstand and pick up another square packet. He handed it to Kelly, who ripped it open before inserting his hand between their bodies. To Cooper's surprise, he felt Kelly put the condom on him. "Are you sure?" Way back in law school they switched too sometimes, but Cooper always had the feeling this was because Kelly felt he needed to reciprocate, not because Kelly actually wanted to do it.

"You'll have to take it easy. It's been ages. Fifteen years, to be precise." Kelly looked at him without shame or shyness.

Cooper kissed Kelly briefly. "You opened up just fine when I was rimming you."

This time Kelly blushed. "That has been fifteen years too."

"You mean Nina never…?"

"Could you leave Nina…?" Kelly let out a frustrated grunt. "Nina was my best friend. She was my wife, but she was never my lover. I loved her to bits, but our sex life…. Why am I telling you all this?"

Cooper ran his hand over Kelly's hair. "I don't need to know. It's none of my business."

"Sex was… perfunctory." Kelly turned to his stomach and away from Cooper.

Cooper tried not to feel the rejection and instead let his hand caress Kelly's beautifully sculpted back. He moved his hand across one of his shoulder blades, staying purposely above the belt. When Kelly didn't flinch, he lined his body up with Kelly's.

"Nice," Kelly commented softly. "Warm."

"Cozy?"

Kelly chuckled underneath Cooper. "Yeah, that too."

Cooper kissed the back of Kelly's neck, again inhaling the scent he couldn't get enough of. It made Kelly moan.

"I mean it," Kelly said in a breathy voice. "I want to feel what you felt when you came last night while I fucked you."

"This morning," Cooper corrected him.

"I wasn't looking at my watch, Coop. I just saw you lose it completely, and I wanted it too."

Kelly spread his legs, opening up just enough for Cooper to be able to rub his cock between Kelly's butt cheeks. Although the feeling was glorious—and judging from Kelly's moans, it felt good to him too—Cooper couldn't indulge too much for fear of ripping the condom. He backed away, reaching for the lube. As he coated his fingers and then Kelly's entrance, he remembered Kelly's plea to take it easy. When he inserted a finger and Kelly easily opened up, he smiled. Kelly eagerly leaned into the touch, and Cooper couldn't wait to push into the tight heat, but he kept his promise as he pressed against Kelly as slowly as he could manage.

Kelly inhaled sharply, and Cooper kissed the smooth skin between Kelly's shoulder blades, both to take his mind off the raging heat between his legs and to distract Kelly from the discomfort. Kelly's skin was salty from the sweat, and Cooper couldn't resist using his tongue when he kissed it, just to savor the taste. How was he ever going to get enough of this man?

"Go on," Kelly grunted more than said. "Want to feel all of you."

Cooper pushed forward with slow rocking motions, taking his cues from the noises Kelly was making. Despite gaining entrance, Kelly was still tight like a vise, and Cooper had a hard time staying in control. Cooper's hips made contact with Kelly's bubble butt, and Cooper couldn't resist thinking they fit well together in no matter what configuration. He gripped Kelly's shoulder and pulled himself even deeper.

"Oh God, yes!" Kelly hissed. "That's it. Right there."

Cooper's instinct was to up the tempo, but he resisted. He knew if he did it would all be over in ten seconds flat, and he wanted to make it last. The fact he'd come twice already over the course of the last hours definitely aided his stamina. He rocked back and forth slowly, losing himself in the hypnotic rhythm of his movements and Kelly's response in the form of moans.

"Hang on for a moment," Kelly asked, his voice pinched. "I want to see you."

Cooper held onto the condom as he pulled back and let Kelly lie down. When Kelly spread his legs, Cooper couldn't resist licking Kelly's dark, hard cock all the way to the tip. He was just about to move to his balls when Kelly asked him to stop. He moved higher so he could kiss him. "You okay?"

Kelly nodded. "Just didn't want to come that way."

"Fair enough. You ready for this?" Kelly nodded. "Relax. Push back."

Kelly was just as tight as the first time, but now Cooper had Kelly's facial expressions to go by as well as his moans. It made it somehow feel more intimate, more connected—less like sex and more like making love—something Cooper had rarely allowed himself to do before. Now he couldn't resist and didn't want to either. This was his man, his lover. He'd waited fifteen years for them to get back together, losing hope along the way until he'd seen Kelly again in that clothes shop in town. Now he was determined not to let him go again, no matter what. The sex was just the cherry on the cake.

"Is this what you wanted?"

Kelly arched his back. "You need to ask? Fuck! Coop."

Cooper slowly continued rocking in and out, never upping the ante, never changing his rhythm, because by God he never wanted this to end.

Kelly's skin started glistening, and Cooper dove down to lick it, then felt his head seized by two strong hands that pulled him up so they could kiss. It wasn't the easiest of positions. Kelly was a big guy and not exactly a contortionist. Luckily, Cooper was long and lean and fit perfectly between Kelly's thighs, but they couldn't keep kissing and fucking at the same time for long.

"Too much," Kelly groaned as he pushed Cooper out of the kiss. "But don't stop."

Although he wasn't exactly concerned about Kelly's ability to stand his weight, Cooper pushed up on his arms. "Better?" he managed to squeeze out.

"Touch me," Kelly begged.

Cooper scooted up onto his knees, pushing them underneath Kelly's thighs so they were holding Kelly's legs up. Although it made the thrusting angle more awkward, it gave him the free hand he needed to help Kelly out. Kelly, in turn, arched his back more and pushed the back of his head into the pillow with a low groan. As soon as Cooper began rubbing Kelly's erection, he started to leak, and it didn't take long for Cooper to feel the contractions in Kelly's muscles as pearls of cum started to become streams and Kelly came all over his own stomach. Cooper was close as well, but not close enough to miss Kelly's contorted face and choppy breathing, or the white knuckles on the hands that grabbed at the bedding. Cooper pushed in a few more times, giving Kelly aftershocks until he filled up the condom to the point where he thought it might not hold.

Kelly pulled him into his arms and kissed him as soon as he'd caught enough breath.

"The condom," Cooper warned. He held onto it as he pulled out and quickly discarded it next to the bed. They'd clean it up later.

Cuddling and kissing, they lost the battle to stay awake.

—39—

WHEN Cooper walked back into his room from the bathroom, Kelly was sitting on the windowsill, one leg up and the other resting on the floor to keep his balance. He was naked, oblivious to Cooper's unashamed stare as he looked out between the trees and toward the mountains Cooper was so used to he didn't even notice their beauty anymore. Even now he didn't follow Kelly's gaze.

"Here you go," he said, handing Kelly one of the two cups of tea he'd gone to the kitchen for. "Just sugar, right?"

"Hhm," Kelly acknowledged, turning his gaze as he took the cup from Cooper. "You remembered."

"It's easy to remember. Since you always used to drink my cup instead of getting your own from the kitchen."

"I liked drinking from your cup," Kelly said with a smile. "Somehow it always tasted better."

Cooper moved a little closer, into Kelly's personal space. He wanted to feel Kelly's warmth, his proximity, and hoped Kelly would feel the same and pull him closer. He didn't. Instead, he took a sip from his cup, hissed at the heat of the tea, and then grabbed Cooper's cup before Cooper could react.

"Hey!"

Kelly smiled broadly, then his expression turned softer. "Yours still tastes better."

Cooper offered him his cup to drink, and Kelly drank from it like a child, licking his lips as Cooper removed it. They looked into each other's eyes for a moment, and then Cooper looked away. He stayed close, though, feeling the pull of Kelly's body, the need to stay close to his lover. "So what are we going to do today?" he murmured, his lips ghosting over Kelly's shoulder.

"I thought we could go for a ride."

Cooper looked up with a start. "I don't know about you, but the thought of mounting a horse after... you know... isn't exactly enticing."

Kelly laughed. "You're so easy to tease these days."

"Aren't you... sore?"

Kelly put his hand at the back of his neck and pulled him closer until their lips were touching. The kiss started soft and chaste but soon escalated until Cooper felt hot liquid touch the skin of his hand, and he pulled away.

Cooper smiled and rolled his eyes as he took another sip of his cup, but Kelly grabbed it and pulled it away from him.

"Yes, I'm sore," Kelly said as he put the cups down on the sill and pulled Cooper between his legs. "But I know why I'm sore, and it's the most exquisite pain I've ever felt."

Cooper had to swallow the emotions away. He felt his eyes starting to sting and only knew one way to hide it from Kelly: by moving close enough to kiss him again. Pushing his groin against Kelly's taut belly did nothing to hide his arousal, but he ignored it. Tasting the sugar in Kelly's mouth was more important now. He moved his hands to cup Kelly's face as they continued seducing each other with kisses, and as Kelly enveloped Cooper's more slender frame in his embrace, Cooper felt warm and safe, although neither was wearing a lot of clothes.

They didn't do much more than kiss and touch, and in his moments of lucidity, Cooper wondered how their dynamic had changed from Cooper being the dominant, older one, to Kelly holding him in a very protective way. Was it the years that had passed? Or could Cooper attribute it to Kelly's bigger bulk or added maturity? The only thing he could be sure of was that he *let* Kelly take on the more mature role. Fifteen years ago, Cooper would have fought Kelly for it. Fifteen years ago, Kelly automatically took on the weaker role, looking up to Cooper for guidance. Cooper didn't want to dwell on it, but did find himself wondering.

As Cooper touched the cold glass of the window, he realized how frosty it was outside. "Aren't you cold?"

Kelly shrugged. "Hadn't noticed."

He let his hands slide down over Kelly's shoulders and arms. "You are cold."

"Don't want to get dressed yet," Kelly said, pulling Cooper even closer by grabbing his buttocks.

"We could crawl under the covers again."

Kelly pursed his lips as if he wasn't convinced.

"Unless you need to be somewhere?"

Shaking his head, a smile broke on Kelly's face. "I am allowed the occasional day off work. They have my cell phone number in case of emergency."

Cooper nodded. He took half a step away from Kelly but didn't let go of his hand. Kelly pushed himself away from the windowsill.

Kelly followed Cooper's tentative move toward the bed. "We're going to have to get out of bed at some point today."

Cooper shrugged, feigning innocence. "We're out of bed now."

"Not for long!" Kelly shouted before crawling under the covers.

They continued to kiss and touch each other without upping the ante. Cooper found he didn't mind. It felt so amazing to have this man in his arms again, and to feel how willing and eager he was, that he had the feeling they had many more days like this left to them. Slowly but surely, hope was starting to grow that maybe they had a shot at a future together. If out and proud wasn't an option, Cooper knew he would gladly settle for this: cuddling and kissing in between lovemaking, all in the privacy of Kelly's house.

AROUND ten, they decided it was time to join the real world, since Cooper reminded Kelly he'd promised to tell Calley about Bill signing the papers.

They showered—separately—and got dressed.

"Don't know when you found the time, but thanks for washing these," Cooper said, unfolding the shirt and jeans he'd left there four days earlier. "At least I have something clean to wear."

"The benefits of a laundry service," Kelly replied. "I've been bringing my stuff to the Laundromat near Calley's since Teo left."

"Be sure to thank them for using non-floral scents. I wouldn't want to go out smelling of lilacs," Cooper quipped. "Ready to go?"

Kelly handed Cooper his hat, put on his winter coat, and opened the door.

Cooper blinked at the onslaught of light and flashes. He instinctively dipped his head to let his hat shield his eyes.

"Sheriff Freed, what is your reaction to the pictures posted this morning in *The Post*?"

Cooper felt his chest go cold.

"I'm not aware of any pictures," Kelly told the woman reporter calmly.

She pushed a copy of the newspaper—if it could be called that—in Kelly's direction. Cooper didn't need to come closer to recognize what the front page depicted. The main spread was a picture of the two of them, from the back, walking toward the construction site on Gable's ranch. They were clearly holding hands. Some of the smaller pictures were taken here, on Kelly's porch, and were of Kelly smiling at him as he approached. There was another one, taken through the kitchen window, of the two of them kissing. It didn't matter that Cooper wasn't recognizable in any of them. Kelly's identity was clearly established, and the person he was kissing was undoubtedly male. The headline didn't lie either. "Newly elected sheriff replaces dead wife with male lover."

Cooper took a step back, but he knew it was too late. The news and tabloid cameras had picked him up, and that was all the confirmation they needed. The feeling of déjà-vu was overwhelming. He'd managed to ruin another life. He wanted to run, hide, get away from the scrutiny of the press, but he had nowhere to go. The driveway was packed with news vans, and his truck and Kelly's car were surrounded by people trying to catch a glimpse of them.

And through all this, Kelly was the epitome of calm.

"Some of these pictures clearly violate my privacy. I will be talking to my lawyer about this, and I will issue a statement later in the day. That will be all you will get from me at this time. Please clear my driveway so I can get to work."

"Sheriff Freed, can you tell us who your lover is?"

"How long have you been together?"

"Were you together when your wife was still alive?"

"Did Mrs. Freed know about him?"

The barrage of questions made Cooper sick to his stomach. There was a time when he thrived on attention like this, played the press like they were eating out of his hand, but the tabloid attention had never been directed at him personally. Ever since the business with Martin, he'd lost the stomach for it.

"I have no further comment. Please let us leave for work."

Kelly looked at Cooper. "You're leaving with me. Leave the truck here. We'll pick it up later," he said in a subdued voice.

Cooper didn't argue. They got into the sheriff's car, and the crowd parted to let them leave. Cooper didn't know what to say as Kelly drove into town. "I'm sorry" wasn't going to cut it, although he *was* sorry.

"Will you come to the station with me, Coop? I need to draft some sort of statement, and I need a second lawyer with me."

"Maybe it's best if you're not seen with me."

Kelly stopped the car by the side of the road. "I don't care, Cooper. The cat's out of the bag. I'm not going to deny it. If you don't want to be a part of this media circus, I understand. You don't need to be there. But I won't let them ruin us. I've waited too long for this."

"You've waited a long time for this job too." Cooper couldn't look at Kelly, afraid his emotions would betray him.

"Cooper, look at me."

Cooper turned his head but couldn't keep eye contact for longer than a few moments.

"If the people that elected me don't want me as their sheriff because I'm gay, then they can come and tell me or run me out of town, I don't care."

"Don't say that, Kelly."

"I'm serious. I'm going to give them a statement, and if they don't like it they can tell me to leave, but if they don't do that, I'll continue to be the do-gooder I've been for the last year."

"I can't have you throw away everything you've worked for in the past twelve years."

"I can't give *you* up for that."

Kelly grabbed Cooper's hand, and it took a few moments for Cooper to turn his around so he could entwine their fingers. He squeezed the hand but couldn't look the man in the eye, because he knew if he did, he'd cry.

"Let's drive to my office, and we can talk there."

Cooper nodded and let go of Kelly's hand so Kelly could drive his car to work.

—40—

KELLY felt surprisingly calm as he prepared to stand just outside his office to read a statement. He'd talked to Jennifer, explaining to her that he was going to step out of the closet a lot faster than he'd anticipated, and to his surprise, she'd not only given him her support, but had suggested she do the introductions.

He'd called in all his deputies—on and off duty and voluntary reserves as well—and had explained to them what was going on. He'd survived the first test when he asked them to resign if they felt they could no longer work for him. A few of them had grumbled a bit, but all of them were still on the roster.

Cooper had helped with the wording of the statement. Next to finding the right words to say to the press, they'd also agreed that Cooper would stay inside the sheriff's office and not be a part of this because he feared that his old scandal would cast a shadow over the real issue.

At exactly 1:00 p.m., Jennifer stepped outside. The cameras were clicking, but as soon as they realized it wasn't Kelly, they shut off.

"My name is Jennifer McCarthy, and I am Sheriff Kelly Freed's assistant. In a minute he will read a statement to you, and after that he will answer questions, as long as you can keep it respectful and orderly."

Jennifer stepped aside, and Kelly took a deep breath before braving the flashes of the cameras. Kelly tried not to squint too much, but after being patient for what felt like a long time, he held up his hands to make them stop.

He took the printout of his statement and started to speak in a calm, steady voice.

"More than a year ago, I came to this town to work as a deputy under Sheriff Hanson. My late wife found me the position because she knew Hanson would retire after his term, and becoming his chief deputy would give me a chance to get to know the people who could vote for me if I signed up for the election.

"I could have found better paid jobs in more prestigious counties, but there was another reason for me to come here, and my wife knew about this even before she married me, because she was present when I met him.

"Nina and I shared a very loving marriage of understanding for twelve years. She was my rock and my most loyal supporter. I didn't think twice about standing by her when she got sick, and moved heaven and earth to give her the best care available. As a result, she lived well past the three years the doctors gave her when she was first diagnosed.

"I will not stand by and let so-called news reporters ruin the character of a woman who was the most caring, inclusive, and supporting woman I ever encountered, nor will I let them drag my name or the name of the man I've loved since law school through the mud. I may be a public figure because I am an elected official, but he is a private person, and I respectfully ask you to allow him his privacy whether he is on his own or in my company."

Kelly took another deep breath as he felt the anxiety rise.

"I am a gay man. I always have been and always will be. I never lied about this, but I was not forthcoming with this information either. Essentially, I am still the same man you elected. I am still committed to making this county a safe and warm place to live. I am still in this to help the people. If, however, you no longer wish me to serve as your sheriff, my office has opened a registry where you can sign in and make your objections heard. We have a population of almost eleven thousand adults. If the registry collects five thousand five hundred signatures by the end of the year, I will step down. If it doesn't, I will see this as a vote of confidence and continue to serve this community to the best of my ability.

"Thank you for your attention."

The room was silent for a moment, and even the flashing lights had ceased. Behind the reporters, Kelly saw he had a silent support team. Hunter and Grant were there with Matty, Gable and Flynn with the twins and Calley. Tim held up his hand, entwined with Rory's. Kelly almost lost it, but then the reporters broke loose, all asking questions at the same time.

Kelly held up his hands yet again. "I cannot understand a word you're saying. Please show each other a little respect by asking one question at a time. Who knows, maybe someone else will ask a question you might be interested in knowing the answer to."

Chuckles rose above the crowd, and then the first question came.

"Kaitlyn Evers. Channel Ten news. Why did you not come forward with this before?"

Kelly smiled. "Miss Evers. When I announced my candidacy for sheriff, your news channel questioned my ability to invest the necessary hours into my job because I had a sick wife at home. All it took was for me to make a statement that I had a live-in housekeeper who took care of both my house and my wife. The other news outlets picked up both the story and my answer and that was the end of it. I was never asked again. Now I have a partner who earns his own money, has his own life, and who has been a part of this community for the last ten years, yet all of a sudden, this reflects on my ability to do my job? I don't think so. Next question?"

"David Chalmers. *Boise Examiner*. The other man in the pictures has been identified as Cooper Nelson, a former lawyer who was disbarred for a conflict of interest, since he had a tryst with a married DA from this county, eight years ago. When the affair went public, the DA killed himself. Would you care to comment?"

"On the name, the affair, or the fact this man was pushed into such a tight corner he saw no other way out?" When the reporter didn't immediately answer, Kelly continued. "I will say yes to the name and ask you again to give him his privacy. The very nature of this question should explain to you why this is necessary."

"But he works on one of the ranches locally known as the queer ranches, right?" the same guy asked.

"You're from Boise?"

Chalmers nodded.

"Then permit me to explain to you that these ranches are two of the most successful horse ranches in the county. They offer employment to locals and people passing through. They are owned by men who were born and raised on this soil, but I don't believe the fact these men are in committed long-term relationships with other men reflects on how these ranches operate. The fact these men are respected in their community and by their clients says enough." Kelly looked past the reporters at Hunter, who tipped his hat at him, and Gable, who had a shy smile on his face. He let his eyes trail back to the first rows. "Next!"

"Lisa LaDure. *WebLegalNews*. What will you do if the people vote you out of office?"

"I always wanted to organize sightseeing tours of the Tetons. I've flown over them numerous times in my helicopter, and they are gorgeous. And I'd buy some horses and add sightseeing on horseback to that."

"You'd stay in the area?" she added to her question.

"Yes, of course I would. My life is here. I like the area and I like the people."

"Even if they vote you off?"

"This is why we have elections, Miss LaDure. So people can decide which person they trust the most to serve them. Everyone is entitled to their opinion." Kelly saw only a few hands in the air and cleared his throat. "I think you all have something to write about, and I have a county to serve, so I thank you for your orderly conduct and your questions." With this he turned around and walked back toward the parts of the office not meant for the public. There were a few people in the waiting area, and he nodded at them before making a beeline for his office. He'd barely closed the door before he was enveloped in a tight hug.

"You went off script."

Kelly squeezed Cooper tightly. "I'm sorry, but that question was downright vicious, and all I could think of was that there were three children who were going to see this, and I had to say something in Martin's defense."

"Thank you."

Over Cooper's shoulder, Kelly could see the direct news bulletins with Kaitlyn Evers "reporting from the scene." "Did you see they were all there? Gable and Hunter and everyone else?"

"They all came out to support you."

"Did you call them?"

"I believe Jennifer did."

"She's too efficient for her own good."

"I think she's perfectly suited for her job."

—41—

"MERRY Christmas!" Kelly shouted as he entered the main house of the Blue River Ranch. He was holding bottles of champagne, and Cooper was following close by with several pots of poinsettias. They were greeted by a whole gaggle of kids running around before they met up with Izzie.

"Come here, you guys," she said, arms open. She hugged both of them. "It's chaos here, as usual. Are you sure you're up to a loud, messy, chaotic family Christmas?"

Kelly looked at Cooper, who shrugged. "Guess we are. We can always run when it gets too much."

"Sure you can," Izzie said, grabbing hold of Vicky, who was running too fast across the hardwood floors.

Kelly smiled at the picture and took Cooper's hand. They rarely did this in public, but here, among friends, was the one place where they could show themselves as a couple.

"There's food all over the place, but leave space for dinner," Izzie said with a wink as she disappeared in the direction of the kitchen.

"There's Calley," Cooper pointed out. She was sitting by herself, hand lying protectively on her growing bump, so Cooper sat next to her and Kelly across.

"You two look radiant," she said. "Moving certainly did you well," she said to Cooper.

"I didn't move yet," Cooper corrected her.

"No, you just sleep there every night. Kelly, haven't you asked him yet?"

Kelly put his hand on Cooper's knee. "He knows he's welcome." He winked at Cooper. "I never invite him over anymore. He's just there every evening, a late dinner ready, our laundry picked up from the

Laundromat, my fridge stocked. I don't miss my housekeeper anymore."

"Bet Teo didn't provide the warm body at night, the hand that isn't your own...."

"Calley!" Cooper cautioned.

"Now come, darlings. One of the benefits of being sick is that I can speak my mind whenever I want to. And you two are made for each other. Everyone can see that."

"So how are you doing?" Kelly asked.

"The rooms all of you built for us are amazing. It's nice to be there with the kids and know that if I'm tired I can just take a nap, because the guys are there to look after them. Which reminds me. Cooper, Sadie needs to talk to you."

"She here?"

Calley shook her head. "The shop closes at six. Sadie will bring Ryan, so they'll be here for dinner."

"But how are *you* doing?" Kelly asked.

"I'm okay. This one"—she petted her belly—"is growing like there's no tomorrow. The doctors are keeping a close eye on him, but so far he doesn't seem to feel any effects of the treatment I'm getting. Once he's born, they're really going to let me have it, but we'll see that when we get there."

"So it's a boy? I'm sure Flynn is thrilled."

Calley rolled her eyes. "I can't believe the mother hen that man is. Sometimes I just shoo him out of my room so he'll leave me alone!" Her face softened. "But it's nice to know that if anything should happen to me or if I need to be in hospital for longer than a few hours, he'll be there to take care of the kids, and I can trust him with the baby too." She looked up. "There he is with my drink."

GABLE walked outside to the porch. It was almost time for dinner and already dark outside, but he had to get out of the noise for a moment. A car stopped in the driveway, and two people got out. As they walked up the porch and into better light, Gable recognized Sadie. Her companion didn't join her through the front door, but instead he walked around the side of the house to where Gable was standing.

"The good stuff is inside, you know."

Ryan jumped but calmed down as soon as he recognized Gable's voice. "Didn't see you there. So if the good stuff is in there, what are you doing out here?"

"Getting out of the noise."

Ryan chuckled, and Gable thought of the long road they'd traveled together. Ryan still wasn't the most communicative kid, but since he'd moved to Blackwater, they had cultivated a quiet understanding, and Gable had the feeling he was getting through to Ryan. At least occasionally.

"Shop busy today?"

"In spurts. I filled shelves while Sadie worked the till."

Gable nodded. "So did you get a chance to drive up to Kaye's house?"

Ryan's face clouded over. He nodded.

"Did you wish him a Merry Christmas?" Gable knew he was fishing, but ever since he'd found out about Ryan's infatuation with Kaye Simmons and the fact feelings were being returned, he'd worked hard at keeping the channels of communication open. He knew from experience that telling him not to see the teacher twelve years his senior would only draw them closer. On top of that, Ryan would stop talking, and Gable didn't want that.

"He's leaving, Gable." There was a crack in his voice, and Gable felt his pain.

"Where's he going?"

"Seattle. He found a job there."

"Well, there's e-mail and Skype. You can stay in touch."

Ryan turned to him and looked like he was about to ask him whether he was stupid.

"Until you're eighteen, Ry. It's safer this way. Right now he could be sent to jail for what you're doing."

"We're not doing anything!" Tears were streaming down Ryan's face, and he wasn't even trying to cover it up.

Gable put his hand on Ryan's shoulder and gestured for him to sit down on the steps of the porch. He sat down next to him.

Ryan looked defeated and miserable.

"Did I ever tell you about the time I was about Kaye's age?"

Ryan shook his head and sniveled.

"I was single at the time and hadn't really had a relationship with anyone. As far as I was concerned, I was the only gay man around here. It wasn't something they talked about, and I didn't have anyone to ask. Before the Handle Bar opened, I'd sometimes go to Idaho Falls or spend the weekend in Boise, because I knew where they had gay bars there." He looked at Ryan, who had stopped crying and was just staring into the darkness now. "I got help at the ranch from one of the neighboring places, and he was sixteen, like you. He was a hard worker."

"Like me."

"Yeah, like you, but he was a real country boy. He'd wear these carpenter jeans and boots that used to belong to his brothers. Most of the times he was gregarious and loud, but sometimes he'd grow quiet. One of those quiet days I asked him what was wrong, and he told me about this girl in school who was pursuing him. And then he told me he didn't want this girl. He wanted me."

Ryan nodded but didn't say anything.

"I liked him a lot, but I was scared. I told him he was too young, but he wouldn't listen to me. He'd come by the ranch every day, and one day I caved."

"You had... sex?"

Gable nodded. He hoped it would inspire Ryan to tell the truth about what he'd done with Kaye, but Ryan remained silent.

"What... was it like?"

"Between him and me, Ryan."

"Okay, I get it."

"It's not a sin what happened between you, Ry, but the law is strict. The day of your eighteenth birthday is the first day Kaye won't run the risk of going to jail over this. So it's for his own good that he moved away."

"I told you, nothing happened."

Gable didn't respond. He didn't believe Ryan, but he understood why he lied.

After sitting together quietly for several minutes, Ryan inhaled audibly. "Kaye didn't want to. He said the same things you did. That he loved me but didn't want to go to jail. He said Cooper knew what was going on and so did Kelly. I guess he didn't love me enough."

"No, Ry. He loved you enough not to. It shows he had a lot of respect for you."

"Fat lot of good that does me. He's not going to wait two years for me, Gabe."

"You don't know that."

"And if he has *so much respect for me*, then what does that make you? Does it mean you didn't have any respect for whatshisname? Who was he, anyway?"

"Again, that's between him and me."

"I bet you made him up."

Gable bit his lip. "I didn't, but if you choose not to believe me, then that's your problem, not mine." He clapped his hand on Ryan's shoulder and got up from the porch step. "Let's go inside and have dinner. Put on your happy face, Ry."

Ryan followed him inside, where most people were already around one of the big tables. Flynn gestured at him, and he walked over. He was glad to see Tim was seated at their table as well. "Mind if I sit next to Tim?" he asked Flynn. They switched places as Flynn was dishing out food for everyone.

"Can I ask you a favor?" Gable asked Tim. "Could you have a talk with Ryan?"

"What about?"

"About getting over your first love."

Tim chuckled. "What did you tell him, Gable?"

"The truth. But I didn't give him your name."

"He's a smart kid. If I go and talk to him, he's going to figure it out."

"Is that such a bad thing?"

Tim smiled and shook his head. "Fine, I'll talk to him."

AT THE other side of the room, Kelly and Cooper were seated at the same table as Hunter and Grant.

"How's the petition going?" Hunter asked. "Are you still going to be our sheriff in the next year?"

Kelly swallowed his sweet potato. "Looks like it. Unless about four and a half thousand people show up in the next week."

"Congratulations," Grant said. "I knew you'd be okay. You give one hell of a press conference. How do you stay so calm?"

Kelly looked at Cooper and smiled, then turned back to Grant. "Cooper taught me that."

"Wait! Imagine them naked?"

Kelly shook his head. "I used to be so nervous every time we had to present closing arguments in mock court, I'd stutter and stammer my way through it. So one day Cooper told me how he did it. He'd tell himself that all was lost and nothing I would say or do would make a difference. But that I had to go out there and show my client I still believed in him. So if I bombed, then it didn't matter, and if I succeeded, I would cause a landslide."

"That wouldn't work for me. Take away all hope? I'd give up." Hunter sat back, patting his belly.

Cooper laughed. "Never worked for me either, but Kelly's Andy Griffith. His primary motivation is lost causes."

Kelly squeezed Cooper's knee under the table. "Bastard."

"Well, ten thousand concerned, but very silent, citizens seem to like their gay sheriff. Andy Griffith or not."

"I'm up for serving the people for the next four years."

Now it was Cooper's turn to squeeze Kelly's thigh.

"So are they still picketing the station?" Hunter asked.

"Nope." Kelly smirked. "They lasted about two days. Then came the hate mail, but that's died down to about one or two letters a week too."

"That's still a lot to take."

Kelly shrugged. "Jennifer opens them for me, and Len, my chief deputy, follows up any letters that actually threaten with something, but most of them are pretty general. I have a great team, and that counts for something too."

"And the reporters?"

"Not a word. There was one more article with a full frontal picture of Cooper on the front page and the headline 'The sheriff's dish on the side,' but that's it."

"Full frontal?" Grant sputtered.

"A face shot, Grant," Cooper explained. "But I liked the background. It was a picture of us riding horses on your ranch. Kelly requested it from the newspaper and got it too, right?"

Kelly nodded.

JUST after dessert, Kelly walked outside for a breath of fresh air.

"Here you are." Kelly put his arms around Cooper and squeezed him. "Thought you'd left without me."

"Wouldn't dare. My sheets in the crew house haven't been slept in for over a month."

"Maybe you should clean out your room?"

"What are you saying?" Cooper asked.

"Nothing I haven't asked before. You have a key, and you basically live at my house anyway. Wouldn't it be easier if you moved your possessions there?"

"You have no idea what you're suggesting, Kells. I have all my law books in storage too."

"Maybe you should take them out and study for the bar again. We'd make a great team."

"I can see the conflict of interest waiting to happen. You arrest a guy and I defend him. Not going to happen, Kells."

"We'll see." Kelly kissed the neck of the man he loved and inhaled the scent he was so happy to have found again. Then he looked at the moon and the stars. "Did you bring them out just for me?"

Cooper lifted his hand and blew over it. His breath was visible in the cold night air. He then flicked away some imaginary specks. "Just need to get rid of the occasional cloud and flick a few stars on to shine a little brighter. Anything for my man."

ZAHRA OWENS is a multilingual globetrotter who loves big cities but also has a weak spot for the wide-open spaces that are so rare where she lives.

She likes her men every which way they come and never tries to change them. Men who are tough on the outside but have a huge soft center get extra credit, though, as do the strong, silent types who think they hide their damage well… but don't. She makes it her personal goal to find them their happily-ever-after, even if the road toward this leads via hospital beds, villas with gorgeous vistas, or ranges full of horses.

Zahra is a proud member of the Rainbow Romance Writers, a special interest chapter of the Romance Writers of America, and won't quit until M/M romances are treated like every other romance story. RWA allowed her into its Professional Authors Network, but she hasn't quit her day job yet since it allows her to work in a man's world. And what girl can resist that?

If Zahra had her wish, a day would have at least thirty-six hours, because how else would she find the time to finish all the novels still inside her head?

You can find Zahra at http://zahraowens.com.

Read Gable and Flynn's story in

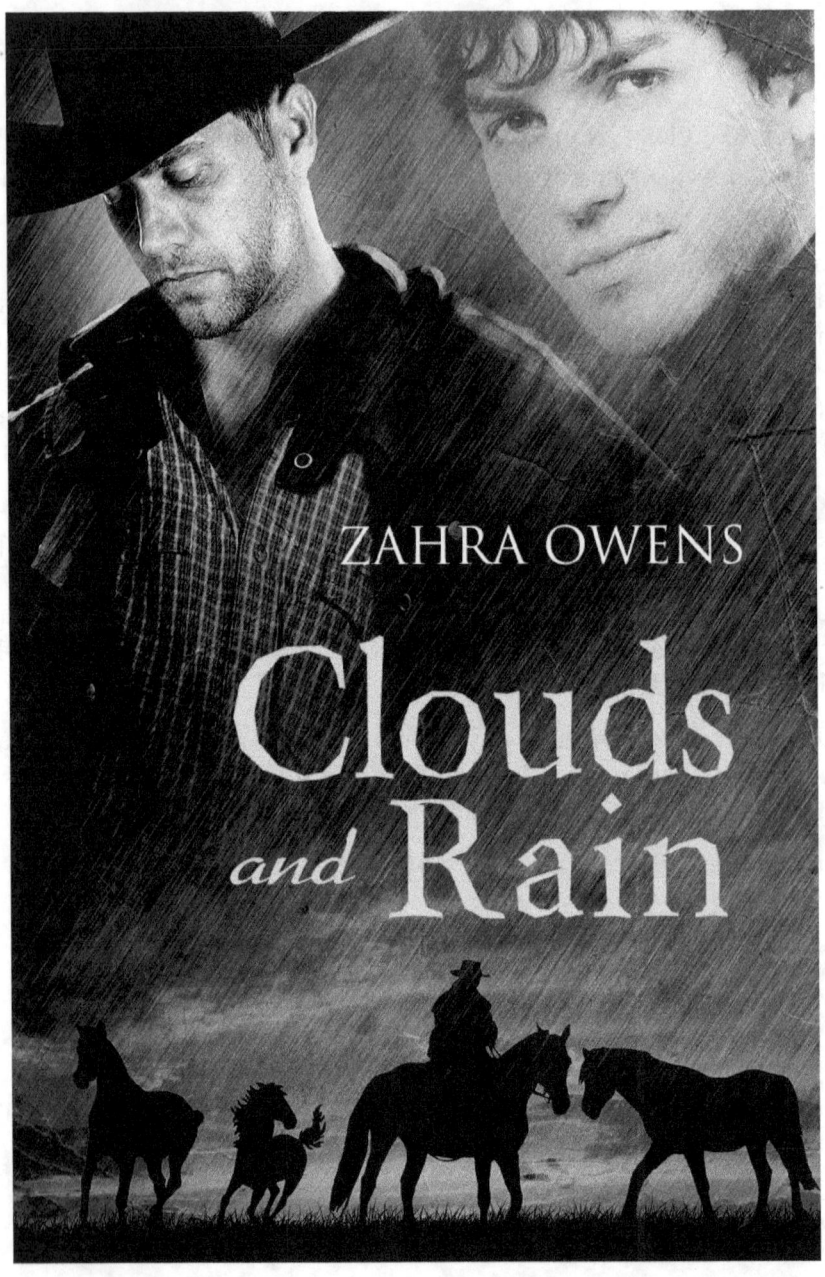

ZAHRA OWENS

Clouds
and Rain

Enjoy Hunter and Grant's story in

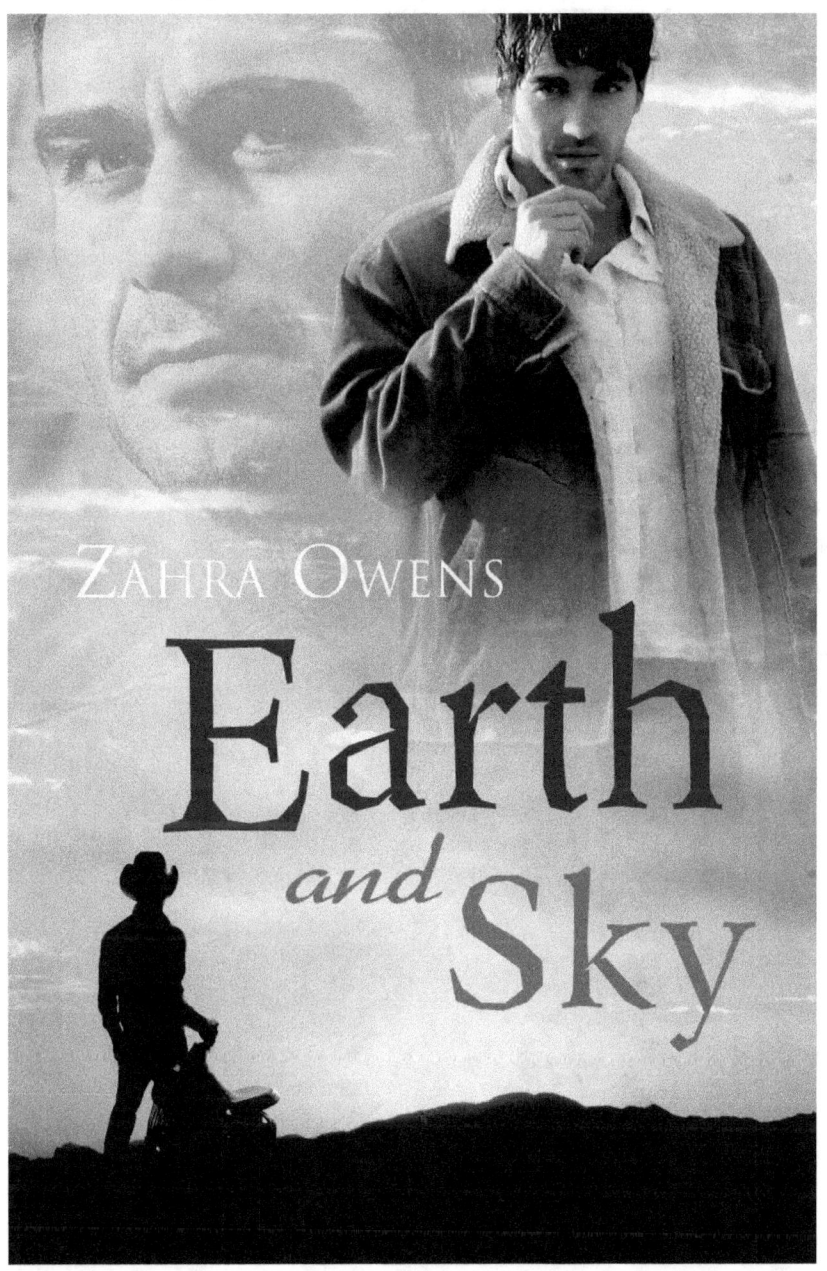

ZAHRA OWENS

Earth and Sky

Curious about Tim and Rory's story?

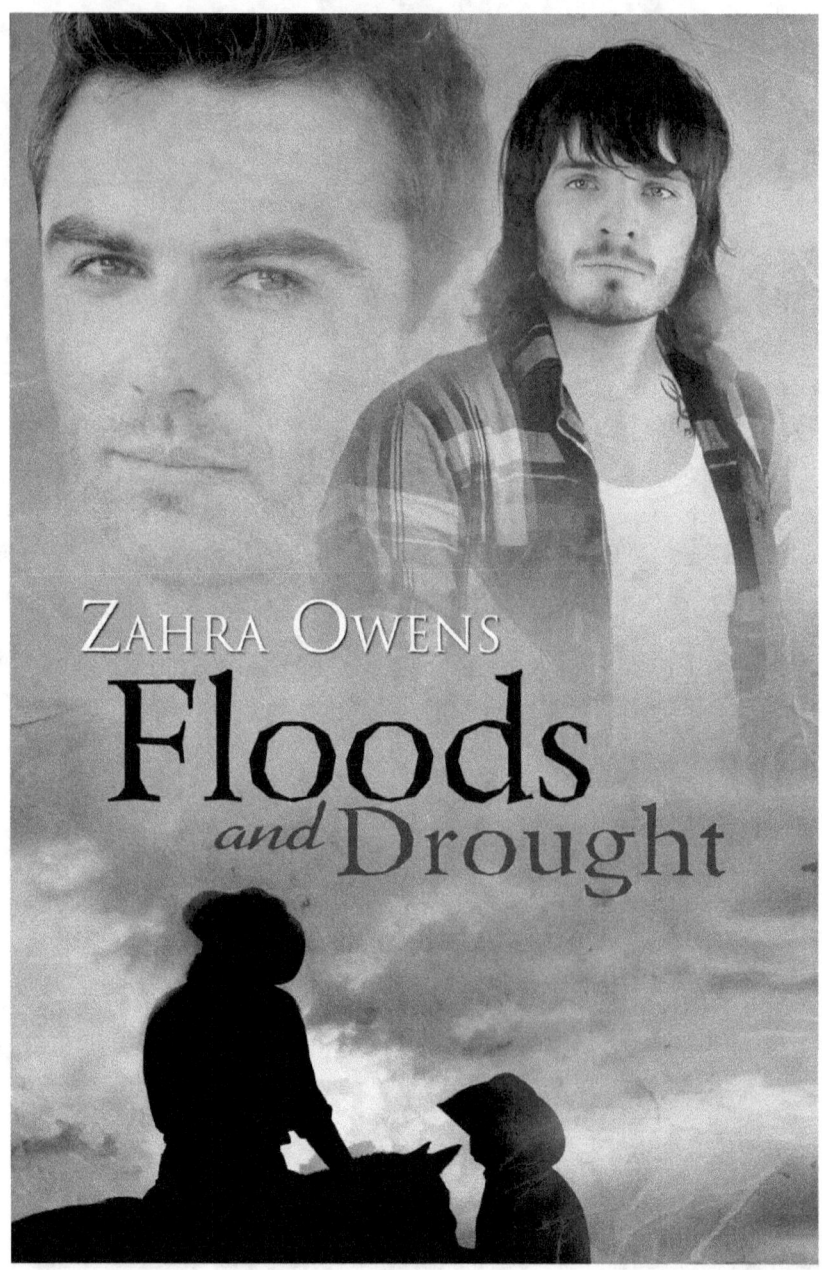

ZAHRA OWENS

Floods
and Drought

Romance from ZAHRA OWENS

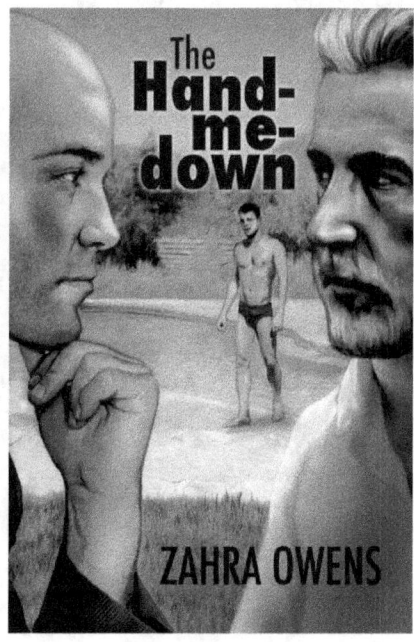

http://www.dreamspinnerpress.com

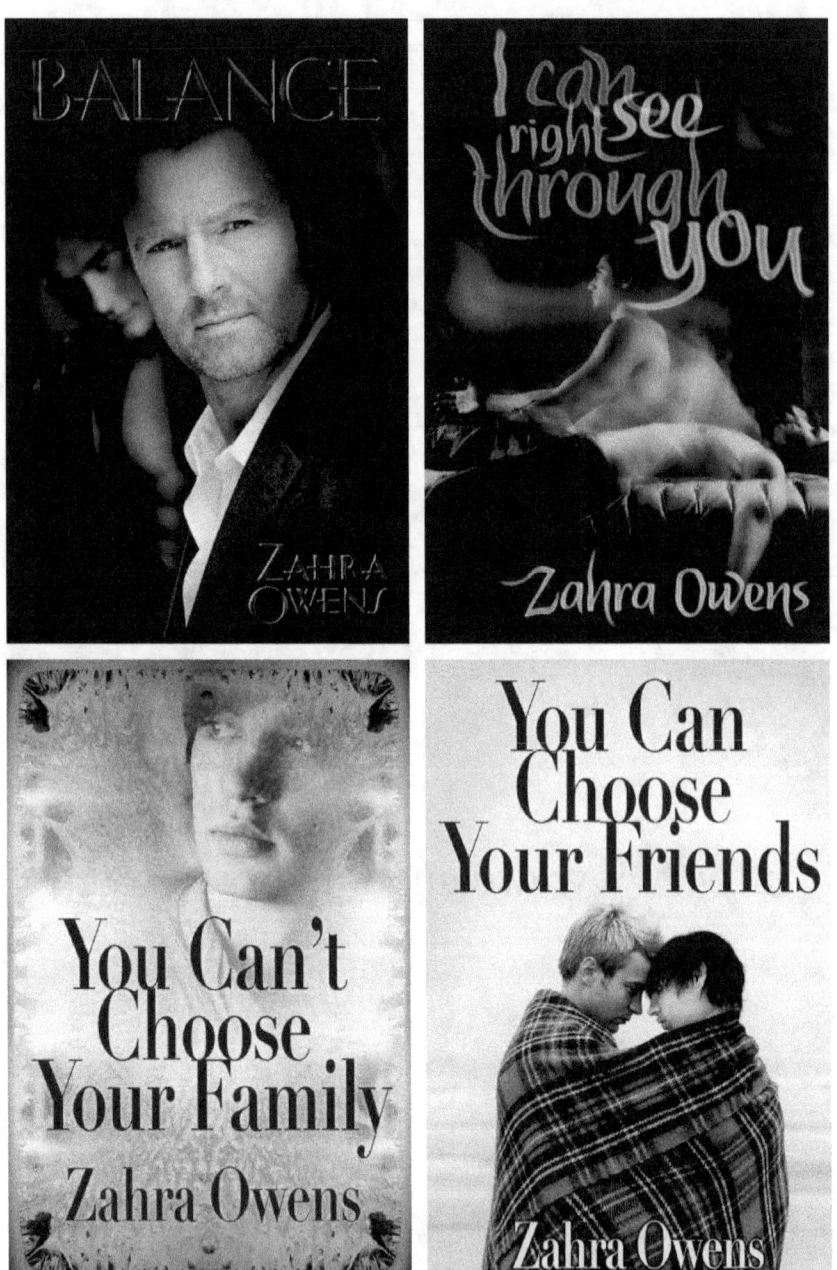

Also from ZAHRA OWENS

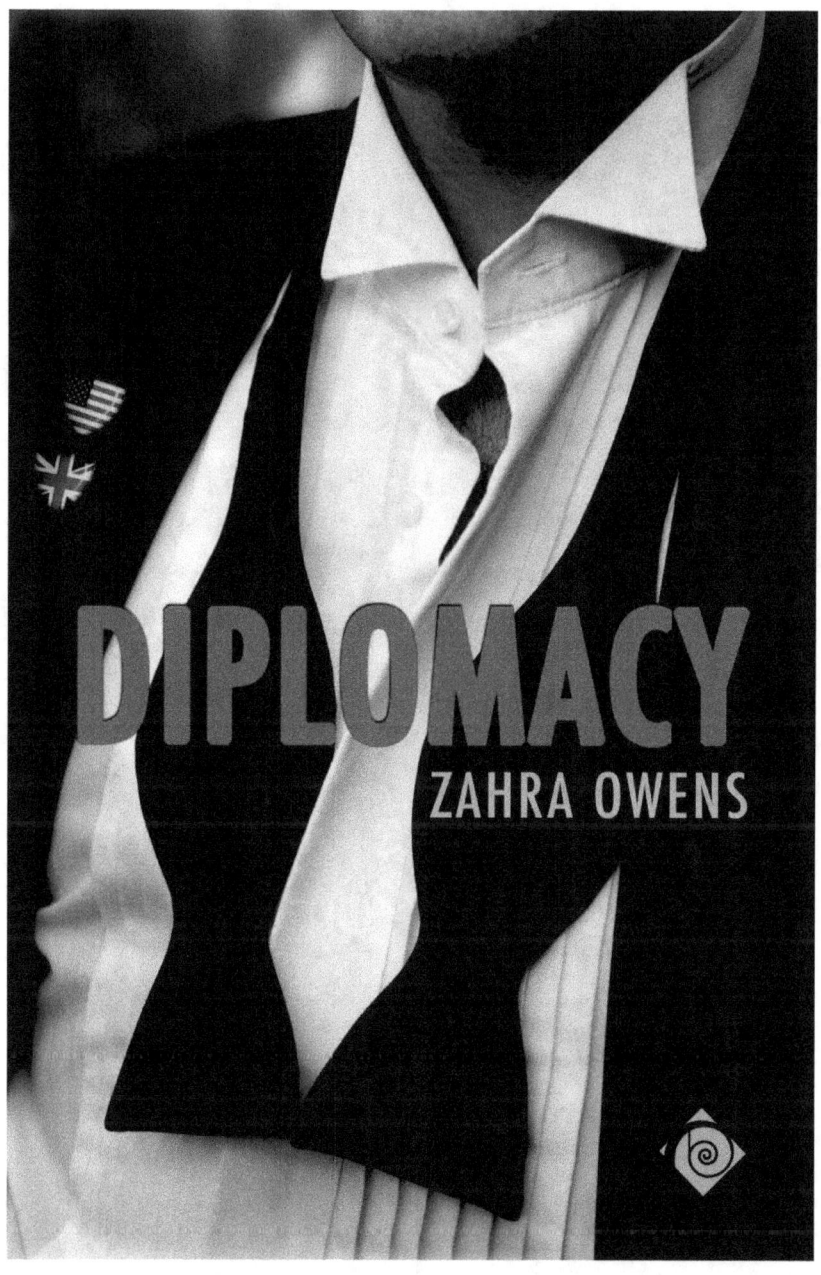

DIPLOMACY

ZAHRA OWENS

http://www.dreamspinnerpress.com